THOSE MISSING YEARS

Jenny Rea

© **Jennifer Rea, 2025. All rights reserved.**

This novel, *These Missing Years*, is protected under international and national copyright laws. No part of this work may be reproduced, distributed, or transmitted in any form or by any means, including photocopying, recording, or other electronic or mechanical methods, without the prior written permission of the author, except in the case of brief quotations for review purposes.

JENNY REA

Dedication

I dedicate this book to my beloved husband, Hugh – thank you for believing in me and having faith when I doubted myself.

To my beautiful daughters, Zowie and Amber, and my wonderful granddaughters, Courtney, Summer, and Darby.

With all my love, forevermore. xxx

Table of Contents

Dedication..iii
Chapter 1 1
Chapter 2 15
Chapter 3 34
Chapter 4 45
Chapter 5 59
Chapter 6 68
Chapter 7 75
Chapter 8 84
Chapter 9 91
Chapter 10 103
Chapter 11 114
Chapter 12 124
Chapter 13 143
Chapter 14 152
Chapter 15 161
Chapter 16 174
Chapter 17 187
Chapter 18 195
Chapter 19 208
Chapter 20 220
Chapter 21 241

Chapter 22	249
Chapter 23	259
Chapter 24	276
Chapter 25	291
Chapter 26	299
Chapter 27	313
Chapter 28	321
Chapter 29	330
About the Author	337

Chapter 1

Rose sat in her basement flat in Chelsea, London, on that snowy January evening. She glanced out of the window and noticed that another foot of snow had fallen since the day before. Silently, so as not to be overheard, she murmured, "It won't be long now. I don't have much time, but I have to do this."

She was in the scullery, preparing dinner on what seemed to be just another day. She hadn't smiled in months. Exhausted and downtrodden, she stared vacantly into space. Suddenly, she let out a yelp, snatching her hand away after accidentally touching the hot stove. Quickly, she ran it under cold water to soothe the pain, then wrapped it in a cool, damp cloth. She cradled her injured hand, wincing slightly as the initial sting began to subside.

Dinner was always on the table promptly at seven o'clock, even though her husband, Tom, didn't always come home. When he did, and there was no dinner, his temper would flare. The last thing Rose wanted was another shouting match.

Despite working long hours, Tom's wages were meagre, making it hard for them to make ends meet. Rose couldn't shake the gnawing suspicion that he was keeping some of his earnings back. She was plagued by uncertainties about his whereabouts and activities, leaving her feeling trapped in a loveless marriage.

Over time, she had stopped asking where he had been. The weight of feeling unloved, unwanted, and unappreciated bore down on her. She withdrew into a world of her own, creating distance between herself and everyone around her, even resisting closeness with her daughter, Cosuda.

Rose's once boundless love had faded, eclipsed by the weight of her past. Beneath her weary exterior, her beauty endured, though it was a truth she neither thought about nor cared for any longer. Her slender frame, long dark curls, and captivating brown eyes, fringed with thick, lustrous lashes, still drew attention.

Yet the scar that traced its way down her left cheek, just below her eye, served as a permanent reminder of her pain. She resembled her father, with his thick, curly hair and deep brown eyes—a likeness that hinted at an untapped strength within her. But it was her mother's gentle, nurturing heart that defined her most enduring legacy.

Seated by the open back door of the dark scullery, Rose pondered the crossroads of her life and the decisions she had to make. Her thoughts drifted back to where it all began. After losing her mother and enduring the declaration of the Second World War, she faced one ordeal after another. Now, however, she was determined to prioritise herself.

Rose was born in London in January 1932. Her father, Neville, was a French officer from Normandy. He was a tall, strong-built man with a thick black military buzz cut, and the stern expression he wore in uniform was etched into her memory.

Her mother, Maggie, was born in 1913, shortly before the start of the First World War. At fourteen, Maggie left school to work in a hat factory, crafting military sun helmets for export. Two years later, seeking better opportunities, she left the factory to work as a domestic servant in the grand 'Big House' near her home in Chelsea. It was there that she met Neville, a dashing young paratrooper.

They dated for three months before he persuaded her to marry him.

Soon after their marriage, Neville was ordered back to France for training, but Maggie, an only child, decided to remain in Chelsea with her mother. After completing an apprenticeship in electronics,

Neville became an invaluable member of his squadron. Though he loved his wife, he was eager to leave the confines of domestic life and put his skills to use on the front lines.

Not long after their marriage, Maggie received instructions to join Neville in France. The prospect of leaving her home, however, left her distraught. Her traditional mother insisted that a wife's place was with her husband, reminding her of her marital duties. Yet, in a bold act of defiance, Maggie refused to leave.

Two years later, when Neville returned home, Maggie was soon pregnant. Rose was born when her mother was just nineteen years old. For the first few years, their life seemed almost idyllic.

Seven years later, in the summer of 1939, Maggie, then twenty-six, fell gravely ill with pneumonia. Her health declined rapidly, and she passed away, leaving Neville and Rose in a state of shock. Their lives were forever altered. Neville, overwhelmed and uncertain, faced the daunting reality of raising his daughter alone. He knew he needed to make decisions quickly, but the weight of his grief and the urgency of a world on the brink of war made every choice a struggle.

Despite his devastation over Maggie's sudden death, Neville forced himself to compartmentalise his emotions. His responsibilities as a Flight Sergeant demanded focus and discipline. Determined to provide for Rose, he sought assistance through the Women's Voluntary Service (WVS), which helped find suitable carers for children whose parents had been called up in the Second World War.

"I need to hire a lady to take care of you, Rose," he said gently. "I have to work, do you understand?"

Tears filled Rose's eyes. "No! I want Mummy back," she cried, her small voice trembling.

Neville knelt to her level, his expression etched with pain. "That's not possible, sweetheart. I want Mummy back too. Please understand this is what we need to do. We need someone to help."

Rose clenched her small hands into fists, her frustration evident. "OK," she muttered before turning and bolting to her room.

Lying on her bed, she stared at the ceiling, memories of her mother flooding back. She recalled Maggie's radiant beauty and the soft, comforting scent of lavender that lingered in every corner of their home. Each night, she would fall asleep to that aroma, often after listening to her mother's stories about her own childhood.

Maggie had been caring, kind, and endlessly cheerful. She loved Rose dearly, always finding moments to sing and dance with her.

"You will be a wonderful dancer one day, my beautiful girl," her mother would say, her eyes shining with pride.

"Just like you, Mummy," Rose would giggle, twirling in her slippers.

The first few carers who came after Maggie's death were inexperienced, fumbling through their duties and leaving Rose feeling even more alone. However, the agency eventually found someone with years of experience working with children. Her name was Mary Clarke.

When Mary arrived, Neville greeted her with a firm handshake. "Rose," he called, his voice echoing down the hallway.

Rose hesitated, peeking from behind the hallway door. Her past experiences had left her wary, unsure of what to expect this time.

Mary stood at the entryway, a rounded woman in her late fifties with a kind, motherly demeanour. Her short brown bobbed hair was neatly pinned back. She wore a plain grey dress, a crisp apron, and a cardigan buttoned snugly at the waist. Despite the hardships of the war, Mary valued order and routine, which provided a stable environment for the children in her care.

When Mary smiled at her, it eased some of the pain, but Rose knew no one could ever replace her mother.

"This is my daughter, Rose," Neville said, introducing her.

Rose hesitated, then stepped out and forced a small smile.

"Hello, Rose. It's lovely to meet you," Mary said warmly.

Rose looked up at her, her wide eyes a mix of curiosity and sadness. "How long will you be here for?" she asked in a whisper.

"As long as your father needs me, Rose. We'll get through this together," Mary reassured her gently, crouching slightly to meet Rose's eye level.

Neville showed Mary her room and left her to unpack while he went to speak to his daughter.

"Mary will look after you while I am away," he said. "You must do exactly what she says and study hard."

"OK," Rose replied softly, her voice tinged with sadness.

Mary, who was also a French tutor, would teach Rose the language at home along with her other academic lessons. Neville was determined for Rose to speak his native tongue and had a serious conversation with Mary about his expectations before leaving for France. He trusted her implicitly to care for his daughter and fulfil the role he could not.

Over the next few months, however, Rose became increasingly withdrawn. She refused to eat and grew alarmingly weak.

THOSE MISSING YEARS

One cold December afternoon, under an overcast sky, the front door suddenly flung open to reveal Neville, home earlier than expected. His face was lined with exhaustion, and his uniform was worn from travel. He paused in the doorway, taking in the sight of Mary in the kitchen.

Mary looked up in surprise. "Hello, Mr Azpax. This is unexpected," she said, wiping her hands on her apron.

Neville gave a tired smile. "Hello, Mary. It's good to be home." He moved over to the fire, held his hands out to the comforting blaze, and then asked, "How's Rose been doing while I've been away?" His voice was rough but full of concern.

Mary glanced over at Rose, who lay curled up on the sofa, fast asleep under a thick blanket. "She's not very well if I'm honest," Mary admitted. "I called the doctor a few days ago. He came to see her and prescribed some medicine, but it didn't seem to be helping. She seems to be getting worse. He's due to call in again later today."

Neville walked over and placed his hand on Rose's forehead. "She's burning up!" he exclaimed. "We need to get her temperature down quickly."

Being medically trained, Neville immediately took charge. Mary fetched a basin of cool water and undressed Rose down to her underclothes. She gently sponged her with a flannel until her temperature began to drop.

Rose stirred, her voice faint and confused. "What's happening? I want Mummy."

"You've been ill," Mary said softly. "But don't worry. The doctor will be here soon."

Mary stayed by Rose's side while they waited. Her heart swelled with both affection and concern as she watched over the fragile child. She couldn't help but wonder if Rose's illness was rooted as much in grief as in her physical condition. With Neville often away, Rose seemed to lack the comfort and stability she so desperately needed.

It was late when the doctor arrived, having been delayed by an emergency call-out. After examining Rose, he assured Neville and Mary that they were managing her condition correctly by keeping her cool and hydrated.

"Her symptoms are physical but stress-related," the doctor explained carefully. "The upheaval from losing her mother and her father being sent away has taken a toll on her. She needs time, care, and stability to recover fully."

The doctor's visit was brief, as he had other patients to attend to.
"If there is any change for the worse, you must call me immediately," he instructed firmly.

The army was of paramount importance to Neville, and he had no intention of allowing what he perceived as a minor illness to interfere with his duties.

Mary stayed by Rose's side all night. The next morning, she was relieved to find that the fever had broken. Although Rose was still deathly pale, she seemed more herself.

On 1 September 1939, Neville received a telegram informing him that war had broken out. World War II had begun. Neville was immediately posted to France, with no indication of how long he would be away. There was no time for long farewells. He had to tell Rose that, for her safety, she would be evacuated to another part of the country.

Rose, still grieving the loss of her mother, now faced her father's sudden departure. Watching him pack his suitcase with no clear explanation, her confusion deepened.

"Evacuated?" she said. "What does that mean?"

Neville knelt down to her level, trying to explain gently. "Yes, Rose. Evacuated. You'll be sent somewhere safe until I can come back. You must do as you're told and not complain. It's a tough world out there, and this is for your own safety."

He sighed deeply and added, "Remember, the host families looking after you are not your parents."

Neville handed Rose a piece of paper with an address. "Write to this address as soon as you know where you're staying. It will reach me through the military postal system. I need to go now. You'll be OK. Goodbye, Rose."

And just like that, he was gone, disappearing from her life as suddenly as her mother had.

Rose immediately noticed the worried look on Mary's face.

After Neville left, Mary couldn't shake the heavy feeling that Rose's life would change forever. Although she understood that Neville had no choice but to serve, it pained her to see the little girl face yet another upheaval.

For Rose, the wounds cut even deeper. Having already lost her mother to pneumonia, she now had to endure the absence of her father. Her once happy home felt emptier than ever, and the silence was filled with a gnawing uncertainty.

Her memories of her mother were still fresh and vivid. To Rose, her mother had been a perfect figure—warm, loving, and full of life. Without her parents, Rose found it difficult to imagine what her future might hold.

"What does 'evacuate' even mean?" she asked herself repeatedly, her mind racing with questions.

That evening, Mary sat her down at the kitchen table to explain.

"I'll tell you what's happening, Rose," Mary said. "There's a war now, a big one, called World War II. It started because a man named Adolf Hitler in Germany wanted to make his country very powerful by taking over others. He told people in Germany that they were better than everyone else and should rule the world. Now they're trying to invade other countries, but many nations are working together to stop them and keep everyone safe."

"So, it's a very bad thing?" Rose asked, her voice small.

Mary didn't want to frighten her but knew honesty was important. "Yes, it is a bad thing," she admitted.

"Do the Germans drop bombs and shoot people?" Rose pressed.

Mary nodded gently. "Yes, it's like that."

Rose sighed heavily, then leaned into Mary's comforting embrace. Within moments, she was fast asleep, her small form nestled in the arms of the only person she could trust.

Two days after Neville had left for France, Mary was cooking when the Prime Minister's announcement came over the radio, causing her to stop in her tracks. The eerie sound of sirens warning of impending bomb attacks echoed through the house. The Prime Minister provided information about the air raid warnings and advised against using tube stations as shelters, warning that people might be reluctant to return to the surface and resume normal life.

Despite the government's advice, the ban was largely ignored. Each night, just before the sirens blared, hundreds of people made their way to the nearest underground station, carrying thermos flasks filled with tea, magazines, and bedding.

"Dinner is ready, Rose," Mary called. "Come and sit at the table, or it'll go cold." She placed their spam hash and mash on the table.

Rose sensed Mary's unease and ate her dinner in silence. Mary knew she needed to be truthful and reassuring without frightening her daughter.

"I want to explain a little more about the war, Rose," Mary said gently. "You'll notice shelters being built along the streets on your way to school. Those shelters are where you should go if any bombs are dropped."

"Don't bombs go through the shelters?" Rose asked, her eyes wide.

"No, the shelters will protect you," Mary replied firmly. "Just make sure you go to one whenever you hear the sirens. They can sound at any time, day or night, but if it happens at night, you'll be here with me."

"Yes, all right," Rose said quietly.

After they finished eating, Mary told Rose to go upstairs to her room and read her books while she tidied up and did the washing. Obediently, Rose made her way up the staircase, but once she reached her room, she couldn't resist approaching the window.

As if sensing her thoughts, Mary called out, "Don't look out of the window, Rose, and make sure no light escapes from your room."

Turning away, Rose shouted back, "I won't, but why does it matter if a little light shows?"

"It's because we're expecting German planes to fly over London," Mary explained patiently. "If they see any light, they could target us with their bombs."

Rose sighed and flopped onto her bed, her thoughts turning to her absent parents.

She wondered why her mum and dad used to argue so often, and whether her father loved her as much as her mother seemed to love him. Then she remembered the times her mother had a split lip or other injuries. Whenever Rose asked about them, her mother would always claim she'd walked into a door or a cupboard. Even as a child, Rose had noticed how unhappy her mother had been.

Seeking an escape from her gloomy thoughts, Rose picked up her *Mary Poppins* book and began reading by the light of a small torch. Despite her efforts, she struggled to concentrate.

"Are you in bed now, Rose?" Mary called up the stairs.

There was no reply, but the faint sound of sniffling and crying reached her ears. Concerned, Mary climbed the stairs to check on her.

"Come on now, it's very late. You get some sleep, and we'll see what tomorrow brings," she said, her voice gentle and optimistic.

"Goodnight, Mary. I'm glad you're looking after me. I wish it were my mummy, but I like you too."

Mary's heart ached at Rose's words. As the little girl nestled her head into the pillow, her thoughts turned to her mother and the uncertainty of what lay ahead now that her father was off at war.

"Goodnight, sweetheart," Mary said softly.

She sat beside Rose until she was certain the girl had fallen asleep. Then, carefully, she eased her arm away, tucked the blanket around her, and tiptoed downstairs.

The following day, Mary ventured into town to buy blackout material to line the back of all the curtains in the house. Luckily, there was a market that day, and she managed to buy enough fabric at a reasonable price.

While in the shop, she overheard a conversation about ration books being issued for groceries, bacon, and ham. Supplies had been scarce for weeks, so the introduction of rationing wouldn't make much difference; most of the shelves were already bare.

Mary spent the next two days sewing the blackout material onto all the curtains in the house, ensuring no light would escape at night.

On Monday morning, Rose walked to school with her friend Anna and Anna's mother, their gas masks slung across their shoulders. Rose grumbled about having to carry hers everywhere.

They all wore identity discs around their wrists, bearing their names, addresses, and school details.

"Why do I have to wear this, Mary?" Rose asked, fidgeting with the string tied to her wrist.

"Everyone has one," Mary explained patiently. "Even adults. It's in case you get separated during an evacuation. Now, off you go. Stay with your teachers unless I've arranged for someone to pick you up."

"OK, I will," Rose replied nervously before hurrying to join her friend.

When Rose arrived at school, she was surprised to see that several of her classmates were absent. She wondered if they had already been evacuated, but no one said anything, as the children hadn't been informed. Instead, they played together on the playground as though nothing unusual was happening in the world outside.

Later, when Rose returned home from school, she noticed a large, corrugated structure at the bottom of the garden.

"What is that?" she asked Mary.

"It's called an Anderson shelter," Mary replied. "It's where we can protect ourselves when enemy planes fly over and drop bombs."

Rose recalled seeing several lorries on the streets during her walk home.

"Is that why there are lorries everywhere? Are they building shelters for everyone? I asked Anna's mum, but she didn't know," Rose said.

"Yes, they're Anderson shelters," Mary confirmed. "They're putting them up in everyone's back gardens. Hopefully, we won't need them, but it's safer to have them, just in case. It's all part of preparing for what might happen."

"What's going to happen?" Rose asked, her curiosity piqued.

"Hopefully nothing," Mary replied with a forced smile, but Rose caught her mumbling under her breath.

"What are you saying, Mary?"

"Nothing, nothing at all," Mary said quickly.

"That's all right then," Rose said, a hint of relief in her voice. "It can't be too bad."

For the first few weeks of the war, not much seemed to change. The sun continued to shine over their home, and Rose settled well into school. They received their ration books and tried to get by, though like everyone else, they had no idea what lay ahead.

Whenever the wail of the air raid sirens echoed in the distance, they dutifully made their way to the shelter. Rose never grew used to that haunting sound.

One evening, Mary left Rose in the garden shelter with some of the neighbours and decided to see for herself what the underground station was like. Despite its reputation for safety, the scene inside horrified her. People were crammed together on every available surface, with bodies lying in every corner. The lack of fresh air made the stench almost unbearable. Mothers sat feeding their babies, who sprawled across their parents due to the lack of space.

Stumbling back to the garden shelter, Mary fell to her knees, burying her head in her hands. Fear gripped her as she wondered if they would be the next to be bombed.

"What's wrong, Mary?" Rose cried, running to her and wrapping her arms around her waist. "Where have you been? What happened? You're scaring me!"

Mary tried her best to reassure her, though the truth weighed heavily on her shoulders.

"It's the war we talked about," she said gently. "But there's nothing to worry about right now."

"Damn war," Mary muttered under her breath.

The shelter grew silent, but Mary resolved to stay strong. As long as she could keep Rose safe, she would cope with whatever came next.

Chapter 2

In June 1940, German troops swept into Calais and Normandy, encountering fierce resistance. The skies darkened with German planes, their shadows looming ominously below. Meanwhile, in London, air raid sirens wailed almost every night from September to May 1941 during the Blitz, each sound a chilling reminder of lives hanging in the balance.

For Mary, the sudden reality of war was overwhelming. Her heart pounded as the sirens grew louder, their piercing cries shattering the stillness of the night. Like so many nights before, she lay awake, terrified and unable to sleep, the passage of time reduced to a blur. There were moments when she couldn't tell what was happening, let alone what day it was.

The sirens became an unwelcome rhythm of daily life. Each time they sounded, everything stopped, and people rushed to the nearest shelter. Despite the danger, schools remained open, with lessons continuing underground. Families were urged to send their children to the countryside for safety, though many hesitated to part with loved ones.

As the bombings intensified, one evening, after dinner, she ushered Rose to the shelter for the night. The space was dark, lit only dimly by the faint glow from the entrance. Outside, searchlights cut through the night sky, while the deafening buzz of falling bombs filled the air. Mary lay awake, gripped by fear, worrying about Rose and what the future might hold.

The next day brought devastation close to home. A bomb exploded alarmingly near their house, reducing neighbouring homes to rubble. Outside, the sky glowed an eerie, vivid red—a sight that was both haunting and unforgettable. That night was one of the worst they had endured, with bombs continuing to rain down, leaving destruction and tragedy in their wake.

Amidst the chaos, the laughter of children playing in the shelters offered a bittersweet contrast to the horrors above. Mary watched them, drawing a small measure of comfort from their innocence. During the day, life somehow continued. Shops opened with whatever goods they had left, men and women climbed over rubble to reach work, and children attended lessons in makeshift classrooms within the shelters. Even in the face of massive loss, the resilience of the community shone through.

The following morning, as Rose prepared for school, Mary glanced out of the window and noticed that Anna and her mother weren't at the corner to join them as usual. Concerned, she suggested they check on them before heading to school. When they arrived at Anna's house, they were shocked to see only a flat area where the house had been. Mary wondered where Anna and her mother might be. With no other option, she walked Rose to school.

During the morning assembly, the Head Teacher addressed the pupils solemnly. She explained that some children were missing due to the recent bombings, detailing the devastating effects on families and homes. Despite the sombre news, she urged the remaining children to carry on with their lessons.

Rose struggled to concentrate in class, her thoughts consumed by Anna. Was she one of the missing children? When the bell rang for break, Rose wandered into the playground, her worry mounting. She overheard Anna's friend, Patricia, who lived nearby, speaking to a group of children.

"Anna's house has been bombed," the girl said.

Rose's voice trembled as she approached the group. "What happened to Anna's house?" she asked, dreading the answer.

"I noticed her house just wasn't there anymore when we were walking to school this morning," Patricia said tearfully.

"Mary and I went round this morning to see why she hadn't turned up to meet us, and saw the flat area," Rose said.

Rose's heart sank as she listened to her friends talking. The news that her best friend's home had been destroyed by a bomb was devastating. Later that evening, Mary gently told her the grim truth—Anna, along with her mother, father, and brother, had all been inside when the bomb struck. They hadn't had a shelter of their own and, tragically, hadn't made it to the public shelter in time. The weight of this revelation crushed Rose, and she couldn't help but wonder if the other missing children had suffered the same fate. That night, sleep eluded her as fear and sorrow consumed her thoughts.

The next morning, Rose woke up early, ate her usual porridge and milk, and met her friends to walk to school. Mary, busy running errands for neighbours whose homes had been bombed, was grateful that Rose had friends to accompany her. Rose knew that if the sirens sounded, she'd have to make a quick decision—run home, continue to school, or head to the nearest shelter, whichever was closest.

At the start of the school day, the children gathered for assembly. Once again, Rose noticed there were fewer children present than the day before. Whispers circulated among the children, many wondering if the missing children had been victims of the bombings.

The school's underground shelter, built beneath the playing fields, had become a second classroom. Rose spent hours sitting on the hard benches, surrounded by the murmur of fearful children. Each day brought a new wave of anxiety, especially as she realised the increasing likelihood of Mary sending her away for safety. Rose recalled her father's words about evacuation—how she might be sent to a safer part of the country.

During the break, Rose overheard a conversation between the Head Teacher and Mary as she passed the school office. They were discussing plans to evacuate another group of children to Yorkshire. Mary's expression was resolute as she left the office. Rose suspected what this meant—Mary had decided she would join the next group of evacuees.

At the end of the school day, Rose chose to walk home alone, hoping to meet Mary on the way. The streets felt eerily quiet at first, but as she turned a corner, the distant hum of planes grew louder, sending a shiver down her spine. Suddenly, a bomb fell nearby, the deafening explosion shaking the ground.

Panic erupted as people ran for the nearest communal shelter. Rose's heart raced as she followed the crowd, her legs propelling her forward as fast as they could. Suddenly, a shop collapsed in front of her, the impact filling the air with dust and smoke.

"Mary! Where are you?" Rose screamed, her voice trembling with fear.

The acrid smell of smoke filled her lungs, making her cough and struggle to breathe. Bombs continued to fall around her, and the sight of bodies buried under rubble added to her terror. She pressed on, her eyes stinging from the smoke until she reached the entrance of a shelter. People were stumbling inside, some coughing, others vomiting from the suffocating fumes. Rose followed them, pushing through the chaos until she found a small corner where she could catch her breath. Her heart thundered in her chest as she prayed Mary would find her.

Meanwhile, Mary was navigating the same devastation, desperate to reach the school and find Rose. The sound of explosions reverberated around her, and the streets were a minefield of debris. As she arrived, she saw teachers leaving the building.

"Where's Rose?" she demanded, her voice laced with panic.

"She left half an hour ago," one teacher replied. "We thought you'd come early to collect her when she said she was going home."

"No, I didn't!" Mary exclaimed, her pulse quickening as fear gripped her.

Mary rushed out into the chaos, desperately searching for Rose. She ran through the streets, leaping over rubble, calling her name, but received no response. Dodging the falling bombs, she searched the shelters and climbed over the bodies that lay scattered on the streets. Shops and houses had been flattened, and debris was strewn everywhere. Rose was just a little girl out there on her own. How would she survive?

Then, another explosion. Mary, along with many others, rushed toward a nearby shelter. It seemed impossible to find Rose in the sea of frightened people. She fought her way through the crowd, stepping over bodies, her voice hoarse from shouting Rose's name. Just as she was about to leave and try the shelter at home, she heard a small, frightened voice calling out.

"Mary, Mary, I'm here, wait for me!"

"Rose?" Mary called out, turning back. The shelter was packed with terrified people, crying and shouting. She pushed past a group huddled near the entrance, following the sound of Rose's cries. She scanned the dimly lit room, straining her eyes through the panicked faces. Then, finally, she spotted her—a small figure curled up in the corner.

Mary rushed to her, enveloping her in a tight, protective embrace.

"Sorry I didn't wait for you, but I thought I would be fine on my own," Rose sobbed.

Mary could only hold her tighter, too exhausted to say anything. Rose was beginning to understand the danger she had put herself in. They stayed in the shelter, eventually drifting into a restless sleep, wrapped in each other's arms.

The night passed in uneasy slumber, and when the air outside grew quiet, they decided to leave and head home, each of them wondering if their house would still be standing.

As they turned the corner, they saw that most houses were intact, but some of the nearby streets had been devastated by the bombs.

When they arrived home, relief washed over them as they saw that their house had not been bombed. They entered the house, and Mary silently thanked the Lord that Rose was safe. She knew she would never have forgiven herself if she had to tell Neville that Rose was one of the bodies on the ground.

Rose peeked through the curtains, but Mary quickly urged her to step away from the window.

"Come on, darling, read your comic while I make dinner," she said, trying to sound cheerful.

The blackout curtains blocked out all light, and while the darkness would usually have been comforting, tonight it was a reminder of the danger lurking outside. Mary's main concern was keeping Rose safe. Though her father had warned her about the evacuation, Mary wanted to make the evening special. She needed to talk to Rose about her departure, which was only a few days away. It was the best decision for her safety, but telling her broke Mary's heart.

After dinner, they cleared their plates. Mary sat Rose down, her voice soft but firm, and explained the situation the best way she could.

"Rose, I'm going to have to send you away," she said gently. "It's the safest thing to do. You'll be able to return after the war ends."

"No, please don't send me away, Mary. I promise I'll be good," Rose pleaded.

"You are good, Rose. That's not why I'm sending you away," Mary reassured her. "It's just too dangerous for you to stay in London any longer." She took a deep breath, her heart heavy. "Come on now, let me get you washed and tucked into bed, and we can talk about all the reasons I have to send you."

Rose reluctantly allowed herself to be tucked into bed, and as Mary pulled the covers over her, the warmth of their embrace was the only comfort in a world growing darker by the day.

"Tell me why then, Mary," Rose asked, her voice small.

Mary took a deep breath. "Okay, so the next group of children will be sent to Yorkshire because it's considered much safer than London. You'll be well cared for, and you'll make new friends at school. And as soon as this war is over, you'll come back home to your father."

Rose listened quietly, her eyes growing heavy with sleep. She fell asleep shortly after Mary began explaining, clutching her comic tightly in her arms.

The government had developed an evacuation scheme, and the assembly points had been announced. It was also made clear that the trains in the capital were running for only nine hours a day. Rose would leave with the next group from the railway station at Sloane Square.

By the end of July, Mary had made all the necessary arrangements for Rose's departure. The children had a checklist of essential items, which included a gas mask, food for the journey, a change of underclothes, a warm coat, and all necessary toiletries. On the lapel of the coat was an identity card with their names, the names of the schools, and their destination pinned to it.

"I feel like a parcel," Rose said sadly.

"You'll be fine, Rose. I know how hard it is to be away from home, but if you listen to the carers and follow their rules, I'm confident you'll do well. And one day, when this war is over, you'll come back home to your father," Mary reassured her gently.

Rose had no idea when the war would end or what might happen next. She was frightened and confused about what was going to happen to her.

"Will I see you again, Mary?" she asked, her voice trembling. "I want to, and I'm going to miss you."

Mary's heart was breaking as she thought about what was to become of them all. "Yes, I'm sure I'll see you again one day."

Mary closed the front door and took Rose's hand as they walked to the railway station together. Rose carried her small, brown, shabby suitcase, with the gas mask flung over and around her neck. She looked back at the home she had shared with her beautiful mother and father for the last time before boarding the train to be evacuated to the countryside.

At the station, there were crowds of children with their parents, all searching for their assigned groups. Led by teachers and volunteers, the children were ushered onto the train. Some were crying for their parents, while others were excited about the train journey. Rose looked tiny and confused among the group under the care of Miss Thomas. Her expression reflected the innocence and vulnerability of the children during such uncertain and dangerous times.

"Don't forget to send me your address as soon as your teacher gives it to you, Rose. I've put a postcard inside your case." Mary hugged her tightly, a tear trickling down her face. Neither of them was ready for what was about to come. Rose was about to start a new life, away from the bombings and dangers of her home in London.

"Quickly, children, we need to get into the carriages," the teachers urged, smiling in an effort to calm the children, though they were clearly trying not to worry them any more than they already were.

Miss Thomas almost had to pull Rose away from Mary, but eventually, the children were all seated. The train grew quiet, but their small faces were filled with fear and uncertainty. Rose looked out the window, her gaze lingering on the officials shouting and the sobbing parents left behind.

Rose was saddened when she saw Mary, tears in her eyes, trying to speak to her through the window. But Rose couldn't hear what she was saying. As the train began to pull away, Mary hurriedly walked along the platform, frantically waving and blowing kisses to Rose.

The children eventually relaxed and, to calm their nerves began to sing *"It's A Long Way to Tipperary,"* with the teachers joining in.

About two hours into the journey, a man in uniform quietly entered the carriage, carrying a small step ladder and a torch. He began removing the bulbs from the overhead lights, one by one, making the train darker. The children, already tense, shouted in protest.

"What are you doing, Mister? It's so dark!" they cried in confusion and fear.

The man's face was grim, his expression determined.

"German planes are flying overhead and, in the distance," he said in a calm, steady voice, "No lights can be seen during air raids. It's all for your safety."

As he drew the blinds on the train windows, he painted the remaining bulbs blue to reduce visibility from the air above. Rose peeked through the edge of the black blind and, sure enough, saw the flashes of explosions in the distance, lighting up the night sky with a haunting glow.

"Do not open the blinds, children!" Miss Thomas shouted.

Despite the warning, Rose's curiosity got the better of her. She needed to see what was happening outside.

Miss Thomas walked over to where Rose sat. "Rose, did you hear me?"

"Yes, I know. Mary told me everything."

"Then remember what Mary told you," Miss Thomas said, her voice gentle but firm.

The children sat in near darkness, the silence punctuated only by the sounds of railway workers running up and down the carriages. It was a long and difficult journey for the children and everyone involved.

One of the younger boys sat next to Rose, trying to offer some comfort.

"Hello, you look sad. But think of this as an adventure. I'm sure we'll have fun," he said, his voice soft in the dim light.

Rose smiled at him. "Most of the children seem happy and are smiling."

"Well, only rich people go on holiday, so I'm thinking of it like that. You should, too. My name's Teddy. What's yours?"

"I'm Rose. And thank you for making me feel a little better."

"Sure thing. We might meet again if our host families are nearby. But for now, goodbye." With that, Teddy returned to his seat.

Eventually, the train came to a stop, and the children were ushered onto coaches. These took them to a large hall in Yorkshire. The billeting officers lined them up on a stage in the village hall and invited potential hosts to choose their evacuees.

Rose looked around at all the men, women, and nurses from the Women's Voluntary Service (WVS) waiting for the children. She hung her head, tears running down her face. She didn't want to go with anyone.

Then a gentle voice broke through her sadness.

"I'll take that one."

Rose looked up to see two nurses standing side by side, smiling warmly at her. She was relieved. Some of the other hosts looked unkind, but the nurses—who looked after people when they were ill—had to be lovely.

The nurses were older, but their smiles were kind and warm. They took Rose's hand and told her to wait a little while until more groups of children were ready to board their coaches.

THOSE MISSING YEARS

An hour later, some children had joined their hosts, while others were still waiting. Finally, the children were on their way to their new homes.

The first stop was in a town called Ilkley. The coach pulled up in front of a large building with big wrought-iron gates, a sign reading 'Middleton Hospital' hanging outside.

Miss Thomas told the children that this was only a temporary stop, and they would stay there for a few nights until more permanent host families could be found. Miss Thomas and several volunteers stayed at the hospital to supervise the children and continue their schooling until their new homes were ready.

The coach left again, carrying other groups of children accompanied by the WVS. It travelled just five minutes down the country lanes to their host families.

Rose decided she would send Mary a postcard as soon as she got to her new home.

The first few nights passed slowly, and the children were kept busy with cleaning to earn their keep. After two weeks, they were told they would be moving again. Once more, the children packed their cases, put on their coats, and waited in the hallway until the bus arrived.

When the bus came, they took their seats, looking scared once more at the uncertainty of what was ahead.

"Where are we going?" some of the children asked.

Miss Thomas spoke softly, "You're leaving for your new homes, and we'll stop at different places to make sure each of you has a safe place to stay. The first stop is an English stately home, run by nurses who will take good care of you."

The bus stopped in front of a grand building. Miss Thomas turned to Rose with a gentle smile. "Rose, this is where you'll stay for the foreseeable future. I know it's a lot to take in, but the nurses here are wonderful, and they will look after you well."

Rose looked up at Miss Thomas, a mix of apprehension and hope in her eyes.

"Will I be safe here?" she asked.

Miss Thomas nodded reassuringly. "Yes, Rose. You will be safe and well cared for."

Rose picked up her small suitcase. As she got off the bus, she turned to Miss Thomas and said, "Thank you, Miss Thomas. Goodbye."

Miss Thomas smiled. "Goodbye, Rose. Take care of yourself."

Rose noticed that the other children remained seated, each waiting for their turn to be dropped off at their new homes.

Teddy waved goodbye. "Maybe we'll see each other soon, Rose," he called out.

"Goodbye," Rose answered sadly.

Rose looked up at Miss Thomas with teary eyes. "Why are the other children not coming with me?" she asked.

Miss Thomas knelt down to her level. "Most of you will be going alone now, Rose, but you may bump into your friends from time to time, as you'll all be fairly close together. Be brave, Rose. You're not alone, and you'll be safe," she said with a warm smile.

Rose walked to the main gate, where she was greeted by a smart elderly gentleman. He bid Miss Thomas goodbye and told Rose to follow him to meet the nurses.

Though Rose knew why she had been evacuated, she still looked sad as she met Nurse Valerie. Valerie had been assigned to take care of Rose and had received details about her, noting that Rose had lost her mother, and her father had been sent to France.

Sensing that Rose might be missing her father, Valerie's face softened, and she smiled gently as she introduced herself.

"It's quieter than London, and there are far fewer bombs falling here. Your father wanted to make sure you were safe while he went to France to work," she explained.

Nurse Valerie took Rose under her wing, sharing that she was born in France. Rose mentioned that her father was also French, and Valerie offered to help her continue learning the language that Mary had started teaching her back in London. Valerie had once dreamed of becoming a linguist, but life had taken her in a different direction. Now, she saw an opportunity to pass on her love of language.

The stately foster home also served as a sanctuary for wounded soldiers, who were cared for by the nurses. Whenever there was a chance, after tending to the soldiers, Nurse Valerie would sit with Rose and teach her new words. They used an old, tattered English-French dictionary. The pages were brown, the ink faded, but they held a treasure trove of words waiting to be discovered.

Rose stumbled over the words, but her determination never wavered. Valerie taught her not only the language but also the stories behind it—the history and the nuances that made it come alive. Rose's vocabulary expanded, and she began to string sentences together.

Valerie's heart swelled with pride at Rose's progress. She saw in Rose the promise of a brighter future. At night, Rose cried, thinking about how quickly her life had changed. She always dreamed of her mother and how much she missed her. Occasionally, she wondered about her father, but she didn't miss him as much. He used to shout at her mother and was hardly ever home.

The next day, she asked Valerie if she could send her postal district and address to Mary in London, so she would know she was safe. Rose guessed Mary would be wondering why she hadn't already sent the address. Valerie agreed and took it to the post office for her.

Rose struggled to fit into her new surroundings, particularly at the local school she attended. The local children referred to the new arrivals as 'vacuees' and, at first, regarded them with suspicion.

Every day, she would tell Nurse Valerie all about her day, knowing how much she cared. In turn, Valerie always made time to talk to her, understanding how lost and scared she was. Day by day, Valerie's support helped Rose gain confidence, and their relationship blossomed to the point where Rose trusted her completely.

It was Christmas 1942 when a telegram from the government was sent to the local official where Rose had been evacuated. The message informed her that her father had gone missing in action and that she should wait for further updates from the military.

Valerie, having received the message, went to inform Rose as gently as she could. However, she found her hysterical, hugging her pillow to her stomach as tears flowed down her face. Valerie recognised that Rose was overwhelmed by the memory of her parents. With the war underway and her life in a constant state of uncertainty, it was hard for Rose to think about much else.

Valerie stayed with her, and they talked about how much safer Rose felt being in the countryside compared to London. Rose was feeling a little better, but Valerie knew she needed to tell her about her father.

"The military will keep us informed of any changes," Valerie said finally.

Rose handled the news well, but she was clearly in shock. "Okay, hopefully, they'll find him."

Two weeks later, Valerie received a letter from the National Service, notifying her that she was to work at St Thomas' Hospital in Southeast London. She was to join a group of women who would tend to the wounded, but before anyone else could inform Rose, Valerie wanted to speak to her first.

Valerie tried to explain why she had been called away and how much the hospital in London needed her. The look on Rose's face when Valerie said she would be leaving immediately was heartbreaking. She tried to hold back her tears at the thought of yet another person leaving her, but Valerie had no choice. There was no other option. Valerie hugged her tightly and apologised, promising that Rose would be cared for by the home in her absence.

A week after Valerie left, Mr Bailey, the man in charge of the home, called Rose to gently inform her that the foster home was closing down, and she would be moving to live with new foster parents, Mr John and Mrs Joan Wilson, on a farm not far away.

Rose was sad to be moving again. After two years, she felt as settled as she could be. The following month, a coach arrived to transfer Rose and the other remaining children from the foster home to their new host families. Rose had almost become accustomed to being moved around, and she hardly reacted. After a half-hour's journey, Rose was the last child to be dropped off, although all the homes were close together.

She saw John and Joan Wilson, an elderly couple, standing by the barn door, waving to the driver. They did not attempt to walk over to greet her or take her suitcase. Their expressions were filled with reluctance, as though they saw her as a burden. They didn't want her—or any child, for that matter. With the war raging on, anyone with spare rooms was expected to accommodate evacuees. The government's payment of ten shillings a week made it more attractive and worthwhile.

"Come here, child," the woman said curtly. "We'll show you where you'll be sleeping, and then we'll explain the rules."

"Rules?" Rose asked curiously.

"That's right. Rules. And don't question us. As long as you're here under our roof, you will follow our rules. Our names are Joan and John, but you will call us Mr and Mrs Wilson. Always remember that you're only here until the war is over. We had no choice but to take you in; we were forced to by law."

"Okay," Rose said timidly, giving her name in a quiet voice.

"We know your name. It was given to us yesterday when it was confirmed that we'd be taking you. Just follow me."

She was taken to a small, dark room that was more like a large cupboard. There was a bed frame with a sheet to lie on but no mattress, and a thin blanket with holes through it to cover her.

"This is your room," Joan said. "Do not turn on any lights."

"Thank you," Rose replied.

Over the next few weeks, Rose was given strict instructions to do exactly what she was told. She was made to scrub floors until they shone, do all the housework, clean out the barn, and eat food that was either out of date or that she didn't like. Every day, she had to walk miles to carry chickens to feed in the cornfields, and it was hard going back to the house because she also had to carry the eggs without breaking any.

Rose was always afraid to return to the house in case she got into trouble for doing something wrong.

"There's always something I do wrong," she mumbled quietly.

It became harder for Rose as she was beaten, mistreated, and verbally abused, simply because they did not want her there. They stole her rations and enjoyed good food, while Rose was given nothing more than mashed potatoes and water. One day, Rose dared to ask for more food, and she was horsewhipped for speaking out, leaving her bruised and bleeding. She could only manage to get through the days by reminding herself that she would return home one day, but the nights were dark, and she cried herself to sleep.

Several months later, in June of the following year, the radio was blaring in the kitchen of the farmhouse, as it often did. Rose, who was over the sink washing dishes, sighed. *I'm sure they're deaf*, she thought, trying to drown out the relentless noise.

Joan sat at the kitchen table. "When is this war ever going to end so that we can get rid of the brat?" she asked John, her voice tinged with frustration.

"One day, one day," he replied, trying to sound reassuring, despite the uncertainty in his eyes.

"Scarper, girl! Get out of my kitchen and stop listening to our conversation," Joan screamed, pushing her towards the back door.

"I was doing my jobs like you asked me to," Rose dared to say.

"Go clean the pigs and be fortunate to be away from the bombs."

It crossed Rose's mind that she would rather be with the pigs than with them. That night, she went to bed in her dark room, which she thought of as her sanctuary—her place to forget about the bad things going on in her life. She could sleep and let the night pass without consequences. The friendly darkness allowed her to rest her eyes and dream of her mother.

Chapter 3

May 8th, 1945, was a date Rose would never forget. She was scrubbing the backyard on her hands and knees while John and Joan listened to the wireless updates on the bombings in London, as usual.

"It sounds like it's all over, Joan," John said excitedly. "Churchill has just announced that the war is over."

"Yes, yes!" Joan shouted.

Rose always listened to the broadcast while doing her chores or whenever she had the chance, hoping one day to hear that the war was over and she could return home. On this particular day, she was outside in the backyard, the sound of the crackling radio in the background, when she heard Joan and John laughing and cheering.

Her heart racing, she dashed into the house and came to a sudden halt, her breath catching, when she realised it was Joan and John who were making all the noise.

John had tears of joy running down his face as he grabbed Joan in his arms, saying, "We can get rid of that brat now."

Rose watched from the crack in the door and saw how happy they both were, but they seemed happier about getting rid of her than about the announcement that the war was over.

How sad. Am I that bad? she thought. On the one hand, Rose was happy that this awful time was over. But then...

"What will I do, and what will become of me? I don't know where Miss Thomas is, and Mary was in London and would have moved on to care for others."

Rose lay in bed, awake that night, thinking about her parents and the best path forward. The announcement still ringing in her ears—the war is over. She had held onto this hope for years, but now that it was here, she felt more lost than ever. The room was cold, and the sounds of the night only heightened her anxiety. She decided she was going to leave. Miss Thomas had been a beacon of hope during the war, a figure she had relied on. But now, with no means to contact her and the uncertainty of the future weighing heavily, Rose felt she had no choice but to run.

"Anything is better than this life," she whispered into the darkness.

While Joan and John were sleeping, oblivious to her turmoil, Rose quietly packed her small bag. She grabbed a torn blanket and gathered what little food she could find in the pantry. She discovered a few shillings wrapped up in paper in a glass bowl on the sideboard and tucked them into her pocket, feeling a fleeting sense of security.

As she closed the door behind her, she took a deep breath, bracing herself for the challenges ahead. She didn't look back, because the weight of the memories and the uncertain peace were too much to bear. Rose ran and ran for all she was worth, her little legs moving as fast as they could. Each step was fuelled by a mix of fear, hope, and the desperate need to go home.

The next morning, Joan went outside and searched the backyard, calling for Rose but couldn't find her anywhere. Puzzled more than worried, she asked John if he had seen her. When he shook his head, Joan sighed with exasperation.

"The lazy brat is probably still sleeping. I'll go and drag her out of bed." But Rose wasn't there either.

"Where are you, ragamuffin?" Joan shouted.

THOSE MISSING YEARS

John stormed through the house, shouting, "The money has gone! The brat has stolen last week's ten shillings we were paid for having her," his face red with anger.

Joan, standing by the kitchen door, folded her arms and scoffed. "She won't get far. She'll be back, just wait and see. She will live to regret what she's done."

"Good riddance, wherever you are," John muttered under his breath, his eyes narrowing as he stared at the front door.

After a moment, Joan sighed. "We should let the authorities know she's run off. We can't have them thinking we did anything wrong. Besides, what if something happens to her?"

John grumbled, "Fine, but don't expect me to care. Let them deal with her."

"Too right," Joan agreed.

As Rose began her long journey back to London, she slept rough in shop doorways or anywhere else that would shield her from the cold. It had been several days on the road, and she knew it was going to be a tough and arduous journey. There was cheering and celebrations all around her, with people dancing, singing, and shouting from the rooftops. The war had just ended, and the streets were alive with relief and joy as people celebrated their newfound freedom.

Curled up on dirty street corners, Rose would peer over the top of her blanket, looking out at the happy people passing by. She heard the upbeat sounds coming from the church and thought about those who wouldn't be returning home from the war. During the journey, which spanned several days and nights, she moved from town to town.

Some friendly people stopped to talk to her and gave her food, drinks, and money, which she put straight into her bag. But others were not so nice, throwing abuse at her and making her feel worse than she already did. After walking for hours through unfamiliar streets, she propped herself up against a wall for a rest, her legs aching from the long trek.

"Little tramp," a young boy and girl, about her age, called out as they walked past her.

Rose ignored them, remembering what her mother had told her about bad people—that two wrongs don't make a right. She didn't know how many days had passed since she left Joan and John's, but after what felt like an eternity on the road, she was hungry, thirsty, desperate for the toilet, and very dirty. When she noticed a public toilet, she hurried inside and washed as best as she could.

As soon as she came out, she went to buy food, but the money was almost gone, despite her efforts to make every penny count. She found a small grocery store and bought a cheese sandwich, which she ate outside, sitting in a corner on the pavement. Her feet were aching, and she could feel the blisters forming. When she got up to resume her journey, the blisters burst, causing her to limp in pain, but she knew she needed to keep going.

Along the way, she stopped some people to ask for directions to get back to London. She couldn't afford to take public transport, like trains or buses, so she thought it was better to save her remaining money for food and drink. After what seemed like a long time of walking, she found herself under a bridge, where she discovered a pile of folded cardboard boxes.

Rose took a couple from the pile, and after making them up, crawled inside, clutching her bag tightly. Surprisingly, with the small, ripped blanket she had stolen from Joan wrapped around her, she was warm and, within minutes, fell asleep.

The next morning, Rose crawled out of her damp box and looked around at the homeless people, most of whom were inside cardboard boxes or dirty sleeping bags. The reality of what she was doing frightened her, but she knew it was better than being at Joan and John's, so she had no regrets.

She resumed her journey and soon came across a public toilet, where she had a quick wash and used the facilities. Feeling a little better, she stopped at a small café for a buttered roll and some water before moving on. Rose had been walking the streets for days, and her blistered feet were sore and painful.

It felt like another world from the one she shared with her parents. People were milling everywhere, shopping, laughing, and having fun. Continuing to walk through unsavoury streets, Rose held onto her bag and hurried past them, scared of pickpockets. She trudged on with no idea where she was, but with road signs and by asking people along the way, she knew she was heading in the right direction.

There were times when she lied and said she was meeting friends but had gotten lost, ensuring that no one would alert the police. By late afternoon, with her aching feet and rumbling stomach, she noticed a five-pound note lying by the bins. Not believing her luck, she picked it up, her eyes scanning the street lined with cafés and restaurants.

She stopped at a small tea house and bought some cheap homemade carrot and potato hotpot. Outside, she sat in a doorway and hungrily tucked into the piping hot meal. At that moment, Rose felt more alone than ever before, but she had made that break, and there was no turning back now.

Sometime later, she stood up, grabbed her bag, and was about to leave when she noticed a young woman walking toward her. She was dressed smartly, with her hair neatly tied back, and she approached Rose with a sympathetic look. Rose thought she wasn't much older than her.

"Why are you out alone, you poor darling?" the girl asked.

"I'm fine," Rose said. "I'm meeting someone soon, so nothing to worry about."

"Well, just be careful until your friend turns up. These streets are not safe for young girls. My name is Ellen. What's yours?"

"I'm Rose."

"That's a pretty name. Are you sure you're meeting your friend soon?"

"Yes, I am. They'll be here real soon."

"Okay, if you're sure, stay safe," the girl said before going on her way.

It had been a long day, and Rose was exhausted. As she headed in the right direction, she knew she needed to find somewhere safe to spend the night. She walked on until she reached an old railway station and decided to settle there. Shivering, she wrapped herself in the ripped blanket, trying to find some warmth. Suddenly, she heard laughter from a group of boys approaching.

Without any warning, they walked towards her, pulled the blanket off her, grabbed her bag, and started tossing it around like a ball, laughing and jeering.

"Please, can I have my bag back?" she asked politely.

"What can we have in return?" one boy asked. He then offered her money, but she refused, scared of what it might mean.

Her mother had spoken to her regularly about safety and being streetwise. Luckily for Rose, the boys didn't bother to look inside her bag, where she kept the little money she had left. They threw the bag back at her, then began kicking her, calling her a tramp.

She pulled the blanket over her head and shut her eyes, waiting for them to kill her.

"Leave her," one of them finally said. "She's no good to anyone."

Before they left, another boy knelt over her and delivered heavy blows to her stomach and sides, calling her vile names. The others laughed and cheered him on.

After what seemed like forever, the torture stopped, and the world grew quiet again. She was sore all over and could feel blood running down her face.

A kind old lady stopped to talk to her. "Can you hear me, my child? I need to get you to a hospital."

Rose could barely speak. "No, don't take me. I need to get back home to London," she whispered, her voice barely audible. The lady could see how weak she was, and Rose didn't have the strength to argue. Luckily, there was a working telephone box nearby. The lady quickly dialled 999 for an ambulance.

The ambulance didn't take long. The lady explained that she had been passing by when she noticed Rose lying in a ball, covered with a bloody rag. She went with her in the ambulance, informing the paramedics of what she knew and insisting that she wanted to stay until Rose regained consciousness. Rose was ill from malnutrition and had been beaten so severely that she almost died.

After a full examination, the doctors discovered she had a few broken bones in her back. The nurse informed the lady that Rose wouldn't have lasted one more night on the streets, and it was because of her that Rose would most likely survive. The lady was asked to fill out some necessary forms, and before leaving her in safe hands, she kissed Rose on the forehead and then prayed for her.

Rose was looked after by the nurses while she drifted in and out of consciousness. They said that, because she was young, she would be able to fight through it. As she awoke, she overheard a nurse and a doctor discussing her case, commenting on how young she looked and wondering where her parents were. She just wanted to get back to London and hope that her father had been found and returned home safely.

It was difficult for her to think about everything she had been through, and she had no idea how long she had been in the hospital or how she even got there. The nurses told her that a kind lady had brought her in by ambulance, and it was because of her that she survived. But Rose had no memory of any of it.

Days turned into weeks as Rose lay in the hospital bed, her body gradually healing. The nurses were kind, always checking in on her and bringing small comforts, such as warm drinks and extra conversations.

"When I leave, could you please tell me where to find the lady who brought me in, so I can thank her?" Rose asked one day.

"I'm sorry, Rose, but because of confidentiality, we are not able to provide any more details. I don't want you to worry about that now; you need to focus on getting better," the nurse replied with a reassuring smile.

Rose turned her mind to other concerns, trying to distract herself from the pain and uncertainty.

"Where am I?" Rose asked one afternoon.

"You're in the hospital, Rose," the nurse replied.

"Where is the hospital? Am I near London?" she mumbled.

"Yes, you're not too far from London," the nurse reassured her.

Before she fell back asleep, they promised to speak with her in greater depth the following morning.

Over the next few weeks, her strength slowly began to return. She often stared out of the window, imagining what life might be like once she was well again. She spent some time reading the books the nurses brought her, trying to occupy her mind and avoid dwelling on the trauma she had experienced.

The blisters on her feet had healed, the bruises on her body faded, and her bones had mended. But the emotional scars were harder to heal. She often woke up in a cold sweat, haunted by nightmares of the boys who had attacked her and the fear she had felt.

Rose gradually regained her strength. She had made some lovely friends at the hospital, especially Sister Victoria, who bore a striking resemblance to how her mother had described her grandmother. She was tiny, with tight, curly, blue-tinted hair and sparkling blue eyes. Rose wondered if she dyed it to match her eyes.

With the support and care she received, Rose was soon well enough to continue her journey home.

Knowing that the day would come when she would have to leave everyone she had grown to care about, she once again wondered what would happen to her. That evening, Sister Victoria went to see her, as she usually did.

"I am going to miss you when I leave," Rose told her. "But I will continue with my journey back to Chelsea."

"I am going to miss you too, sweet child. But as you are only 15 years old and have no one to care for you, we've arranged for you to stay at a youth hostel in the East End of London."

Rose was pleasantly surprised to learn that they had arranged a roof over her head, as she had been sure she was about to start her journey back on the road again. It was even better that the hostel was in London, where she could try to find out more about her father.

Sadly, Victoria told her that many of the houses in the streets of Chelsea had been flattened by the bombings, and Rose's family home could be one of them. She went on to explain that not only Chelsea, but most areas, had been heavily damaged or destroyed. The hospital staff were sorry to see her go, but they had no reason to keep her any longer and were in desperate need of beds.

On the day of her departure, they cuddled her fondly and said their goodbyes.

Victoria, who had spent most of the time caring for Rose, said, "If you ever need me, you can always find me here. At my age, I won't be going anywhere. Goodbye, my angel."

Rose liked being with Victoria and hated saying goodbye, but in a flash, she was gone. Throughout her young life, as quickly as she met some lovely people, they left her. She thought of all the people who had looked after her and grown close to her, beginning with Mary, then Nurse Valerie, whom she adored, and now Sister Victoria.

The regular hospital driver arrived and took her straight to the hostel in Hackney. As they drove, the driver glanced at her through the rearview mirror.

"You must have been through a lot, young lady," he said kindly. "Are you feeling better now?"

Rose nodded slightly, still processing everything. "I'm getting there, thank you."

"You'll like the hostel," he continued. "It's not home, but the people there are good and will take care of you."

Rose managed a small smile, appreciating the driver's attempt to comfort her.

The rest of the drive passed in thoughtful silence, with Rose feeling apprehensive about what lay ahead.

Chapter 4

It had been a long drive to the hostel, but Rose was relieved not to be sleeping on the streets. When they finally arrived at the hostel in Hackney, the driver helped her carry her bag and checked her in before returning to the hospital.

The manager on duty, a stern woman with sharp features and a no-nonsense manner, explained the rules and how the hostel was run. Her firm tone left no room for questions. Rose listened intently, trying to absorb everything despite her exhaustion. After the briefing, she was shown to the dormitory, which she would share with twenty other girls of varying ages. The room smelled damp and sweaty, reminiscent of an unwashed PE kit, but Rose reminded herself that it was far better than where she had spent the last few nights.

The beds were all neatly made with white cotton sheets and grey blankets. Each girl was responsible for washing her own bedding and keeping the area tidy. Shattered from the journey and the emotional strain of recent events, Rose headed to bed. The girl in the bunk across the room was snoring loudly, but after living with Joan and John, Rose felt she could endure anything. Fortunately, the girls and boys at the hostel were friendly and got along well.

Despite her challenging circumstances, Rose was thrilled to be back in the big city after such a long time away. She quickly adapted to her new environment and settled into a daily routine that included cleaning the common areas, helping in the kitchen, and doing the laundry. Though the bustling city was full of distractions, she remained determined to find her way to Chelsea and uncover what had happened to her father.

One evening, Patricia and a group of girls approached Rose with eager smiles.

"Rose, we're going to the local dance hall tonight," Patricia said, her eyes sparkling with mischief. "Get ready and meet us outside by the café on the corner at 7.30."

Rose grinned with excitement. The other girls were already sixteen, while she still had two months to go until her birthday, but she decided to tag along anyway, knowing she wasn't technically allowed inside until she turned sixteen.

Patricia and her friends, toughened by their time at the hostel, seemed to know all the ins and outs of the local scene. When they arrived at the dance hall, Rose could hear the rhythmic thumping of music vibrating through the walls. The air was thick with cigarette smoke, and the sharp tang of alcohol lingered near the entrance. For one evening, she felt she was stepping into adulthood.

Rose was the only newcomer; the others had been before and moved confidently through the space. Some of the group wasted no time dancing and chatting with strangers, while others gathered at the bar to drink and talk. The lively atmosphere swept them up, and they spent hours enjoying the music and camaraderie before heading back to the hostel.

On their return, Rose noticed a couple of the girls had brought new friends back. The dormitory buzzed with quiet chatter and giggles. She felt a sense of belonging as if she had found a temporary escape from her worries.

A few weeks after settling into the hostel, Rose met Tom. He worked in the kitchen, mostly at the back, but occasionally appeared at the counter to serve food. His friendly demeanour caught her attention, and whenever she went to the canteen, she found herself looking out for him.

It seemed as though Tom was waiting for her too. His warm smile and cheeky wink, often accompanied by an extra spoonful when no one was watching, became the highlight of her day.

Rose found herself shy around Tom, but she couldn't help thinking how handsome he was, with his mop of wavy black hair. Neither of them had yet worked up the courage to start a proper conversation.

That week, after finishing school, Rose decided it was time to find a job. She set out job hunting and was delighted to secure a position as a shop assistant at the Co-op department store, working in the hosiery department. Earning £5 a week felt like a small triumph, giving her a sense of independence she hadn't felt in years.

A few weeks into her stay at the hostel, Rose's sixteenth birthday arrived. Birthdays for her were usually quiet affairs, barely acknowledged since her mother's passing when Rose was seven. This time, though, she mustered the courage to mention it to Tom. What better excuse to finally have a proper conversation?

"Let's meet and talk after I finish work," Tom suggested. "Is that alright with you?"

"Yes, that would be fine," Rose replied, her voice barely above a whisper.

"Alright. Be outside at 8 o'clock," Tom added, his attempt at confidence masking his nerves.

He had thought about her often but resisted the urge to seem too eager. That evening, as the time neared, Rose stepped outside to the spot he'd mentioned. Sure enough, Tom was waiting.

They walked to a quiet place to sit and talk. Rose hesitated at first but soon began sharing bits of her past. She spoke of her earliest, happiest memories with her family, her mother's warmth, and the last birthday she'd celebrated properly, at seven years old. She avoided delving into the more painful parts of her past for now, focusing instead on the journey that had brought her to the hostel.

Tom listened intently, sensing the sadness behind her words. Her eyes carried the weight of loneliness, but he didn't press her to say more. Instead, he offered quiet understanding, knowing she would open up when she was piqued.

She seemed so fragile, and all he wanted to do was hold her and protect her. He liked her immensely but hesitated to reveal his age—twenty-four—deciding to keep that detail to himself for a little longer.

Over the next few weeks, their meetings became a regular and cherished part of their days. They spent time talking and laughing, and Rose felt a growing sense of comfort around him. Though they didn't kiss or cuddle, their connection deepened as they looked forward to these moments together, squeezed in between Tom's work, her chores, and her schoolwork.

One day, during one of their conversations, Tom mentioned an old barn not far from the hostel grounds.

"It's been locked up for as long as I've been here," he said, nodding towards a path.

Rose's curiosity piqued. "How long have you been working here, Tom?"

Tom paused, a faint smile tugging at the corners of his lips. "About four years now."

"And before that?" she asked, leaning in slightly, her interest genuine.

He shrugged, attempting to sound casual. "Oh, a bit of this and that. Spent some time on the streets, begging. Then someone kind told me about this place, and I've been here ever since."

Quickly, he changed the subject. "Anyway, enough about me."

Rose felt a thrill at the idea of a hidden spot for them to explore. They made their way to the old barn. She watched as Tom pried away some loose wooden panels at the back, the aged boards creaking as they gave way to reveal a small entrance.

Tom slipped eagerly through the barn's opening, but the unholy stench of manure and filthy straw nearly knocked him back. "Come on, quick!" he called to Rose, motioning for her to follow so they wouldn't be seen.

Despite the overpowering smell, Rose entered, drawn by the excitement of their secret meetings. They cleared a corner and made a small space to sit. Over the next few visits, they spread out some old rags they had found to make it slightly more comfortable.

For Rose, these moments became precious. She valued Tom's company above all else, even if it meant enduring the barn's unpleasant conditions. In time, Tom became her closest friend. One day, he arrived with food and drink he had managed to sneak from the kitchen. As they sat together, he reached into his pocket and pulled out a packet of Woodbines and matches, offering them to her.

Rose shook her head with a polite smile. Tom shrugged, lighting a cigarette and taking a long drag. The strong scent of tobacco filled the air as she watched him, noticing how mature he seemed—more like a man than a boy. She found herself liking that about him.

THOSE MISSING YEARS

They spent hours talking during their meetings. Tom was unfailingly kind, listening to Rose with genuine interest and care. He gave her his full attention as she spoke of her fears, dreams, and emotional turmoil. She confided in him about her mother's death, her father's departure to war, and the heartbreak of being evacuated. The end of the war, which should have brought relief, had instead marked the shattering of her dreams of becoming a ballet dancer, a path she had longed to follow in her mother's footsteps.

Tom offered unwavering support. He didn't judge her or dismiss her pain; instead, he encouraged her to keep striving and to hold onto her dream of dancing, even when she felt it was out of reach.

The barn, with its weathered wooden beams and dusty corners, became their sanctuary. The faint scent of straw mingled with the warmth of shared laughter and whispered dreams. Each meeting brought them closer, their connection deepening into something unspoken yet profound.

One afternoon, as golden light filtered through the cracks in the barn's walls, Tom finally gathered the courage to tell Rose his age. The tension in the air was palpable as he braced himself for her reaction. But Rose just smiled, her eyes full of understanding. "It doesn't matter," she said simply.

Reassured, Tom felt their bond grow even stronger. One day, as they sat together in the barn, he leaned in and kissed her for the first time. It was a moment of tenderness, yet it also carried the weight of something far more complicated.

Their meetings continued, each one a lifeline for both of them. Tom often brought small tokens of affection—food, drink, and his quiet support. He enjoyed watching her as she worked on her homework, feeling at peace simply being in her presence. Over time, they began holding hands and sharing more kisses. Rose, however, reminded herself and Tom that she wasn't ready for anything too serious.

One evening, as they sat close in the barn, Tom looked at her with a mix of tenderness and hesitation. "You're so beautiful," he said softly. "I think I'm falling in love with you, Rose."

Her heart fluttered at his words, but she knew their situation was far from simple. Tom was aware of the risks too—she was only sixteen, too young to fully grasp the consequences of a deeper relationship.

Despite his growing feelings, Tom sometimes struggled to control his emotions. One evening, as their connection deepened, he leaned in, unable to resist. Rose, though flattered by his attention, knew they had to stop. She gently pulled away, explaining, "Tom, I can't. I'm afraid of getting pregnant. A baby isn't something I want in my life right now."

Though naïve in some ways, Rose was acutely aware of the dangers of having sex. Yet, despite her clear boundary, Tom didn't listen.

Tom repeated softly, "I love you, Rose."

"You said you think you're falling..." Rose began, her voice uncertain.

"I meant I know I am," he interrupted, his tone steady and sure.

"I care about you too, Tom. But let's just enjoy our time together and not rush into anything." She smiled faintly, though her thoughts swirled with questions. She liked him deeply, but did she love him? She wasn't sure. Still, she didn't stop him, even though the last thing she wanted was a baby. They had been careful to keep their meetings discreet, always hoping no one would notice them.

Just six weeks later, Rose started feeling unwell. Nausea greeted her each morning and stayed with her throughout the day. Certain smells made her gag, and her body felt heavy and different. When she missed her period, the realisation dawned on her, and she finally confessed her symptoms to Tom.

His reaction was a volatile mix of fear and frustration. "We need to go to the drugstore and ask them. They'll know what to do," he said, his voice firm but laced with anxiety.

Rose nodded, her heart pounding. "Yes, of course."

They walked in silence to the nearest drugstore, each step heavy with unspoken fears. Upon arrival, Rose asked to speak with the pharmacist, hoping for discretion and understanding. She couldn't shake the feeling that someone might recognise them, and the mere thought made her stomach churn.

"He's busy at the moment," said a young female assistant, her tone clipped and impatient.

"This is important and private. Could you please ask him to see me?" Rose asked nervously.

Tom's frustration boiled over. "This is important. Get him now," he snapped, his voice sharp.

The assistant stiffened, her expression turning icy. "Shouting at me won't help," she replied calmly. "Wait here, I'll speak to him."

Rose was startled by Tom's outburst but reasoned it was his nerves getting the better of him. While they waited, she paced the aisle, her hands trembling. Finally, the pharmacist emerged—a stern-looking man with greying hair wearing a crisp white coat. He glanced at Tom, his disapproval plain.

"Young man," he said firmly, "do not shout at my staff. It's unnecessary and won't get you anywhere." Then, turning to Rose, he added, "Come round to the back."

Rose followed him into a small room behind the counter. The faint smell of old medicines filled the air, intensifying her unease. The pharmacist shut the door, his expression softening slightly as he addressed her.

"Now, tell me what's troubling you," he said gently.

"I... I think I might be pregnant," she admitted, her voice barely above a whisper. "I've missed a period and... I'm not sure what to do."

The pharmacist sighed deeply. "I see. Look, I can offer some advice, but you need to see a doctor. They won't usually examine you until you've missed two periods, but it's still important to take care of yourself. Rest, eat well, and try to avoid stress."

Rose nodded, tears welling in her eyes. "Thank you. I'll go to the surgery now."

He offered a small, sympathetic smile. "If you need someone to talk to, there are support groups for women in similar situations. It can help to share your worries with people who understand."

"I'll think about it. Thank you," she said softly.

As they returned to the shop floor, the pharmacist turned to Tom. "Young man, I expect you to apologise to my assistant."

Tom's jaw tightened. He looked away, refusing to apologise.

Rose quickly intervened. "Tom, I'm going to see a doctor to confirm everything."

"I need to get back to work," he said abruptly. "Come and see me when you're done."

"I will, Tom." Rose leaned in to kiss him, but he pulled away, turning on his heel and rushing out the door.

She stood frozen for a moment, a confused frown crossing her face. His reaction gnawed at her, leaving her to wonder if something else was weighing on his mind.

"Bye, Tom," she called after him, her voice tinged with uncertainty.

As Rose set off for the surgery, a mix of fear and determination surged within her. She didn't know what the future held, but she resolved to stay strong for herself—and for the life she might be carrying.

When she arrived, she approached the receptionist, a woman with a warm yet preoccupied expression.

"Can I see a doctor? It's important. The pharmacist advised me to come here," Rose said quietly.

The receptionist nodded. "Take a seat in the waiting room, please. There's only one doctor on duty today, so it may take some time."

Rose thanked her and entered the waiting area, where ten other patients were waiting. Despite the long queue, she didn't mind. Time felt like a blur, her thoughts consumed by uncertainty.

Two hours later, her name was called. She rose quickly, her legs trembling slightly as she walked to the doctor's office.

Knocking gently, she opened the door to find the doctor engrossed in his paperwork. He was middle-aged, with dark hair flecked with grey and spectacles perched on his nose, giving him an air of quiet authority. Without looking up, he gestured toward the chair opposite his desk.

Rose sat down, clasping her hands nervously in her lap. The silence was heavy until the doctor finally looked up, his piercing eyes softened by a hint of curiosity.

"What brings you here today?" he asked, his voice even and professional.

Rose took a deep breath. "I've missed a period, and… I don't know what to do," she admitted, her voice trembling.

The doctor studied her for a moment before nodding. "Lay on the examination bed behind the curtain," he instructed his tone slightly gentler.

Her pulse quickened as she complied, the crinkling of the paper-covered bed loud in the silent room.

The doctor performed a brief examination, his touch professional yet kind. "I can't confirm anything just by this. We'll need to run some tests to be sure," he said, his tone matter-of-fact but not unkind.

Rose's heart raced. "What should I do next?"

He began scribbling on a form. "I'll schedule an appointment for you at the local hospital. But before that, you'll need to register as an expectant mother."

"Thank you, doctor," Rose said, her voice shaky but sincere.

She left the surgery and returned to the hostel to find Tom on his break, leaning against the wall in a quiet corner.

"Go straight to the hospital and register. We'll talk later," he said briskly, his tone betraying a mix of concern and impatience.

The hospital wasn't far, and Rose made her way there with a sense of urgency. The staff, already aware of her referral, worked under the assumption she was pregnant. She filled out the necessary forms, her hands shaking slightly.

A nurse guided her through the next steps. "We'll conduct a pregnancy test to confirm everything," she explained, handing Rose a prescription for iron tablets. "We'll also schedule you for prenatal clinic visits to monitor your progress."

The weight of her situation pressed down on her. As the nurse measured her blood pressure and offered nutritional advice, Rose's thoughts drifted. What would it have been like to tell her mother? Would her father have been angry or supportive? She ached for the guidance she couldn't have.

Her second visit to the hospital confirmed what she had feared—she was pregnant. The news felt both surreal and terrifying.

That evening, Rose met Tom at the barn. The space that had once been their sanctuary now felt heavy with unspoken tension.

Sitting together in the quiet, Rose finally broke the silence. "Do you love me, Tom?" she asked, her voice barely above a whisper.

Tom looked at her, his expression unreadable. "Yes, of course, I do. And we'll get married if that's what you mean."

Although Rose believed marrying Tom was the right thing to do, something felt missing. It wasn't the way she had imagined it. He seemed different—distant, even. She liked him, but was he her "knight in shining armour"? She knew neither of them wanted a baby right now, but it was too late to change that.

While staying at the youth hostel and searching for housing, they continued meeting in the barn to plan their future. The decision to marry seemed inevitable. Their wedding at the Chelsea Registry

Office was brief and understated, with only Tom's older brother and his wife as witnesses.

Afterwards, they moved into a damp basement flat in a poverty-stricken estate in the East End of London. The neighbourhood was bleak, but it was all they could afford. Tom left his job at the hostel and took work as a trainee chef at a nearby restaurant, though the pay was meagre.

Tom was hardworking and dedicated, rarely taking a day off, even when he was sick. Every Friday night, he handed Rose his pay packet after keeping back a small amount for tobacco and beer. At first, he seemed supportive, frequently asking about her health, patting her growing belly, and talking about their future as parents.

But over time, something shifted. His once-loving demeanour hardened into indifference. He stopped asking about her day or showing her affection. He began spending more time at work and came home irritable, snapping at her over small things. Sometimes his words stung deeply, though Rose tried to dismiss them as signs of exhaustion and stress. When she asked why he was so sharp with her, he dismissed her concerns, accusing her of imagining things.

It wasn't just the absence of physical intimacy that hurt—it was the absence of attention, the lack of warmth. She began to see how shallow his love for her truly was.

Rose tried to focus on her own responsibilities. Her body was changing rapidly, and she was struck by how much she had grown. Her waist had disappeared entirely, and she felt heavy and cumbersome. Soon after moving into the flat, she left her job at the Co-op and found work in a factory as a machinist, sewing underwear. The job paid seven pounds a week and allowed her to sit during the long hours, but the work was exhausting.

THOSE MISSING YEARS

She kept at it until the baby was born, knowing every penny mattered. Life was already difficult, and motherhood would bring even greater challenges.

One morning, a letter arrived in the post from the Chelsea and Westminster Building Society. Rose opened it with curiosity and was stunned by its contents. The letter revealed that her late mother had left her a small sum of money, which she could access on her eighteenth birthday.

Three months later, when that day arrived, Rose made an appointment with the building society. There, she learned the exact amount—£1,000. The news was bittersweet. The money was a gift from her mother, a reminder of the love she had lost too soon.

Rose decided to keep the inheritance a secret from Tom. She felt uneasy about their relationship and knew she might need the money someday—for herself or her child. She asked the building society to hold onto the funds for her, leaving them as a hidden safety net for an uncertain future.

Chapter 5

It was September 1949 when Cosuda was born. Rose looked at the fragile bundle cradled in her arms as if it were someone else's child. Instead of the overwhelming love and selfless devotion she expected to feel, there was only a void. She provided all the necessities—food, clean clothes, and care—but her heart remained closed. The issue was not with Cosuda; it was with her. Rose wasn't sure if she was longing for her old life with her mother or grieving the loss of Tom's interest in her.

Her pregnancy had been easy, and the birth straightforward, but she knew she had become a mother several years earlier than she had planned. Consumed by guilt and shame, she didn't feel prepared for the role. She saw less and less of Tom and convinced herself that his absence was the cause of her postnatal depression. In those early weeks, Rose found no joy in staying home with her baby. When Cosuda cried, Rose would cover her ears and cry as well.

A year later, when Cosuda's final immunisation was due, Rose took her to the GP's surgery. There, she broke down in front of the practice nurse. It was a relief to express her feelings openly. Over time, something shifted. One day, Rose noticed the vulnerability in her daughter's eyes—a need for acceptance that mirrored her own childhood. She remembered how much her own mother had loved her. Overwhelmed by a sudden warmth, she picked up her child and cradled her against her chest. The warmth of Cosuda's little body melted the ice encasing her heart. Looking into her daughter's eyes, she whispered, "I love you, my sweet girl." At that moment, Rose finally bonded with her baby. While she loved her deeply, she always worried it might not be enough.

Her marriage, however, was in tatters, and Rose knew it would never recover. For the next few years, she endured her unhappiness, doing her best to create a stable life for Cosuda. Her daughter was a cheerful little girl who loved music and danced happily around the house with her player always on. Rose was a full-time mum, housewife, cook, and cleaner, just as Tom had always wanted. He never wanted her to work, meet people or have independence. Increasingly controlling, he became a bit of a bully.

The £1,000 her mother had left her in inheritance, was a secret Rose never wanted Tom to know about. They had little money and could barely survive on Tom's wage, so she told him she needed to go back to work, which was easier now that Cosuda was in school.

Tom grudgingly allowed her to take a part-time at the factory, though this meant Cosuda had to take on more household chores.

Rose taped a list of tasks to Cosuda's bedroom door, and her daughter dutifully completed them every day, never missing a single one. Rose would inspect the furniture, running her finger across its surface to ensure no speck of dust remained. This rigid standard of cleanliness had been ingrained in Rose during her own childhood under Joan and John's strict rules, and she passed it on to her daughter without question.

With her marriage crumbling, Rose once again found herself failing to give Cosuda the love and attention she deserved. Yet Cosuda remained a happy, lively girl, proud to help her mother keep the house immaculate. Outside of school and her chores, Cosuda ran errands and learned to fend for herself while her mother was at work. She completed her tasks with a quiet hum, often dancing as she worked. Her dream was to become a dancer, just as her mother had once longed to be.

"I'm going to dance in front of lots of people on a stage," she told herself one day.

She was gifted with a natural grace that dazzled anyone who saw her. Her petite, slender frame was perfectly suited to dance, and her striking blue eyes and long, dark, curly hair framed a delicate, pretty face. At home, however, she wore simple, patched-up clothes—a long, thin cotton dress held together with safety pins and clumsy black shoes with holes in the soles. There was no money for new clothes or luxuries, and even food was a constant struggle.

That evening, after Rose had finished work, she sat Cosuda down for a talk.

"I would like that," Cosuda said, smiling lovingly at her mother.

Rose hesitated before speaking, her voice soft and full of emotion. "I'm sorry I haven't always told you this, my darling girl, but please know that no matter what happens, I love you very much."

"I love you too, Mummy," Cosuda replied, wrapping her arms around her mother in a tight cuddle.

Rose began to share memories of her own mother, describing how Cosuda reminded her of her grandmother. She told stories about how wonderful her mother had been—how beautiful, graceful, and adored she was by everyone. Her grandmother's hair was always neatly tied in a bun, and her smile seemed to light up every room. Rose recounted how her mother had danced beautifully, with a promising career ahead of her, before falling ill and passing away suddenly. Her death mirrored that of her own mother, although Rose's grandmother had lived to an old age.

Even though Cosuda had never met her grandmother, her mother's vivid stories made her feel as though she knew her. Each word revealed how deeply Rose cared for her daughter.

"What about Grandad?" Cosuda asked curiously.

THOSE MISSING YEARS

Rose's expression softened. "He went missing during the war, sweetheart. That's all I know for now."

"That's sad," Cosuda said, her face thoughtful. "Your daddy and my daddy are both missing."

"It is sad," Rose agreed. "But maybe one day, we'll find out what happened to him."

Over the following month, Rose and Cosuda grew closer. Rose became more affectionate, and Cosuda seemed happier than ever. Gradually, Cosuda stopped asking about her father and why she never saw him.

"He's busy at work right now," Rose would say, trying to mask her unease.

One evening, Rose came home from work looking pale and exhausted. Cosuda, noticing her mother's weariness, approached her with concern.

"Are you okay, Mummy?" she asked.

Rose looked into her daughter's small, earnest eyes, feeling a pang of sadness and guilt. "Yes, I'm okay. Don't worry about me. Thank you for cleaning and preparing dinner, sweetheart."

"That's okay, Mummy," Cosuda said brightly, skipping away.

Before she left the room, Rose called her back. "You're a good girl, Cosuda. Don't ever let anyone tell you otherwise." She kissed her daughter on the forehead, and Cosuda skipped off, smiling.

But as much as Rose cherished her daughter, she couldn't shake the feeling that something was missing. She knew she would have to uncover the truth about her father someday. She wouldn't rest until she did.

Later that evening, Rose lay in bed, her mind swirling with thoughts of the future. "It won't be long now," she whispered to herself. "I need to leave Tom and go to France to find out what happened to my father." Nervous but determined, she felt a mixture of sadness and excitement.

Over the years, Rose had come to realise that her relationship with Tom had been a mistake. He was more of a friend than a partner, someone who had offered comfort after her mother's death. But they should never have pursued anything further. As she drifted off to sleep, she stirred when she heard the key turn in the front door.

She never knew whether Tom would come home or not. He opened the bedroom door and slid into bed, assuming she was asleep. She smelled the alcohol on his breath as he turned his back to her and fell asleep almost immediately.

Rose lay awake, as she often did, thinking and planning her escape. Her mind wandered to how much had changed since they'd first met at the hostel. The next morning, as she began to clear the dinner left uneaten on the table, she noticed Tom approaching her from behind.

"Morning," Tom said curtly.

"You were late last night, Tom, and you didn't eat your dinner."

"I was working late," he replied flatly, offering no further explanation before leaving for work. As he slammed the door behind him, Rose jumped, startled, and was jolted from her thoughts. Tom's late nights and the stench of alcohol on him had become all too familiar. She wondered if he was having an affair or if he wasn't well, but to him, a possession rather than a partner. The lack of communication over the years confirmed what she had already decided—leaving him was the right thing to do.

THOSE MISSING YEARS

The next morning, Rose went to the library to search for orphanages where Cosuda could stay temporarily while she went to France. She found several addresses and spent the morning writing letters to each one, which she promptly posted.

Over the next few days, replies began to arrive. However, none of the homes seemed suitable. They offered basic shelter and food, but the staff-to-child ratio was low, leaving Rose uneasy about the care Cosuda would receive. Then, two days later, she received a response from a children's home in Yorkshire. It had a ballet school attached, catering to gifted children or those with wealthy parents.

It seemed perfect for Cosuda. She was talented and loved to sing and dance. Although Rose couldn't afford ballet lessons with the modest amount of money her mother had left her, this home might provide her daughter with the opportunity to watch ballet, if not train in it. Rose comforted herself with this thought, trying to ease the guilt of her decision.

Some children at the home would be adopted, others might pursue a career in ballet, and some would simply leave when they reached the appropriate age. But Rose had no intention of leaving Cosuda there indefinitely. She told herself she would return for her one day—she just didn't know when that would be.

Rose made up her mind. This was the best option for Cosuda when she went to France to uncover the truth about her father. It would be a long journey to Yorkshire, and she knew it might stir up painful memories from her own childhood, but her daughter's future came first.

Three days later, she received an appointment to visit the home. Explaining the decision to Cosuda was difficult. Rose told her she needed to find out what had happened to her grandfather and that putting her into care was the best option, as she didn't know how long she would be gone.

"It's the right decision for both of us," Rose assured herself.

The day of their journey arrived, and the train pulled into the station with its rather scruffy carriages. The wooden seats were hard and offered no padding. They boarded, and soon the guard blew his whistle, signalling their departure.

Rose struggled to talk to her daughter during the journey, her guilt weighing heavily on her.

"What if I don't like it there, Mummy?" Cosuda asked hesitantly.

Rose tried to reassure her. "It looks lovely in the leaflet, darling. It's that big house in the country I told you about. There'll be lots of children to play with, and they have a ballet school too."

Cosuda listened quietly, not answering.

The rest of the journey passed in silence, with both lost in thought. Suddenly, the train jolted to a halt. The guard's voice rang out: "Scruton Railway Station."

Rose and Cosuda disembarked, along with a handful of other passengers. Rose asked the guard for directions to St Patricia's Orphanage, and he pointed her down a country lane, explaining that there was no public transport but that it wasn't too far.

As they walked, the light began to fade. The tall, skeletal trees lining the road shivered in the wind, their naked branches creaking above them. Shadows deepened around clusters of twigs, and the cold air seemed to press closer.

THOSE MISSING YEARS

They passed a tall stone tower, its narrow windows aglow with flickering candlelight. The eerie glow cast long, wavering shadows across the ground.

"This must be it," Rose whispered, holding her daughter's hand tightly as they approached the gates.

"I don't like it. It's creepy. What is that building?" Cosuda asked, clutching her mother's hand tightly.

"I'm not sure, but it has lights, so it must be used for something," Rose replied, her voice steady, though she felt uneasy herself.

As they continued down the path, they noticed tall wrought-iron gates looming ahead, their intricate design stark against the darkening sky. The gates seemed to watch them, cold and uninviting. As they stepped closer, the tarnished plaque beside them came into focus. The words etched into it read: *St. Patricia's Orphanage.*

"It's like a prison. Can we go home soon?" Cosuda murmured, her voice tinged with fear.

Rose sighed softly, pushing the gates open with effort. She approached the heavy black door and lifted its ornate knocker. The clang echoed as it fell from her delicate hand, and after a few moments, the door creaked open to reveal a kind-looking young man.

"Good afternoon," he said with a warm smile. "My name is Johnny. I'm the matron's porter and caretaker here at the orphanage. The matron is expecting you. Please, follow me, and when your meeting is finished, I'll show you around the home."

Rose nodded gratefully and followed Johnny into the building. The dimly lit corridors smelled faintly of wood polish and damp stone. Johnny stopped in front of a large oak door and knocked firmly.

"Enter," a stern voice called from within.

Johnny opened the door and stepped inside, gesturing for Rose to follow. "Madam," he said respectfully, "this is Mrs Douglas and her daughter, Cosuda."

"Thank you, Johnny. Please take Cosuda outside and wait while I speak with Mrs Douglas," she instructed her tone firm but not unkind.

"Yes, ma'am," Johnny replied promptly. He turned to Cosuda, "Follow me," he said gently. Cosuda hesitated, her wide eyes fixed on her mother as if silently pleading for her not to leave. Rose bent down and smoothed a stray curl from her daughter's face. "It's okay, sweetheart. I'll be right here," Rose whispered reassuringly, though her own heart ached. Cosuda gave a reluctant nod, glancing over her shoulder at her mother as they left the room. The heavy door closed behind them with a thud, and Rose found herself alone with the matron.

Chapter 6

The matron introduced herself and offered Rose a seat.

"Hello, Mrs Douglas," she said, shaking her hand. "My name is Mrs Hilda Jones, and I am the matron. When I read your letter about Cosuda, I believed she would fit in perfectly."

Mrs Jones was a smart, slightly built woman with silky grey hair and smooth, flawless skin. Rose thought she had kind eyes, but they seemed to expand, giving the unsettling impression that she was looking right through her. Rose decided the matron was trying to weigh her up.

The matron explained that the orphanage was an educational institution, outlining everything Cosuda would need to do to stay there.

"Cosuda will need to work diligently to earn her living and education," she said. "We are funded by public charities, which allows us to provide education, food, and clothing. However, if a child hasn't been adopted or collected by the age of seventeen, they are expected to work and earn their living."

The matron continued, "For example, children are assigned daily chores such as cleaning, gardening, and assisting in the kitchen. Every morning, they attend their academic lessons. We strive to maintain a semblance of normalcy."

We have a ballet school attached to the home for those children with a talent and flair for ballet and dance," she added. They will be evaluated, and some will participate in the lessons. For instance, we have a child who joined us last year, has shown exceptional promise and now performs in recitals that raise funds for the orphanage."

Rose nodded, envisaging Cosuda's potential new life. The matron's words painted a picture of discipline and opportunity, intertwined with challenges and resilience.

The matron made it clear what Rose needed to do to keep Cosuda there, emphasising how fortunate she was because there was only one space left.

"She is used to working hard at home," Rose explained. "She cleans the house and prepares dinner before I return from work, so that will not be a problem for her."

"I will send you my address as soon as I've found a place to stay, and then we will be able to keep in contact."

"Yes, the best option is to write a letter, as the phone line is for emergency outgoing calls only. Not many people have telephones," the matron replied.

"Well, I will be writing frequently," Rose assured her.

Soon after, Rose left the office, followed by the matron, to find Johnny waiting at the end of an exceptionally long corridor. He appeared to be standing to attention. Rose was pleased to see Cosuda smiling up at him.

"He looks like a soldier," Cosuda giggled to her mother.

The matron instructed Johnny to quickly show them around the orphanage and then resume his duties before showing them out.

Shaking Rose's hand, she said, "Good day to you, Mrs Douglas. I will see you in two weeks."

Rose thanked her for her time and said she would be in touch again.

Johnny led them both around the home before taking them to the ballet school at the back of the building. Cosuda was awestruck to find a beautiful building adorned with photographs and paintings of both young and old ballet dancers. When Johnny quietly opened the classroom door, her mouth dropped open at the sight of girls dancing in their elegant pink tutus.

"This could be you one day," he said, smiling in an effort to make her feel comfortable.

"I don't think I'll ever be that good," she replied, her voice tinged with doubt.

He noticed the sadness in her eyes—he had seen that same look before in the faces of other children who had lost so much. Memories of similar moments flashed through his mind, reminding him of the countless times he had tried to bring hope to those in despair. "You never know until you try," he said gently, hoping to build her confidence.

"You'll be part of this magical world one day. Your dreams can dance. Just believe in yourself," Johnny told her with an encouraging smile.

He introduced them to some staff members, who reassured them that, while life at the orphanage would be challenging, Cosuda could succeed if she worked hard. Initially, Cosuda seemed indifferent, but her interest was piqued when Johnny introduced her to one of the ballet teachers. She was listening intently.

"How long have you been working here?" Rose asked Johnny.

"Not long," he replied politely, avoiding any details. He was meant to be working and didn't have time for personal conversations. Yet he couldn't help but focus on cheering up Cosuda and encouraging her to follow her dreams. Work could wait; this moment felt more important.

"Well, it was a pleasure to meet you, Johnny. Come on, Cosuda, we must go. Say goodbye to Johnny; he'll see you again soon."

"I'll see you soon, Cosuda," Johnny said.

"Maybe," she murmured reluctantly.

Although Cosuda struggled to accept that she would be returning to stay, Rose thought Johnny had a good sense of humour and had made an effort to put her daughter at ease.

"Goodbye, Johnny," Rose said as they left.

The train journey home was quiet and reflective. Rose felt a deep sense of guilt, but she reminded herself that it was the best decision for both of them. The matron and the orphanage would provide Cosuda with a temporary home and the opportunity to pursue a career in ballet. Rose believed the matron would soon recognise her daughter's talent. Cosuda was a graceful little girl, and Rose was confident she would one day be grateful for this opportunity.

Two weeks later, all arrangements were complete, and Rose was taking Cosuda back to the orphanage. With no money and few belongings, packing her daughter's small case didn't take long.

When they arrived, the matron greeted them at the door, appearing sterner than Rose remembered. Her grey hair was now neatly plaited, and her bright green eyes were as piercing as ever.

"Welcome, Cosuda," the matron said. "Follow me to my office, Mrs Douglas."

This time, Rose noticed how beautiful the hallway was, adorned with large framed photographs of ballet dancers, both boys and girls.

THOSE MISSING YEARS

Cosuda removed her coat, but she clung to her mother, sobbing inconsolably until they sat in the living area.

"You should leave now," the matron said firmly, aware that the child's tears wouldn't stop until her mother had gone. "Say goodbye to your mother, child, and come with me."

Rose knelt to embrace her daughter tightly and whispered, "I love you. One day, you'll understand. I promise I'll return, and I'll write to you frequently." Tears streamed down her face as she kissed Cosuda goodbye.

Though terrified and unwilling to let her mother go, Cosuda finally let the matron lead her away. Rose assured her that hard work could lead to a great future.

As she walked away, Rose felt an unbearable sense of loss but kept reminding herself that this was necessary for their future.

She hugged her and kissed her lips, as her tears kept coming. Having never been away from her mother before, she was terrified and did not want her to leave her there. But Rose assured her that if she worked hard, it could be a good start to a great future.

"You know I need to go to France, and it's important for you to get to know your grandfather," she told her. "It's not forever; I will be back." Tears blurred her vision as she watched her mother walk away. Rose felt like she was abandoning her, but there was nothing she could say or do to stop it.

The matron walked down the corridor with Rose in silence. When they reached the main outside door, Rose thanked her and repeated, "I will be back, I just don't know how long it will be. Please look after my daughter, she is a sweet girl who will not cause you any problems. I will write as soon as I have an address."

The matron looked at her and nodded.

"We will," was all she spoke.

Walking back down the country lanes, Rose hung her head like a dying flower. The walk back to the train station seemed to last forever, as she blinked away the tears the entire way. She had no time to reflect on what she'd done because she knew she had a short time to pack and leave before Tom arrived home.

With only the money her mother left her, she was able to travel to France, to discover exactly what happened to her father. Once she arrived back in London, she went to a travel agent and booked a flight to Normandy for late that evening. Panic and fear were an instinct, but she needed to relax and focus on her father.

After she arrived back home, she gathered her belongings together in a small brown torn and battered suitcase. She put her money and passport in her bag before sitting down to write a letter to Tom.

Dear Tom

This letter is long overdue. I am sorry to say that I have left you. I have gone to France in search of my father.

I often reflect on the time we met and the fun times we spent together. Our conversations are over; there are no responses to any questions I ask, just a roll of the eyes and a grunt. Sometimes you don't even come home, and you tell me you're working. The pressure makes me want to scream.

Neither of us planned to have a baby, but I accepted it, while you never did. I have taken Cosuda to a children's home in Yorkshire (the address is at the back of this letter), where she will be well cared for. When the time comes, she will be reunited with me.

THOSE MISSING YEARS

The tides have shifted, and what I once believed to be love that would hold us together has now passed. This is why I have decided to leave you.

We were never meant to be together; we should have stayed friends.

I wish you well.

Rose

The wind had been howling all evening, its intensity growing as the hours passed. Now it rattled the windowpanes, a reminder of the storm outside. She walked across the old timber floorboards into her dimly lit bedroom for the final time. The grey-painted walls, once striking, now bore the scars of time. Standing there, her gaze swept across the flat, its air faintly scented with lavender—the lingering aroma of the sachets she kept in her drawers, a comforting reminder of her mother.

Her fingers trembled as she turned the key in the rusty lock, securing the front door. It was the last time she would hear the clunk of the latch. With a heavy heart, she stepped back, leaving the memories—and the life she once knew—behind forever.

Chapter 7

Cosuda was led to the dormitory by one of the older girls, where she would share the space with thirty others aged between five and fifteen. When they turned sixteen, they were moved to a separate dormitory.

She looked around, her eyes wide with a mix of anxiety and curiosity.

The older girl introduced herself as they walked down the corridor.

"My name is Susie," she said smiling. "Let me tell you a little about it here. The matron is in charge of us, and she is the Head of the Home. She's strict but also fair. As long as you follow the rules and do what you're asked, you'll be fine. The matron's word is law." By the time they reached the dormitory, Cosuda seemed more at ease.

Susie gestured around the room. "This is where the girls in your age group sleep," she said, pointing to an empty bed. "This bed is for you." Cosuda followed her gaze to see two rows of small, metal-framed beds lining the room. Each bed had its own small wall cupboard.

"You're expected to keep your area clean and tidy at all times," Susie added. "If not, there are consequences—harsh ones. You might have to go to bed early, do extra cleaning, or even bathe in cold water."

Cosuda nodded, taking in every word. "Okay, I'll be good," she replied, her voice trembling slightly.

She looked around the large, stark room. The white-painted walls seemed sterile, and above her hung a large, ugly ceiling light with a broken bulb. The bedding smelled faintly of unwashed feet and felt as rough as sandpaper. Every bed had the same setup: a single pillow and a dark grey blanket.

At the far end of the room, an elderly woman sat silently. Her skin was thin and papery, and though she smiled faintly, she didn't say a word. Cosuda wondered why she was there, but assumed it was to ensure everyone behaved.

"I'll leave you to unpack," Susie said gently. "Once you're done, I'll come back to help you get cleaned up before you meet the matron."

"Thank you," Cosuda said timidly, still glancing occasionally at the silent women.

As she unpacked her small case, her thoughts churned. Why was this happening? Coming to France to look for her grandfather wasn't reason enough for her mother to abandon her. She hadn't seen her father for days and wondered if he even knew she was there.

"I'm an orphan, then," she whispered to herself, the realisation sinking in.

Her mother had never said she was unhappy at home, but Cosuda had always sensed her sadness. All she could hope for now was that her mother would return soon.

The dormitory was eerily quiet, with the other girls in lessons. The only sounds were her shallow breathing and the ticking of the clock. She watched the big hand move ten minutes forward, feeling a confusing swirl of emotions. All she wanted was for her mother to hold her and make everything better. But deep down, she knew she had to adapt, to survive.

Half an hour later, Susie returned.

"I'm glad to see you've unpacked," she said warmly. "Now, let's get you tidied up before you meet the matron."

Susie guided her to the bathroom, her presence comforting and reassuring. She helped her wash, chatting softly about the daily routines of the dormitory. She plaited Cosuda's long hair neatly down her back and dressed her in a crisp white cotton dress, a black cardigan, black socks, and sturdy lace-up shoes.

"There you are," Susie said, stepping back to admire her work. "You look perfect. Ready to see the matron?"

Cosuda nodded nervously, feeling a bit more at ease thanks to Susie's gentle demeanour.

Susie gestured toward the silent elderly woman in the dormitory. "That's Ethel. She used to be one of the dance teachers, but after losing her husband, she stopped speaking. She's lovely, though, and now she helps keep things running smoothly here."

Ethel stood and motioned for Cosuda to follow her. The two walked down a long, dimly lit hallway until they reached a heavy black metal door. Ethel unlocked it, guided her inside, and pointed to a chair. She smiled gently before stepping back and closing the door with a loud clang.

As Cosuda sat, she couldn't help but wonder about Ethel. She noticed how Ethel's eyes seemed to speak volumes, conveying a depth of sorrow and wisdom. Despite her silence, there was a comforting presence about her, as if she had seen and survived more than anyone could imagine.

The room was dark and musty, the air thick with an unpleasant, old smell. Cosuda coughed, her voice quivering as she whimpered, "Please let me out... I don't like it. It smells."

No one answered. She sat in silence, time dragging unbearably. To distract herself, she began singing softly and dancing—a small comfort in her frightening new reality.

After what felt like an eternity, the door opened, and the matron entered. Cosuda recognised her from a visit with her mother weeks ago. The matron's posture was rigid, her piercing green eyes focused intently on the girl. But there was a subtle softness beneath her stern expression.

"Hello, Cosuda," she said in a serious tone. "Welcome to the orphanage. You'll work hard while you're here—everyone does. Laziness is not tolerated."

Cosuda nodded, too scared to speak.

The matron walked around her slowly, examining her small frame and long legs with a critical eye. After a long, tense silence, she said, "You may not believe it now, but one day you'll love it here. This will become the only life you know."

Cosuda glanced at her warily but nodded again.

"Do you understand what I'm saying?" the matron pressed.

"Yes," Cosuda whispered.

"Good," the matron said. "Now, come with me. Let's visit the classrooms and meet some of the other girls."

Side by side, they walked back into the hallway. Along the way, they passed a girl scrubbing the floor on her hands and knees. She looked up at Cosuda and smiled, despite her exhaustion. Her hands were raw and chapped, her cheeks streaked with dirt, and her tangled hair framed her weary face.

They stopped at several classrooms, briefly peering inside. When they reached the hall, a group of students was rehearsing a dance routine. The matron paused, watching Cosuda closely as she observed the girls' graceful, disciplined movements. Their beauty and strength were mesmerising, every detail of their performance immaculate.

Further down the corridor, the matron showed her the younger group of dancers she might one day join. Cosuda loved to sing and dance, but joining them felt like an impossible dream.

When the matron rang a bell, the dancers and their instructor, Miss Palmer, immediately stopped.

"I'd like to introduce you to Cosuda, who will be living here at the orphanage and may one day join the lessons." The girls exchanged friendly, welcoming smiles, and Cosuda shyly smiled back. Miss Palmer, on the other hand, sent a shiver down Cosuda's spine. The ballet mistress, who ruled the studio with an iron hand, swept her eyes over Cosuda, assessing her lithe frame and delicate features.

Her hair was pulled tightly into a bun, framing her stern face; her sharp eyes took in every detail, and her lips were pressed into a thin line.

"You're new, then?" she said, her voice as sharp as a needle.

"Yes, I am," Cosuda replied, her voice barely audible.

As the girls resumed their lessons, the matron escorted Cosuda to the older girls' studio. Her heart raced as she stepped inside. The room was filled with the gentle sound of a piano, its notes drifting through the air like leaves carried by the wind. The walls were adorned with faded posters of graceful, renowned ballerinas.

The older girls glanced at her with a mix of curiosity and indifference. Some had been dancing for years, their bodies moulded by countless hours at the barre. Cosuda knew she was different; the war had taken her mother, leaving her with a hunger for life that could only be satisfied through movement.

She would have to work extra hard if she ever hoped to join the dance classes and eventually catch up with them.

THOSE MISSING YEARS

The matron introduced Cosuda to Miss Brown, the tutor for the older girls aged ten and above.

Miss Brown smiled warmly. "Welcome."

"Hello," Cosuda answered, thinking how much friendlier Miss Brown seemed compared to Miss Palmer.

The first group of three girls had just finished their lesson, and Miss Brown permitted them to leave.

The matron instructed the three girls to take Cosuda back to the dormitory, show her around, introduce her to the other children, and help her feel at home.

"Yes, Ma'am," Jane said, walking over to Cosuda.

"Hi," she said. "My name is Jane. This is Louise and Betty."

Cosuda looked at them, her eyes wide and uncertain.

Jane, the eldest and tallest of the three, led the way. Her fair hair was pulled into a tight plait, and her blue eyes were bright and focused.

"Follow us, and we'll show you around," Jane said.

The girls took Cosuda to the dormitory and showed her where everyone slept. They pointed out the window, where the moon peeked through the clouds.

"That's our nightlight," Jane said. "It keeps us company when we're scared."

Next, they went to the back of the kitchen.

"This is where you'll spend a big part of your day," Jane explained.

Cosuda listened to their chatter, and for the first time that day, she felt a little more comfortable.

Jane smiled. "You're part of us now," she said. "We take care of each other."

The girls welcomed Cosuda into their fold, teaching her the rules, sharing secrets, and laughing together in the dormitory. They excitedly told her about life at the orphanage and how they had found their way into ballet.

It had been a busy first day, and as evening fell, Cosuda waited anxiously for the rest of the girls to return. When the door opened quietly, they entered, exhausted but happy.

"Did you have a good day?" they asked, talking over each other.

"Yes," Cosuda answered. "It was a good day."

The girls smiled. "Come, sit with us. We'll tell you more about this place before dinner," they said.

Later that evening, the girls helped Cosuda settle into her new home. It wasn't proper nighttime—it was only 7 p.m.—but it was bedtime, and there was no messing about.

"We have long days with schoolwork, ballet, and chores," they explained.

They reminded her not to break the rules, and Cosuda listened intently, thanking them for their guidance.

She pulled back the thin grey blanket, climbed into the crumpled white cotton sheets, and lay down on the lumpy mattress, her thoughts turning to her mother. The light filtered through gaps in the doors and the thinly drawn curtains. She listened to the creaks of the floor above her and the swooshing of oak branches against the rooftop.

Although she wanted to sit up and look outside, they weren't allowed out of bed, so she lay still, staring at the ceiling. The wind whispered through the cracks in the walls, and her mind drifted to her mother. She wondered if her mother had already left for France.

The thought of abandonment filled her with sadness, and she couldn't help but cry.

Hearing her soft sobs, Lucy, one of the girls, sneaked out of bed to comfort her.

"Hello," Lucy whispered, putting a finger to her lips. "My name is Lucy. I haven't had a chance to talk to you yet, but I heard you crying. We'll get into trouble if we're caught talking, but it's not so bad here. You'll be all right."

"Did I see you scrubbing the floor earlier?" Cosuda asked.

"Yes, that was me," Lucy said, smiling.

Jane and a few of the other girls joined the conversation from their beds.

Lucy explained that she had been at the orphanage for three years after losing her parents. She attended academic lessons, dance classes, and helped with chores to earn her place in ballet. She made it sound almost exciting, and Cosuda listened, momentarily forgetting her sadness.

Lucy's bright emerald eyes and long caramel plait matched the freckles on her nose. Despite her small, undeveloped frame, she radiated inner strength.

They didn't hear the soft shuffle of footsteps approaching.

"What are you doing, girls? You know there's no talking after lights out."

They jumped, turning to see Mrs Burgoyne standing in the doorway, her disapproval evident.

"I'm dreaming," Lucy said quickly.

Mrs Burgoyne gave her an unsure look but decided to let it go.

"Get back to your bed, and next time, dream quieter."

Lucy scurried away, whispering to Cosuda, "We'll talk again."

"Can we?" Cosuda asked hopefully.

"Yes, we will," Lucy promised.

After Mrs Burgoyne left, Cosuda thanked the girls for their kindness. They all said goodnight and snuggled down for the night.

Though her parents had left her, and she longed to go back to the carefree days of her childhood, Cosuda reminded herself that she needed to focus. One day, her mother would find her grandfather, and then she would return for her.

For now, all she could do was pray and work hard, hoping that day wouldn't be too far away.

Chapter 8

Meanwhile, Rose caught the train and headed to the airport. Focusing on the minutiae of travel helped her momentarily forget the fear of the unknown. She was heading to Normandy alone, a place where anything could happen. As soon as she boarded the plane, an image of her father from years ago flashed into her mind: his smart, important uniform adorned with medals that gleamed brightly on his chest.

Once seated, she began writing a letter to Cosuda. She had done it—left Tom, temporarily settled her daughter, and embarked on her mission to uncover what had happened to her father.

After a long journey, Rose arrived in Normandy. The weather was cold and miserable, and she was both tired and hungry. She stumbled upon a small diner and ordered French onion soup with bread. The diner buzzed with activity, full of cheerful people laughing and chatting. Despite being a stranger, she felt comforted by the warmth of the atmosphere.

The soup was delicious and satisfying, and the friendly waitress, noticing Rose's lost expression and a small suitcase, struck up a conversation. Rose explained she had just arrived and was searching for temporary accommodation. The waitress kindly recommended a local agency, a small and friendly English-speaking company that could assist. Rose expressed her gratitude, promising to return to the diner, which was a welcoming, family-run establishment.

At the agency, Rose explained her situation and her need for a short-term let. The agent quickly arranged a viewing for a single furnished room in Bastille, just a few streets away.

The room was small but cosy, with freshly painted white walls, pink floral bedding, and matching curtains. The polished floorboards were softened by a small rug. It was immaculate and perfect for her needs while she searched for work. The rent was reasonable, and after paying a week's deposit and a week's rent in advance, she moved in immediately.

Once the agent left, Rose made herself a pot of tea. The cupboards were stocked with crockery, pans, and utensils, and she unpacked her belongings into the small chest of drawers. Later, she visited a corner shop to buy tea bags and milk. Reflecting on her achievements for the day, and the kindness of those she'd met, she lay down, exhausted, and fell asleep.

After an hour, she woke and wrote a letter to the matron at the orphanage, providing her address and asking her to inform Cosuda that she had arrived safely. She also wrote to Tom, sharing her new address in case of emergencies. Feeling productive, she ran a warm bath and went to bed early, determined to rise at dawn to begin her job search.

The following morning, Rose braved the chill of the early air and walked to the library. There, she discovered an area dedicated to job opportunities, marked by a large noticeboard with the words 'Employment Agency'. Approaching the desk, her heart raced. A kind-looking lady greeted her, and after a brief conversation, handed Rose an application form.

She completed the form meticulously, every stroke of the pen a step toward a new beginning. While the clerk reviewed her application, Rose browsed the job listings. Memories of simpler, pre-war times drifted through her mind.

Forty-five minutes later, the clerk called her back to the desk. Rose's palms were damp with anticipation.

"Mrs Douglas, after reviewing your application, I've identified two jobs that could be perfect for you," the clerk said with a smile. "One is full-time, and the other is part-time. They only came in yesterday, so you're the first person I've discussed them with."

Rose smiled. "That's wonderful. Thank you."

The clerk continued, "The first is a part-time position at a post office just down the road from where you're staying."

"I was hoping for a full-time role, but I'd be happy to attend the interview," Rose replied.

"The second position is full-time, based at the archives department in Seine-Saint-Denis, where they hold national military personnel records. It's a more senior role, but it's about a twenty- to thirty-minute bus journey from here."

Rose's heart leapt. This role sounded ideal—both for her career and her personal mission. She assured the clerk that she was more than willing to travel for the opportunity. The clerk arranged an interview for the following morning, and Rose left the library feeling optimistic.

On the day of the interview, Rose prepared carefully. She tied her long curls neatly away from her face and applied light makeup. She wore her only blue printed dress with navy blue heels, feeling both professional and confident.

At the archives department, a polite young receptionist escorted her to the personnel office, where she was offered a seat. After a brief wait, a tall, severe-looking woman in a black dress introduced herself as Miss Lacoste, the personnel manager.

"Good morning, Mrs Douglas," Miss Lacoste said, shaking Rose's hand. She led her into the office, where two senior staff members awaited.

Mr Jackson, an older man with thinning hair, sat at the head of the table, his expression serious. Beside him was Mr Simons, a younger man with a warm, approachable demeanour.

As Rose settled into her chair, her thoughts briefly wandered to the room's décor. The faded elegance of the wallpaper and the worn plush carpet spoke of a bygone era.

Mr Jackson leaned forward, breaking her reverie. "Mrs Douglas, could you tell us about your experiences during the war?"

Rose took a deep breath, carefully considering her response. How could she encapsulate years of fear, loss, and resilience in a few sentences? She decided to keep it concise.

"I'm originally from England," she began. "I was evacuated to Yorkshire in 1940 when my father was posted to Normandy. In 1942, we were informed he was missing and presumed dead. Afterwards, I worked in a factory in London. Now, I'm here in Normandy to uncover the truth about what happened to him."

Mr Jackson nodded thoughtfully.

Rose confidently told the panel that she had strong spoken and written French, a skill she had learned as a child from Mary and later perfected under the tutelage of Valerie, a French nurse at the stately home.

"I'm pleased to hear that," Mr Simons said with an encouraging nod. "Most of our employees are French, and the language is essential for this position."

"They mentioned it as a requirement at the job centre," Rose replied.

Miss Lacoste, elegant and poised with her perfectly styled victory roll held in place by gleaming bobby pins, leaned forward. "And now you're seeking employment here. Why our company?"

Rose hesitated, carefully choosing her words. "I believe my resilience and attention to detail can contribute significantly to your projects. I've learned to adapt, overcome challenges, and persevere—qualities I can bring to this role."

The room fell silent. Rose worried she had said too much—or perhaps too little.

"Resilience and attention to detail," Miss Lacoste repeated thoughtfully. "Admirable qualities, Mrs Douglas."

Mr Simons maintained his kind expression. "Mrs Douglas, determination and adaptability are traits we value highly. Your wartime experiences speak to those qualities, and we need people like you on our team."

The interview process was challenging, with a range of questions about data structures and administrative practices. Rose felt her palms grow clammy, but she held her ground, answering with conviction.

When asked about her experience, she candidly replied, "While I may not have years of formal experience, I've spent countless hours managing finances and learning from previous roles. I believe my enthusiasm and hunger to learn more than compensate for any gaps."

Her sincerity shone through. Miss Lacoste nodded approvingly. "Confidence is often missing in candidates," she said. "You've got it, Mrs Douglas."

After the interview, the young receptionist gave Rose a tour of the grand building. It was as magnificent as the agency had described, with intricate chandeliers hanging in every room. The space exuded history and elegance, but Rose's focus remained on the role's potential to help her uncover the truth about her father.

Back in the office, Miss Lacoste informed Rose she had been selected for the position. "You're a suitable candidate, Mrs Douglas. We'd like you to start your induction next week," she said with a rare smile.

Rose accepted without hesitation, reminded that sometimes the perfect job wasn't about ticking boxes but about finding a deeper connection.

The following Monday, Rose rose early to prepare for her first day. Selling herself as the right candidate during the interview had been one challenge; proving herself on the job was another. Her real hope lay in the archives—one way or another, they could lead her closer to answers about her father.

She joined two other new starters for the induction. Feeling slightly overwhelmed, she took in the vastness of the building and its beautiful gardens, though they mattered little to her mission. The atmosphere was formal and serious, but Rose kept her focus on the work and the income she needed to survive.

After finishing the induction, Rose went to a local grocery store, purchasing only the essentials until her first week's pay arrived. Back in her small room, she wrote to her daughter, sending her new address again to ensure it reached her. She reassured her daughter that she had found work and hoped she was settling in well at the orphanage.

Blinking back tears, Rose sealed the envelope. She missed her daughter fiercely but reminded herself it was temporary. Rushing to catch the last post, she returned to her room feeling a pang of loneliness. Undressing for bed, she reminded herself that she was doing this for their future. Sleep came quickly, and her alarm jolted her awake at 6 a.m.

THOSE MISSING YEARS

Eager not to be late for her first full day, Rose showered, had a quick bowl of cereal, and left for the bus. Thoughts of her daughter lingered—was she being treated well? What was she doing?

As the bus approached, Rose sprinted to catch it, waving her hand just as it was about to pull away. She entered the office building determined to familiarise herself with the archives and, when possible, locate the sections on WWII records.

By the end of her first week, Rose had soaked up knowledge like a sponge. She asked countless questions, sought guidance from colleagues, and refused to let doubt creep in. Her confidence wasn't an act; it was genuine. She belonged here.

More importantly, she knew she was inching closer to uncovering the truth about her father.

Chapter 9

Cosuda woke several times during the night, afraid of what might happen if she overslept. The girls were woken at 6 a.m. and given their chores.

Cosuda's day began before the sun shone through the misty windows. She crossed the room and picked up the broom leaning in the corner, old and tatty from years of use. With quiet steps, she hummed a tune while sweeping the floors and completing her tasks. She had always imagined herself on a stage, the star of the show, performing in front of a large audience.

Moving to the window and gazing out, the world seemed distant. For now, she was at the orphanage, where dreams were impossible and hope was rationed.

And then, the dancing. Cosuda loved to dance more than anything. Her small body moved gracefully, holding the broom as if it were her dance partner. She twirled through the dust on the floor, forgetting her troubles. In that moment, she was free. Closing her eyes, she made a wish—to be back home. But until then, she would keep dancing and humming her tunes.

She never tried to shirk her duties, even the most disagreeable ones, and took pride in keeping her area clean and tidy. She made her tiny, narrow bed to perfection, ensuring the old white sheets and blankets were tucked in straight. She understood little but followed orders diligently, working like a little trooper.

One Saturday morning, while scrubbing the corridor, her small fingers bled. The sharp smell of bleach clung to her, but she was numb and no longer felt the pain.

As she turned, she caught the matron's eye. For a fleeting moment, there was a glimmer of softness in her face and a strange light in her eyes.

The matron played a crucial role in the orphanage. She was tough but fair, ensuring the children's emotional and physical well-being while keeping them safe. Strict about discipline, she commanded admiration from her staff and enforced the rules without exception. Any wrongdoing was met with punishment—hours of scrubbing floors with a stiff-bristled brush or polishing shoes to a shine without the aid of polish. She reinforced discipline with daily ridicule.

The younger children who wet the bed would rise before the others, shuffling to the communal bathroom in their nightshirts to wash their soiled sheets in secret.

After the morning chores, Cosuda gathered the bedding piled on the dormitory floor. Susie led her through the narrow corridor, guiding her to the laundry room tucked away at the back of the kitchens. Some of the other girls were already working, but there was always more to be done.

As Susie opened the door, the air was thick with dampness. A row of heavy industrial machines lined the wall, and washboards were stacked in a corner. The domestic assistant, Mrs Saunders, moved gracefully across the marble floor.

"Good afternoon, Mrs Saunders. This is Cosuda, she hasn't been here long, but you'll be seeing her often," Susie said.

"Hello, Cosuda, I'll show you what needs doing, and you can follow the other girls," Mrs Saunders instructed.

Cosuda nodded.

Mrs Saunders was a strong, broad woman with a crown of silver-grey waves pinned back from her face. Her sharp green eyes missed nothing.

"There's your pile," she said, pointing to the corner of the large room.

"Jane, show Cosuda how the machines work."

"Yes, Miss."

"Make sure all the marks and stains are removed," she added.

"Yes, Miss," Cosuda replied eagerly, not wanting to disappoint as she couldn't risk ruining her chances.

The sheets were badly stained, making it hard work to remove the marks. One of the girls glanced at Cosuda, smiled, and raised her eyebrows, trying not to be noticed. They kept their heads down and carried on. With sweat running down her face, she finally finished scrubbing the stains, the sheets were ready for the boiler.

When the whistle sounded, the girls followed Mrs Saunders back to the dormitory, where they were allowed outside for some fresh air before dinner.

Over the months, the matron kept a close eye on Cosuda. She noticed how gracefully the girl moved, but remained unsure whether she could handle the structured demands of dance classes. Cosuda had the perfect physique for a dancer, strong yet light on her feet. More importantly, the matron recognised her discipline and work ethic.

The following Monday morning, as she passed through the dormitory, the matron caught Cosuda staring longingly out of the window. Pausing for a moment, her expression softened.

"Cosuda," she said gently, "would you like to watch the beginners' dance class today?"

Cosuda had overheard the other girls whispering excitedly about the class earlier that day.

"Yes, I would love to! Thank you," she replied eagerly.

"Good. Come with me," the matron said, leading her down the corridor.

As they entered the hall, the door creaked loudly, catching the girls' attention. They turned to see who had come in and were delighted to spot Cosuda alongside the matron.

She took a seat on a wooden bench at the back of the hall, her eyes widening in awe. As she watched the girls dance, she was transported into another world. This was where she belonged. She couldn't wait for the day she would be allowed to join them. Cosuda knew she would have to earn her dance lessons through hard work, but she was willing to do anything for the chance to be part of the class.

Despite the kindness she had received at the orphanage, after six months, she longed to hear from her mother.

A week later, after finishing her academic lessons, she clutched her tattered notebook and pencil, her brow furrowed in concentration. Her progress was evident; her once shaky and uncertain sentence structure now formed neat lines across the page. Miss Compton, her academic teacher, had noticed her transformation. Cosuda, who once struggled with reading, had turned it into a strength.

"You're doing great, Cosuda," Miss Compton said, patting her shoulder. "Keep going as you are, and you will go far."

"Thank you, Miss," Cosuda said with a small smile.

She returned to the dormitory and changed into her scrubs.

While scrubbing the corridors on her knees, she neared the matron's office and paused as a smartly dressed couple entered. The door clicked shut, muting their conversation, but one word stopped her in her tracks—adoption.

She held her breath. It had been a long time since anyone had been adopted in the orphanage.

She strained to hear, pressing closer to the door.

"Thank you for coming today," the matron's voice said. "We appreciate your interest in adopting one of our children. Let's begin by discussing the age and gender you're looking for."

Then, she heard the man speak.

"We've been considering adopting a slightly older girl, perhaps between the ages of eight and twelve. We believe that would be the right fit for our family."

Suddenly, she heard footsteps and faint voices approaching behind her. Keeping her head down, she continued scrubbing.

"Keep working, Cosuda," the matron's deputy, Miss Thompson, said as she walked past with two other teachers.

Cosuda nodded. "Yes, Miss," she replied, but her ears remained focused on the conversation in the matron's office.

"We are good people with a good home," the woman said. "For years, we have longed for children, but we have never been successful. Adoption is our last hope, and we would greatly appreciate being considered."

Cosuda's heart pounded. She needed to hear how the matron would respond.

THOSE MISSING YEARS

"I only have one girl in that age group, and her paperwork has already been completed," the matron replied.

"Does that mean Lucy is being adopted?" Cosuda muttered to herself. "Maybe Lucy doesn't know yet. It can't be me—my mother is coming back." She reasoned that other than Lucy, she was the only girl of that age in the orphanage. Panic welled up inside her. No, no, please don't take me. My mother will return. She needed to speak to Lucy, but first, she had to keep listening.

"I do not have any girls of that age available," the matron continued firmly, "but I have others I can arrange for you to meet."

"But I heard there's a girl here named Cosuda, around that age," the man said.

Shock coursed through her. How do they know my name? How do they even know I'm here?

"I don't know where you heard that," the matron responded, "but she is not available for adoption. Her mother will come back for her, so she is ineligible. The rules require a child to have been in the orphanage for two years with no contact from next of kin before they can be considered for adoption."

"It was a friend of mine who mentioned there might be children of that age range available for adoption," the woman explained.

Cosuda had heard enough. Heart pounding, she slipped away from the matron's office. It must be Lucy. She's been here longer than I have. She needed to find her and tell her everything she had just overheard.

But a troubling thought gnawed at her. Who are these people, and how have they heard about me?

Despite the matron's reassurances, anxiety settled in her chest. She hadn't heard from either of her parents. What if my mother isn't coming back? Her mind raced with questions, and panic clawed at her.

She hurried back to the kitchen and found Lucy, who was about to take her break.

Cosuda approached her with a concerned look. "I need to talk to you, Lucy. Let's go to the dormitory."

"I need to talk to you," Cosuda whispered urgently. "Let's go to the dormitory."

The girls had formed a strong bond, always looking out for each other. In their limited free time, they shared stories about their pasts, their families, and what had led them to the orphanage. Despite being younger, Cosuda felt a deep responsibility to care for Lucy after learning that both of her parents had died.

"What's wrong?" Lucy asked, sensing her distress.

Cosuda relayed everything she had overheard, her voice barely above a whisper.

A look of concern flickered across Lucy's face. "I haven't heard anything about adoption," she said, shaking her head. "Let's just wait and see."

They waited nervously for the matron to call for them, but she never did. Cosuda convinced herself it was because her mother was still coming for her.

They decided to keep it to themselves.

Despite their different circumstances, both girls felt the sting of rejection. Their friendship deepened, and they clung to each other for comfort. In the evenings, they would sit together on their beds, speaking in hushed tones about their pasts, sharing their fears, and quietly praying that they would never be adopted.

"Before you arrived here," Lucy explained, "even though the girls are lovely and friendly, I longed to be adopted and lost hope that anyone would ever want me."

After losing both parents, it had taken Lucy a long time to feel wanted and accepted as part of a family.

"All I ever wanted was for someone to show me love and to be there for me. I watched others being adopted, but it was never me. I wanted a home, a mother and father just like all the other children. The matron has always been kind to me, but as time passed, I stopped thinking about it. Now, after meeting you and being told that my dancing is improving, I don't want to be adopted anymore, because I'm content."

Cosuda held her tightly, determined to be strong. Whatever happened, they could rely on each other. Cosuda felt the same way but didn't want to sound uncaring and deep down, she still believed her mother would come back for her.

"For now, we have each other. At least we can support one another for as long as it takes," Cosuda said.

It had become a routine for the girls to meet in the gardens after their schooling and chores were finished, catching up on the day's events.

A few weeks passed. One afternoon, Cosuda made her way to the back of the dance studio to watch the girls, longing to be as good as them one day. She knew she had to study hard and took every opportunity to visit the studio. Lucy was the most beautiful dancer, and Cosuda couldn't take her eyes off her.

Later that evening, as she approached Lucy, who was sitting on the garden wall, she sensed something was wrong.

"Is everything okay? Has something happened since I saw you in class earlier?" she asked.

"Louise and Betty were called out of class today."

The girls had whispered behind their hands, their eyes wide with curiosity, all concluding that it must be yet another adoption. The two had never returned. Mrs Brown, their instructor, had hesitated, torn between discretion and openness. She wasn't sure whether to announce it to the class, and in the end, she decided it wasn't her place. The students had held their breath, waiting for answers that never came.

"And so, Louise and Betty vanished, leaving us with nothing but questions," Lucy sighed. "I can't complain because the matron treats me well, and I've grown to love it here, but I still wonder why I've never been chosen. There has to be a reason."

Cosuda listened carefully, wanting to tell Lucy that her mother would take her with them, but she hesitated. It wasn't a promise she could make—not yet. The last thing she wanted was to give Lucy hope, only to see it crushed.

"The matron does seem to be especially kind to both of us," Cosuda said thoughtfully. "But maybe it's because I make sure to do everything I'm asked, and I don't want to get into trouble. My future in dance is far too important. It's because of you that I stay strong and keep going, and when I watch you dance, I dream that one day, that will be me. I don't know what I'd do if you left. In some ways, I feel like I don't have parents either. I haven't heard from them in over a year."

Lucy nodded. "I've noticed that we aren't punished like some of the other girls. There must be a reason." She paused before adding, "At least we have each other. If one of us left now, it would be tough, unless we went together." She smiled.

After their break, Lucy returned to the dormitory to do her homework, while Cosuda remained outside, lost in thought.

The evening was peaceful, but tonight, Cosuda couldn't shake the feeling that everything had changed. Nothing felt certain anymore. The world had become a maze, leading to an unknown destination.

As time passed, Cosuda watched more and more of her friends being adopted by families who visited the orphanage. Slowly, she began to understand her place among them. She realised that, unlike them, she was never chosen. It became clearer each day that her parents had abandoned her.

The absence of their letters and their voices caused her heartache.

The next morning, Lucy was already having breakfast when Cosuda walked in. She blinked in surprise.

"You're early?" Cosuda asked, unable to hide the hurt in her voice. Why hadn't Lucy waited for her as she usually did?

"I woke up early and decided to sit here and wait for everyone," Lucy replied. "But I have to go now," she said, her eyes darting towards the clock.

"Of course. We'll carry on talking later?" Cosuda asked, trying to keep the disappointment out of her voice.

"Yes, as always," Lucy said, smiling reassuringly before she left the room.

Later that day, when they both had free time, they met again. Lucy had never talked much about her past until she met Cosuda, but today, she felt the need to share more.

"My parents told me I'd be better off at the orphanage because they weren't good parents," Lucy began. "At the time, I knew they didn't want me, but I didn't understand why."

She paused before continuing.

"I hadn't heard from them in nearly four years when the matron summoned me to her office. The police were there. They told me that both of my parents had died in a motorway accident."

Cosuda's heart sank. "Oh, Lucy…"

"I was fine at first," Lucy admitted. "I hadn't heard from them in so long that it didn't feel real. But two weeks later, the toxicology report came back. It showed that my father had been drunk while driving, he had the equivalent of ten drinks in his system."

She took a deep breath.

"That's when I learned the truth. Both my parents were alcoholics. And as far as I know, I had no other family. I used to wonder why they didn't want me, but now that I'm older, I realise they had no idea what they were doing."

Cosuda listened, her chest tightening. "I'm so sorry you had to go through that alone."

Lucy nodded. At the time, she had been too young to understand. All she had wanted was to be with them because, for better or worse, they were her world. But after hearing the news from the police, the realisation that she was truly alone hit her harder than anything.

THOSE MISSING YEARS

Shocked by what she had just heard, Cosuda reached for Lucy's hand. "You'll never be alone again. I'll always be here for you."

She felt guilty, suddenly aware of how little she understood her own life. It was different from Lucy's, but in many ways, just as uncertain. Wanting to comfort her friend, she shared her own childhood memories. The good times with her mother.

"I barely saw my father," she admitted. "And when I did, I was afraid of him. He was always shouting at my mother, always angry about something. I thought it was normal, but there's always been this deep emptiness inside me that I can't explain."

She hesitated before adding, "Still, I believe my mother or maybe both my parents will come back for me."

She told Lucy about her grandfather, a man she had never met.

"He was allegedly killed in France during the war. My grandmother died when my mother was just a small child."

Lucy let out a breath. "Well, we certainly got a lot off our chests today," she said with a small smile.

Cosuda laughed. "Yes, we did."

"It's good that we can still smile," Lucy said as she wrapped her arms around her friend. Together, they walked back to the dormitory.

That night, as they lay in their beds, they felt a little lighter. The burden of their pasts had not disappeared, but sharing their stories had made it easier to carry.

Chapter 10

Rose had been working in the archives for eighteen months when she discovered some astonishing facts about her father. A dusty old file she stumbled upon revealed a hidden truth, Neville had held a high rank in the army. As she gathered more information, she learned that he had been assigned to command an army group overseeing all ground forces involved in the Allied invasion of Normandy.

She read that he had been taken as a prisoner of war, but there were few details beyond that. He had been captured and detained in an internment camp in Drancy, near Paris. To her shock, she discovered that he had been sentenced to death for factory sabotage. Then she read that, in 1942, he had gone missing and was presumed dead. She vividly remembered the nurse breaking the news to her.

But if he had gone missing, presumed dead, then perhaps, just perhaps he had escaped the camp and might still be alive. The thought ignited a spark within her. This was just the beginning of her search, and she was determined to uncover the truth.

Rose was prepared to spend as much time as necessary to find him, or at the very least, to learn what had happened. Following her initial findings, she read everything she could about those war years, squeezing in research between work and waiting for the right moment. The last thing she wanted was to be caught. She uncovered the names of several individuals who had served with her father, but every attempt to track them down led to a dead end.

Through careful conversations with the archive staff, she learned that many addresses had been destroyed in bombings, leaving nothing but empty, hollowed-out structures. Yet she pressed on, searching at every opportunity. Eventually, she came across an address belonging to Mr Zach George, one of her father's lieutenants.

At first, she considered writing to him—sending a letter to introduce herself and ask if he would be willing to meet. But she quickly changed her mind. His address was close to her apartment, so she decided to visit him in person after work. If he still lived there, he might have answers about her father's fate.

Leaving work promptly at 5 p.m., she made her way to Mr George's address. The street was dark, lit only by a few dim streetlamps stubbornly glowing into the night. The old brickwork evoked a sense of nostalgia—memories of lives once lived under cloudy skies. She imagined children playing, their laughter echoing against the walls. Yet, in the distance, she could almost hear the faint rumble of warplanes and the wail of sirens.

Had this street remembered the joyous celebrations at the war's end? Or did only sorrow remain?

As she approached the house, she let her hand brush against the weathered bricks, wondering if its abandonment was permanent. Taking a closer look, she noticed the black, shiny hinges on the door, a broken window, and tattered curtains shifting with the breeze.

Then, just as she began to think the journey had been in vain, she saw him. A man stood at the side of the window, partially obscured by the shadows.

Her heartbeat quickened. Summoning her courage, she knocked on the heavy oak door, its surface scarred with deep gouges.

Moments later, the door creaked open, revealing a dimly lit hallway thick with an old, musty scent. Her mind raced as she took a deep breath.

Then she saw him properly, his two powerful arms defying the absence of his legs.

Was he the wartime veteran who had known her father?

He looked at her for what felt like an eternity, squinting with suspicion. But beneath his wary gaze, she saw something else, a sadness.

Seated in a wheelchair, he spoke slowly. "Hello… c-can I help? Do I know you?"

Rose offered a polite smile. "Good evening. I'm sorry to bother you. No, you don't know me, but I'm hoping you can help. I'm looking for Mr Zach George."

He hesitated before replying. "Y-you're looking at him."

Relieved, she took a deep breath. "My name is Rose Douglas. I'm not sure where to begin, and this may sound strange, but I've travelled a long way. I'm searching for my father, Neville Azpax. I believe you knew him. He was a General, posted to France in 1939."

Zach's expression shifted. He seemed taken aback, and for a moment, he said nothing. Then, finally, he nodded. "Y-yes, I knew him. We worked closely together during the w-war."

Though cautious, Zach gestured for Rose to come inside. Nervous but grateful, she stepped over the threshold, and he closed the door behind her.

To her surprise, the house had a welcoming feel. The wide hallway, lined with warm wooden panelling, led her further in. The parquet flooring creaked softly beneath her feet, and along the walls, old photographs hung in neat rows. Many featured men in uniform, but one stood out—a man in the centre with medals on his jacket, an attractive young woman by his side, her neatly styled hair framing a gentle smile, a baby nestled in her arms.

"I'll make us some tea if that's all right with you?" Zach offered.

Startled from her thoughts, Rose turned quickly, not wanting him to catch her staring at the photographs.

"Yes, thank you. I'd love that," she replied gratefully.

As he wheeled himself towards the kitchen, his voice took on an edge of curiosity. "So, tell me a little about yourself. What was the last thing you heard about Neville? How did you find my address? And how did you know I'd still be here? How do you know I worked with your father? And what else do you know?"

His words tumbled out, his anxiety clear. Before he could continue, he took a deep breath. "I'll pour the tea," he muttered.

Rose swallowed her nerves. She understood his suspicion, after all, her father had been missing for years, and here she was, turning up out of nowhere. She had spent months chasing leads, desperate for answers. Now, sitting in front of her was a man who might finally hold the key to unlocking the mystery.

"Can I help with anything?" she asked, watching him closely.

Zach noticed her shifting uneasily in her seat, avoiding eye contact. She wondered about his stutter and suspected he had lost his legs in the war. As if reading her thoughts, he swiftly pulled a blanket over the ends of his trousers.

"I c-can make a drink," he said sharply. "I have arms and hands. Just no legs."

Rose flushed with embarrassment. "I'm sorry… I just wondered how—" She trailed off, then quickly apologised again. "I have no right."

He ignored her awkwardness and handed her a mug of tea. His hands, limp over the blanket, trembled slightly. His red-rimmed eyes stared into the distance, and in that moment, she realised how lonely he seemed.

Her thoughts wandered. Did he have a family? A wife? Children? Would someone come down the stairs at any moment?

Zach interrupted her musings. "Tell me more about yourself. And how you lost touch with your father." His tone remained cautious, his suspicion still lingering.

Rose nodded. "Of course. I understand completely."

Rose began at the very beginning, recalling everything she knew about her father, starting from when she was a small child. She spoke of how devastated he had been when her mother, his wife, had died.

"He needed someone to look after me while he was at work, so that's when he employed Mary. Then the war broke out, and that was the last time I heard from him. He was called up to Normandy immediately, and I was left with Mary, who cared for me until I was evacuated. I was seven years old. That was the last time I saw or heard anything about him, until 1942 when one of the nurses where I was staying told me she had received a message saying my father had gone missing and was presumed dead."

She met Zach's gaze, and for a fleeting moment, he saw the echoes of his own grief reflected in her teary eyes. He understood what it must have been like for her, losing both parents at such a young age.

THOSE MISSING YEARS

"I am s-sorry," he said finally, his voice quieter now. "But I needed to know a little about you. I hope you understand. I've lived here since I was released, and I haven't heard anything from anyone until now. I just needed to be sure. Please, carry on."

"Thank you for listening. It must have been a bit of a shock, me turning up like this," she said gently.

She continued, telling him what had happened after the war, how she had been sent to a children's home. She didn't feel it was necessary to go into too much detail about marrying Tom and why she had left him. But she did mention that she had decided it was time to find a job in Normandy and, most importantly, to find out what had happened to her father before returning home to her daughter.

"I arrived here from England just over eighteen months ago and found a small room not far from here. I found the perfect job at the archives. During my first week there, I started searching through files from those missing years, but until today, I hadn't had much success. Then I discovered your name listed as having served with my father. It showed your address, and I prayed you were still here."

Zach listened intently, sympathy evident in his expression. He could only imagine what she had been through, evacuated, treated like an outsider, and eventually left homeless.

Struggling with his speech, he finally said, "You've been through s-so much, Rose, and I'm truly sorry. The war was a terrible time for me. I saw so many friends die, and sometimes I wished I had been one of them. It would have been less painful. But let me tell you what I know about your f-father."

"Yes," Rose said softly, "but please stop if it becomes too much."

He nodded before continuing.

"I was sent to Normandy from London, and that's where I met Neville. We served together until the day we were forced to parachute out of a burning plane. We landed in German territory.

"We were captured and sent to Stalag VIII-B, a German prisoner-of-war camp. The conditions were harsh, we were crammed together like sardines. Neville and I were assigned to work in the mines as forced labourers. They issued us with an ID tag and a lamp to take down with us, but the mines were damp, and water pooled everywhere.

"Whispers spread among the prisoners that the Germans were planning to relocate some of us to another camp. Nobody knew where. We could only hope that it meant better conditions, or a chance to escape."

Maintaining eye contact, Rose said, "Zach, I can't imagine what you all went through." Her heart raced as his words unfolded. She clenched her fists, feeling the weight of his pain.

"The next day, I remember it was bitterly cold. The prisoners were bundled into trucks for transport. Some feared we were being sent to the dreaded Auschwitz. Then, suddenly, there was a deafening roar, the engine was failing. The truck swerved violently and crashed into a deep ditch. The guards shouted orders as we stumbled onto the icy ground. Neville and I exchanged looks, and in that moment, we seized our chance and leapt from the truck and sprinted into the nearby forest."

As Zach spoke, his hands trembled, the memories flooding back—the hunger, the cold, the fear.

Rose could see it on his face; he was reliving that awful time.

"Please stop, Zach. No more for now. There's plenty of time for us to talk, perhaps we can continue another day?" she suggested, hoping he would agree.

"I must carry on. You need to know everything. And now that I've started..." he said, wiping the sweat from his face.

She could see how much he needed to talk, but she insisted he stop.

"I'm sorry to bring it all back, but we should take a break. I can come back another day if you don't mind?" she asked gently.

At first, Zach seemed frustrated, but Rose could tell he was a kind and gentle man. She was grateful for his willingness to help.

He hesitated before mumbling, "I get frustrated, and I'm sorry. I was rude when I first saw you." He explained that he suffered from PTSD, and his speech impediment worsened when he was anxious, especially around new people.

"I'm sorry," Rose said sincerely.

She told him she needed to leave, mentioning an early start the next morning. That wasn't entirely true, but there were things she needed to do.

"I think I've taken up enough of your time, especially in one visit," she added apologetically.

"It was good to have company and to talk to someone after so many years alone. I have often wondered what happened to Neville, but given my circumstances, I was never able to do anything about it."

They continued talking for another hour, sharing stories over tea before Rose finally got up to leave. She could never bring herself to call her small rented room 'home'—her home was in London, with Cosuda.

"Yes, please come back as soon as you can," Zach told her. "I'll continue telling you everything I know. I want to help you find Neville as much as I can."

As she thanked him, she noticed how his face had softened. There was a look of relief in his eyes. Despite the difficult start, the visit had been both helpful and hopeful.

When she returned to her room, she lay on the bed, her mind replaying everything Zach had told her. What a terrible ordeal he and her father had endured.

This felt like the first real step towards finding out what had happened to her father. She needed Zach's help now. She decided to leave it a few days before returning, but she wanted to hear as much as he could tell her without overwhelming him too soon.

She had been working tirelessly, but her heart yearned for her father.

That evening, after preparing a simple dinner, she changed into a cosy pink sweater and black slacks. Without hesitation, she set off once more to see Zach.

Zach opened the door and smiled, pleased to see Rose standing there. Since meeting her, he felt a spark of life return, something he hadn't felt in years. For so long, he had forced thoughts of Neville to the back of his mind, convincing himself there was nothing he could do. But now, with Rose here, he had a reason to remember.

"Come in," he said warmly, stepping aside.

As she entered, Rose confided in him about her work at the archives, emphasising the need for discretion. While her colleagues attended meetings, ran errands, or gossiped during breaks, she cherished those rare moments of solitude when she could sift through files undisturbed.

Zach listened intently. "We have something in common, Rose, Neville. And I w-want to help in any way I can to find out what happened to him."

Feeling more at ease, she thanked him for his support. "I'd love to hear more, anything at all could help."

Zach nodded, gathering his thoughts before continuing where he had left off.

They had been hiding in an outhouse, planning their next move, when they spotted a figure peering through a farmhouse window. They exchanged uneasy glances—was it the farmer's wife? Before they could react, the door swung open, and a young woman stood there, shining a torch in their faces.

"Who are you?" she demanded, suspicion flickering in her tired eyes.

They hesitated for a moment, too weak to flee. Their words stumbled over each other as they tried to explain, but something in their desperate faces must have convinced her. Her expression softened. "Come inside," she said.

They followed her into a dimly lit, rustic kitchen. She handed them bowls of hot soup. As the warmth spread through their frozen bodies, she explained the danger of hiding them. If caught, she would be in serious trouble, but she had seen men like them before, terrified and running for their lives.

She considered hiding them in the loft but decided to wait until she had spoken to her husband. "He's a good man," she assured them. "He'll help you until the Resistance can get you back to England."

But before she had the chance to speak to her husband, they heard the crunch of boots on gravel. The German soldiers spotted them, eyes cold and accusing. There was no time to run. No escape.

The relentless questioning began immediately. Their stories were dismissed as lies. Eventually, they were classified as prisoners of war and transported to Leemdorf, near the German border. From that moment on, they clung desperately to the fading memory of freedom, their spirits fighting against the grim reality.

Rose's heart ached as she listened. "You went through a terrible ordeal, Zach. I can't begin to imagine what it was like." She took a deep breath. "This must have been when Nurse Valerie told me my father was missing, presumed dead. But I was never going to accept it, not until I knew for sure."

Zach gave a slow nod. "I'm glad you knocked on my door last week, Rose. I needed this conversation more than I realised. And I'll tell you more each time you come."

She reached for his hand and gave it a gentle squeeze. "Thank you, Zach. I appreciate everything."

"We'll get through this together," he promised.

Rose smiled, feeling a renewed sense of hope. In that moment, she knew they would face whatever came their way, together.

Chapter 11

Now in her third year at the orphanage and soon to celebrate her tenth birthday, Cosuda's determination to keep practising hard had never wavered. She had a natural gift, but no amount of effort could ease the pain of missing her mother. Her days were filled with chores, lessons, and quiet moments when she would gaze up at the stars, wondering if her mother was watching over her. The stars became her companions as she whispered her hopes and dreams to them. But the ache remained; a bittersweet tune that echoed through her soul.

At night, she dreamt of her mother holding her hand as they wandered through fields of flowers, laughing and singing while the breeze carried them along.

Birthdays at the orphanage were precious occasions. The children would gather in the hall, filled with anticipation. For a fleeting moment, they felt special as all attention was on them. The kitchen staff would bake a simple sponge cake and place it on the bench in the hall, surrounded by paper streamers.

For Cosuda, it was no different, except for the handmade card she received from her friend Lucy, a heartfelt message written with care.

"Happy Birthday, Cosuda. May your hopes and dreams be transformed into reality."

Lucy's words touched her heart, and she marvelled at how her friend always knew just what to say.

The hall buzzed with excitement as the other children flocked around the cake.

Cosuda blew out the flickering candle, closed her eyes, and made a wish.

"Please, let my mother write to me."

As the clapping continued and the cake was cut, Cosuda found herself lost in thought, imagining a letter from her mother. Would she pretend that everything was fine?

Lucy approached, noticing the sadness mingled with gratitude in her friend's eyes.

Yet Cosuda was determined to face her time at the orphanage with grace. Lucy's card was a reminder that friendship could bring joy even in the darkest times.

"I'll keep hoping, dreaming, and moving forward."

"Thank you, Lucy, for your beautiful card. Even though life has dealt us both a difficult hand, I am grateful to be alive."

Lucy nodded.

"There's always hope and the quiet strength of those who learn to dance in the rain." She took Cosuda's hand. "Let's celebrate the birthdays of our dreams together?" she asked, wrapping her arms around her friend's neck.

After a long day of chores and laughter, the girls gathered to clean the hall before retiring for the night.

"Let's make this place shine," Lucy said. The others nodded, gripping their brooms and dusters. Together, they swept away the remnants of the party.

Once they were finished, the girls returned to their dormitories, leaving Cosuda alone to practise her ballet steps. She dreamt of performing before an audience one day. In her mind, she imagined her parents, wherever they were, smiling down at her. Their absence was a void she could never fill, but dance helped to bridge the gap.

From the doorway, the matron watched, a soft spot for Cosuda evident in her gaze.

She admired the girl's determination and the resilience that shone through each delicate movement. The matron couldn't help but feel a pang of protectiveness.

"You have a rare gift. Never forget that."

Cosuda nodded, her gaze lingering. She wanted to make the matron proud, and one day, she hoped, her parents too.

The matron was pleased with her progress. It was no surprise that she had not only caught up with the other girls in her class but had surpassed them.

One warm summer morning, as the sun shone through the library windowpanes, Cosuda discovered an old, crumpled book on the lower bookshelf. Turning its pages, she became engrossed in the stories of prima ballerinas who had danced beneath moonlit skies. She devoured every word, her heart burning with longing. Clutching the book to her chest, she felt its weight press against the rapid pulse of her heart. She wanted to be that girl on stage.

The matron, always watchful, kept a close eye on Cosuda. She had long recognised the girl's potential and believed she could become a great ballerina one day.

One afternoon, after her usual rounds checking on the girls, the matron noticed something different about Cosuda. It was as if she were in another world. Her eyes held a distant look, and she moved with a grace that seemed almost otherworldly. Alone in the quiet studio, she pirouetted effortlessly, lost in the rhythm of her dance.

A sudden movement startled her. A shadow shifted near the studio door. Her heart pounded as she turned quickly. There stood the matron, a stern figure as always, yet her eyes held a warmth that never failed to surprise Cosuda.

"Your dancing is beautiful, child," the matron said. "But are you all right?"

Cosuda thought she glimpsed a rare smile. Being kind didn't come naturally to the matron, who was known for her strict demeanour, but something about Cosuda always seemed to soften her.

For a moment, Cosuda hesitated, sensing an unspoken understanding between them. She had often wondered why the matron treated her with a little more kindness than the others.

She stammered, "Yes, I… I'm fine. I was just enjoying my practice and got lost in the dance."

"Come to my office after you've finished your duties this evening. There's something I need to discuss with you."

Cosuda's heart leapt. "Yes, I will!"

She could hardly contain her excitement, convinced that the matron had received news from her mother. It was difficult to focus on her chores that afternoon; she just wanted to rush through them. But she knew they had to be done properly. Every brushstroke, and sweep was a countdown to the moment she had been waiting for.

Once she had finished, she made her way to the matron's office, her hands trembling as she knocked gently on the door. The corridor seemed to stretch longer than usual, filled with the echoes of her own nervous footsteps.

"Come in," the matron called out.

THOSE MISSING YEARS

Cosuda entered, taking in the smell of polished wood and old books. The matron's desk was neatly organized, with papers stacked in precise piles.

"Sit down," the matron instructed, her voice firm but her eyes gentle.

Cosuda obeyed, her heart racing. She studied the matron's face, searching for any hint of the news she was about to receive.

"I called you here to tell you how pleased I am with your progress." The matron's praise was rare, and Cosuda hung onto every word. "Your dancing is outstanding, and your schoolwork is just as impressive. You've proved yourself in every way since you arrived."

Cosuda's face flushed with pride. "Thank you. Everyone here has been so kind to me," she said softly. She had worked tirelessly to prove she could be that dancer.

Yet, despite the matron's kind words, Cosuda's thoughts were elsewhere. She longed to hear something, anything about her mother.

"Are you happy, Cosuda?" the matron asked. There was often a haunted look in her eyes, a shadow of something unspoken, though she kept it buried deep.

Not wanting to seem ungrateful, Cosuda replied, "Yes, I am. Thank you."

The matron studied her carefully. "Is there anything you'd like to ask me?" she prompted, sensing the girl's hesitation.

Cosuda's heart pounded. She had to know.

"I thought you might have heard from my mother," she said quietly, hope flickering in her voice.

The matron sighed. "I am so sorry, Cosuda. I wish I could say yes. But I'm sure there's a good reason why she hasn't written."

It was a lie. Another lie.

Cosuda's face fell. "Oh… I thought that was why you wanted to see me." Her chest tightened with disappointment, the weight of her unfilled hopes pressing down on her.

The matron quickly changed the subject. "I wanted to see you because you've now been here for three years," she began, her voice both gentle and firm. "You've worked hard and succeeded in all that you do. Because of this, I've decided you're ready to join the advanced dance classes with Miss Brown."

Cosuda gasped. Then, unable to contain herself, she leapt up in excitement.

"Thank you! Thank you! You won't regret it!"

Though her heart ached for the letter that never came, this was the next best news she could have wished for.

Since she was learning so quickly, the matron informed Cosuda that she would be joining the dance classes immediately. The group she would be placed in met every afternoon after academic lessons ended at 3 p.m., and any additional practice beyond that was up to them.

Overwhelmed with excitement and gratitude, Cosuda thanked the matron once more. The matron assured her that she would make all the necessary arrangements so she could ease into the class the following morning. But for now, Cosuda was glowing with happiness. Gracefully, she held out her hand in thanks.

"Thank you, Ma'am," she said, her voice barely containing her joy. She had never expected this opportunity, and relief washed over her knowing she wouldn't have to join Miss Palmer's class.

The matron took her hand warmly, placing her other hand gently on top.

Cosuda had worked hard, absorbing every lesson, and now her efforts had been rewarded. The thought of starting ballet classes immediately sent a swarm of butterflies fluttering in her stomach.

"You've earned it," the matron said with a rare smile. "Now go back to the dormitory, your classmates are waiting."

Cosuda nodded, her pulse racing as she hurried down the corridor, eager to share the news.

But as excitement filled her, reality tugged at her. There were still lessons to attend, chores to complete, and new friendships to nurture. The matron believed in her, and she wasn't going to disappoint her.

Taking a deep breath, she steadied herself, her voice shaking but resolute.

"Girls," she called, standing in the doorway. "I have something to tell you."

The room fell silent as they listened.

"I've been told that I am ready to join the dance classes."

A ripple of surprise and happiness spread through the group. The girls huddled together, their eyes fixed on Cosuda. Lucy and Jane stepped forward.

"We're thrilled for you!" Lucy beamed. "You'll be amazing."

Cosuda smiled at her friends. "Thank you. I won't let you down."

For so long, she had watched from the sidelines, admiring the way the other girls moved so gracefully, their confidence resonating through the dance studio. Now, at last, she could step into their world—into the world of pirouettes and pliés.

The next morning, her alarm rang at 6 a.m., and she was up and ready, her heart full of anticipation. The matron's words echoed in her mind: You're ready.

Yes, I'm ready, she told herself.

That afternoon, after finishing her academic lessons, Cosuda attended her first dance class with Miss Brown. Unbeknownst to her, the matron stood at the back of the studio, quietly watching.

Her eyes never left Cosuda.

She had seen many girls pass through the dance classes, but none quite like her. The matron herself had once been a prima ballerina in her youth, but life had led her away from the stage. Now, she lived on through the students she nurtured.

As she watched Cosuda move, she recognised something rare, an unshakable determination, a deep passion that radiated from her every step. She could see it in the way her body and soul surrendered to the dance. Every pirouette, every plié, was executed with grace and precision. Cosuda was graceful, perfectly proportioned, and moved as if she were floating on air. The more the matron watched her, the more certain she became: Cosuda was born to be a dancer.

Her tutors provided regular feedback, and it was always the same, outstanding and glowing remarks.

Despite the long hours of study and practice, Cosuda never complained. The girls rose early every morning, but Cosuda was always the first in the studio. There, in the quiet, before lessons began, she came alive, losing herself in the rhythm of the dance.

Yet, a small part of her always felt different from the other girls. They seemed like creatures from another world, graceful, poised, and belonging to a life she had never known. She spoke differently from them, possessed fewer belongings, and had never experienced the privileges they often spoke of.

But, to her surprise, she discovered their kindness. They welcomed her into their world, and for that, she was grateful.

Being part of the ballet school felt like a dream come true.

During breaks in the garden, the girls shared their secrets with her. They told her about their privileged lives, their elegant homes, and their holidays in exotic locations. Though their worlds were different, Cosuda realised that, beneath it all, they weren't so different after all.

And most importantly, they had accepted her as one of their own.

"I always feel like an imposter, like I don't belong here," Cosuda confided to Susie.

Susie gave her a reassuring smile. "Cosuda," she said, "we're all outsiders in our own way. Some wear it on their sleeves, while others hide it behind silk. But deep down, we're all searching for acceptance."

As Christmas approached, the girls practised tirelessly for the upcoming show. But for Cosuda, dance was more than just steps and pirouettes, it was her lifeline, a way to escape the harsh reality of loss and uncertainty.

At every stolen moment, she slipped into her leotard, laced up her pointe shoes, and disappeared into the dance studio. The mirror reflected her unwavering determination. Her eyes sparkled, and her arms stretched towards the sky, seeking perfection. Her delicate feet barely touched the ground as she floated, twirled effortlessly, and extended her graceful legs, gliding across the floor like a true ballerina. At that moment, she wasn't just Cosuda the orphan; she was the lead in *Swan Lake*, performing under golden stage lights, the world watching in awe.

But it wasn't all a bed of roses.

Fatigue weighed on her face from long nights of schoolwork. Her hands were blistered from endless cleaning duties. The cough that had plagued her for the past two weeks still lingered. Yet, no matter how poorly she felt or how overworked she was, she never missed a chance to practise. Every ache and pain from relentless chores served as a reminder of her dedication. Gritting her teeth, she pushed forward, refusing to let exhaustion break her.

After finishing her daily chores, if she wasn't dancing, she was studying in the dormitory, determined to succeed in both ballet and her lessons.

And yet, no matter how much she immersed herself in dance and books, there was still a part of her that longed for something more.

As time passed, she found herself lingering outside the matron's office, hoping and praying that one day she would see her standing there, holding a letter. A message. Anything from her absent parents.

But day after day, there was nothing.

The disappointment pressed heavily on her chest, a constant ache that never faded.

One day, she told herself. One day, I will have answers.

With a deep breath, she resolved to keep hoping, keep dreaming, and keep dancing until that day arrived.

Chapter 12

Rose had become a frequent visitor to Zach's, often stopping by during her lunch break or on her way home after staying late at the office. He was always pleased to see her, and she found comfort in his company. Each time she visited, he shared a little more about his time in the war and his connection with her father. Yet, there was always more—more he wanted to say, more he needed to tell her.

As Rose prepared to leave work, she glanced at the clock and decided to visit Zach. It would have to be a quick visit as she had so much to do when she got back to her room, including reviewing military documents and checking for any post from the matron. Every day, she prayed for something from her daughter.

Zach had just finished cooking when an unexpected knock sounded at the door.

Wiping his hands on a tea towel, he crossed the front room, the wooden floor creaking under the weight of his wheelchair. Through the glass, he recognised the silhouette of a familiar woman. Rose. He hadn't expected her, but he was glad she had come.

"Come in, Rose. It's good to see you. Is everything okay?"

"Yes, everything's fine. Sorry for dropping by unannounced, I just needed to see a familiar face."

Zach smiled warmly. "There's no need to apologise. Life has a way of surprising us, doesn't it? Besides, it's always nice to see you. Come through and sit." He gestured toward the settee. "I'll put the kettle on. You can tell me about your job."

"Thank you." Rose perched on the edge of the cushion, her hands clasped together.

"It's going okay," she admitted. "But as you know, I'm only there to find information about my father. Most of the people are friendly, though some keep to themselves, focused on their work."

She hesitated before continuing, lowering her voice. "There's a room in the administration office that I've been curious about for a long time. It's not far from where I sit, but it's always locked. I've never seen anyone go in or out. I need to know what's inside, and I've made it my mission to find out. Once the office is empty for the night."

Zach's expression grew serious. "Be careful, Rose. The consequences could be severe. Not only could you lose your job, but there might be more at stake than you realise."

She smiled, touched by his concern. "I appreciate you worrying about me, but I'm prepared to take the risk. I've been keeping track of when the staff leave, and I know the best time to look."

The kettle whistled, and Zach took out a delicate china teapot, pouring the steaming water inside.

As she watched him, she marvelled at his unshaken composure. Was it simply his nature to put others at ease? Or was it something learned—a way of coping with the past?

She accepted the matching china cup he handed her, the warmth seeping into her cold fingers. "Thank you," she murmured, taking a sip.

The room was cosy, bathed in the soft glow of a single lamp. Zach settled across from her, his eyes attentive and kind. As they spoke, the gaps in their stories began to fill. Rose learned more about how the war had changed everything and how Zach had coped by shutting out certain memories. In turn, Zach listened intently as Rose shared what little she knew of her father—the man who had disappeared without a trace.

Her voice trembled with emotion, and Zach's face softened with empathy.

"Sorry for taking up so much of your time, Zach," she said eventually. "But today was one of those days when I just needed to see you. I should leave you in peace now."

Zach smiled. "I was being a little presumptuous in thinking you'd stay for dinner. There's still so much more to talk about. But perhaps another time?"

She hesitated, torn between the warmth of the moment and the documents waiting for her back at the office. Documents she needed to return unnoticed.

"Another time," she agreed with a small smile. "But for now, thank you for the tea and your company."

She had come seeking answers, but when Zach asked about her job, she realised she needed to take things slowly.

Zach had so much to say, memories buried for years finally surfacing. Talking to Rose seemed to ease his depression, it was as if her presence had unlocked something in him. He had spent years blocking out the past, but now, with her here, the words came more easily.

"As much as I need to go back, I'm sure it can wait a few more hours," Rose said, offering him a small smile. "So, thank you. I'll accept your kind invitation."

The more he spoke about their time in the army, the closer she felt to her father. After sixteen years, she needed any help she could get to find him. She needed closure, and she refused to believe he was dead until she had proof.

Sinking into the fireside chair, Rose gazed into the flames, her thoughts drifting. Zach watched her, noticing the emptiness in her eyes.

He could only imagine how difficult it must have been for her to try to uncover what happened to her father while being so far from her daughter. He wondered if she ever thought about giving up, returning to England to take Cosuda and start a new life, just the two of them. But he knew she must have felt that leaving now would mean everything she had endured these past years would have been for nothing.

Over dinner, she told him she had discovered where some of the old military records were kept. But every time she thought she had an opportunity to look through them, someone needed her. Still, working at the archives was the best lead she had in finding out what had happened to her father, and she clung to the hope that he was still alive.

"The job means nothing to me," she admitted, her voice tinged with frustration. "It just gives me enough to survive while I'm here."

Zach listened intently, his eyes reflecting a deep understanding. "You're doing everything you can," he reassured her.

She often thought about asking Zach about his injuries but had never found the right moment. The pain he carried, both physical and emotional, was something she couldn't begin to compare to her own sorrow. She hesitated to bring up the subject, fearing it might reopen old wounds.

As she rolled up her sleeves to wash the dishes, she became aware of Zach watching her.

"If you feel ready to tell me more, Zach, I'm happy to listen," she said gently, sensing his need to unburden himself.

Zach hesitated, rubbing his hands anxiously. "Yes… Please, sit down. We'll clean up later."

She wiped her hands and nodded. "Of course."

Once she had made another pot of tea, she poured them both a cup and sat opposite him, eager to hear more.

"I need to tell you what happened to me," he began. "I didn't think it was important before, but I want you to know."

His voice was steady, but she could see the weight of the memories pressing down on him. For years, he had tried to block out the past, but now he had decided, it was time to tell her everything.

"In 1943, we were about to leave Leemdorf. We weren't far from camp when the ground shook beneath us. The air was thick with tension, the sky strangely still. We marched forward, exhaustion etched on our faces when suddenly, artillery fire erupted. Three men were killed instantly."

Rose held her breath as he continued, her heart pounding as he continued.

"The war had s-swallowed us whole and spat us out as shadows of ourselves. Another man—his arm was blown off. Neville wrapped his shirt around the wound, trying to stop the bleeding. The smell of gunpowder and blood hung heavily in the air. But when we got back to camp, we realised many of our men were missing."

Zach's gaze darkened. "Later that day, they found the bodies. Among them, Neville's shirt was lying on the ground, and inside the pocket, a crumpled photograph. They must have mistaken it for belonging to one of the dead soldiers. I'm certain that's why they reported us killed rather than captured."

Rose's chest tightened. "You were captured?"

He nodded, his eyes reflecting the pain of the memory. "We were caught trying to help some of the wounded. The next thing I knew, I woke up in a hospital bed, s-surrounded by pain. Men moaning, crying out for their loved ones... It wasn't a place of healing. It was a grim, makeshift sanctuary for the broken."

Zach paused, his fingers gripping the edge of his teacup. "The beds were so close together, stacked one on top of the other. Then I saw him— it was Neville. Lying flat out. I didn't know how long he'd been there, but he was in bad shape."

Rose swallowed hard, waiting for him to go on.

Zach exhaled slowly. "I thought we were both going to die there."

A heavy silence settled between them, broken only by the crackling fire.

Rose gasped, her breath catching in her throat. Tears welled in her eyes as she imagined her strong father lying helpless, broken. It was impossible to comprehend how he must have felt.

"I was delirious," Zach continued, his voice raw. "I couldn't remember why I was there, but I guessed I'd been injured. A nurse told me it was the anaesthetic making me confused, but she was rushing around, tending to the wounded. There was no time to stop and explain. I tried to piece together how I had ended up in that bed."

"I'm so sorry, Zach," Rose whispered. The words felt inadequate even to her own ears, but they were all she could offer. She could hear the weight in his voice, the years of silence, and the memories pressing to be set free.

Rose's eyes widened. "How did you know the photograph was of me?"

"On the back, you could just make out the faded writing... 'Rose, 1939.'"

A tear slipped down her cheek as the memories flooded back.

"I was seven then," she murmured. "He must have taken that picture before he left for France."

A heavy silence settled between them.

"Are you sure you want to keep going?" Rose asked gently. "You don't have to."

Zach's hands traced down his side, his fingers running over the jagged scars hidden beneath his shirt, a permanent reminder of the shrapnel that had torn through him.

"I need to," he said, his voice unwavering.

He told her how, in the hospital, he had called for the nurse, desperate for help. But she had barely looked at him, her voice cold and detached.

"A bedpan will do," she had said, before turning away.

Zach clenched his fists. His anger had bubbled then, just as it did now. He hadn't wanted a bedpan. He had wanted an arm to hold onto, reassurance that he was still human, that he wasn't just another broken soldier waiting to be discarded.

"I asked her why I was in the hospital," he continued, his voice tightening. "Sh-she barely spared me a glance. Said I'd been injured by shrapnel from a nearby explosion. That they had to operate. Then she rushed off, saying the doctor would explain in the morning."

Zach wheeled himself restlessly around the room. Rose could see the tension in his shoulders, the way his jaw tightened with the memories resurfacing.

"Zach, let's take a break," she insisted softly.

He hesitated, then nodded. "Yes… Okay."

They stepped outside into the small back garden. The evening air was warm, with a gentle breeze carrying the scent of flowers. It felt good to be there, to pause for a moment.

"You were right," Zach admitted after a while, exhaling deeply. "I needed that."

Rose gave him an encouraging nod. "Whenever you're ready."

After a moment, he continued.

"The nightmares started almost immediately," he said.

He described how, in the depths of sleep, he was back on the battlefield. His heart pounded as he struggled to move, but the heavy blankets wrapped around him, refusing to let go. Panic surged through him. He fought against the weight, kicking frantically, until—

His eyes flew open, squinting against the harsh hospital light. The sterile smell of antiseptic filled his nostrils.

And there she was. The nurse. Her face was lined with exhaustion, her weary eyes studying him as he tried to sit up. But something was wrong.

His legs wouldn't move. A sharp, cold fear gripped him. "Where are my legs?" he blurted, his voice barely more than a desperate whisper.

The nurse leaned closer, her expression softening. She gently pressed his shoulder back onto the bed.

"Rest," she murmured. "You're in good hands."

But no amount of reassurance could change the truth. He squeezed his eyes shut, willing his mind to accept what had happened, to somehow undo the horror. Sleep pulled at him again, but this time, it came with pain and uncertainty, with the echo of her promise lingering in his ears. 'You're in good hands.'

Rose listened intently, her own eyes shimmering with unshed tears. She could see the agony in Zach's expression, the ghosts of his past still haunting him.

He sighed, running a hand over his face. "I'm sorry for upsetting you. I never thought I'd be able to talk about this."

"You don't have to apologise," Rose said softly. "I'm grateful you're sharing it with me."

Zach swallowed hard. "The following morning, the nurse returned… but this time, she wasn't alone."

He looked at her, his expression unreadable.

"The doctor came in, his white coat stained with spots of blood, like he had just come from surgery."

A chill ran down Rose's spine. She held her breath, waiting for what would come next.

Rose rose from the garden bench, her heart heavy with Zach's pain. She wished there was something, anything that she could say to ease his suffering, but words felt inadequate.

"Zach, promise me you'll rest," she said gently. "Just for a little while. I have to leave now."

This time, he listened. Exhaustion was etched into every crease of his face, and he finally admitted, "Please don't go home tonight."

Seeing how drained he was, she hesitated. He had spent years burying his past, and now that the floodgates had opened, she couldn't abandon him.

"All right," she agreed. "I'll stay. But I have to leave early in the morning; I need fresh clothes for work."

He nodded, gratitude flickering in his weary eyes.

"I'm sorry it took so long to tell you what we went through," Zach murmured. "For years, I thought it would die with me."

"I'm glad you can finally release some of that suffering," she said, her voice gentle. "A little at a time, only when you're ready."

"Thank you for staying." He gestured toward the spare bedroom. "There's clean bedding in the spare bedroom. I have a large shirt you can use to sleep in."

She kissed his cheek softly. "Goodnight, Zach."

That night, she fell asleep the moment her head hit the pillow. The weight of Zach's story, the horrors he had endured, settled over her, but sleep came swiftly.

At 6 a.m., her alarm jolted her awake. She resisted the temptation to linger. There was no point in wasting time when she could freshen up at her own room. As she dressed, her mind raced thinking about the previous night. The pain in Zach's voice, the weight of the memories he had finally let free.

She scribbled a quick note, leaving it on his bedside table. *Thank you for trusting me. I'll see you soon.*

As she slipped out of the house, a nagging thought followed her, would Zach think she had left because it was too much? Would he worry that his past had scared her away?

THOSE MISSING YEARS

When Zach woke to an empty room, he felt a pang of loneliness. His eyes landed on the note.

Rose needed time to process the past. He clung to that hope, longing for her to return.

Back in her own room, Rose immediately checked for post, but as usual, there was nothing. No reply to any of her letters. The silence weighed heavily on her heart. Hugging herself, she stared at the emptiness of her small space.

But she couldn't afford to fall apart. She had a purpose. She had to be strong. For herself. For her daughter.

Shaking off the disappointment, she quickly bathed, got dressed, and sat at the small table with a cup of tea. As she sipped, her thoughts wandered back to Zach. The horrors he had endured. The father she was still searching for. The war that had taken so much.

After he enlisted, her father had left behind one promise, to return.

And she would never stop searching until she found the truth.

After a long, exhausting day at work, Rose didn't hesitate. She went straight to see Zach.

He hadn't been sure she would return so soon, but the moment he saw her, relief flickered in his eyes.

"I needed to see you," she said.

Concern crept into his expression. "Are you okay? Did something happen at work?" He hesitated. "Or was it... yesterday?"

Zach reached across the space between them, his fingers brushing hers. "You don't have to carry the burden alone," he said. "We're in this together now."

She paused before answering, "It's not just that," she admitted. "It's been three years since I left Cosuda... and I haven't heard anything."

His brow furrowed. "Nothing?"

She shook her head. "Not a single letter. I can't even call because the matron told me the phone line is for outgoing emergencies only."

Zach frowned. "That seems... strange. But if something was wrong, surely they would have found a way to contact you?"

Rose swallowed hard. "I don't know anymore. I've written countless letters. Poured my heart into every one. But there's never been a reply." She exhaled sharply, frustration creeping into her voice. "The Matron assured me everything would be fine. She knew I couldn't give a timeframe for how long I'd be gone. But now... I'm beginning to doubt it."

Zach's gaze was steady. "Then the quickest way back to Cosuda is to finish what you started."

Rose listened.

"If you stop now, it'll all have been for nothing," he said gently.

Rose nodded slowly, absorbing his words. He was right. Her daughter was waiting. And no matter how long it took, she would find her way back.

That evening, Zach prepared chicken with roast potatoes, a meal which Rose deeply appreciated. By the time she usually returned to her room, it was late, and more often than not, she wouldn't bother eating. Sitting at the table, the warmth of the meal and the quiet companionship made her feel at ease.

After clearing the dishes, they settled in front of the crackling log burner, exhaustion creeping over them, but content with how things were unfolding. They watched *Ben-Hur*, engrossed in Charlton Heston's gripping performance. The film's epic battles and themes of resilience resonated in ways neither of them voiced aloud. When the film ended, they sat in silence, the intensity of the moment hanging in the air.

Zach shifted in his chair, his expression serious as he turned to Rose. "I think it's time I tell you the last part of what I know about Neville."

Rose straightened, her heart pounding. "Of course," she replied. Anything that could help find her father was invaluable.

Zach's voice was steady, but she could hear the emotion beneath his words.

"The war left Neville broken, disoriented and severely injured. When the world began rebuilding, he was finally released from the prison camp. The hospital became more than just a place to heal his body, it was where he tried to piece himself back together.

There, he met Nurse Susan. She was compassionate and dedicated. She cared for his wounds and listened intently to his war stories. They spent countless hours together, sharing their fears and their dreams. Slowly, Neville realized he had fallen in love with her, captivated by her kindness and strength.

But Neville wasn't just a wounded soldier; he was a man burdened by a past and bound to a family he couldn't forget. And yet, the thought of losing Susan terrified him. He made a decision, one that would change everything. He assumed the identity of Susan's deceased husband, adopting his name and backstory. With this new identity, he could be with Susan without fear of being found.

"We lost contact soon after, long before the war ended. Everything changed. I was sent home, and I didn't hear anything until I spoke with a man in a local store.

Zach struggled to put his thoughts into words. "It's been years, Rose. I never thought I'd hear his name again. But in a small store of all places, I met someone who knew Neville."

The look on Rose's face was intriguing, "Who was it?"

"A man who had been in the same hospital as Neville. His wife, who was a nurse there, worked closely with Susan. They were friends." Zach hesitated before continuing, his voice tightening.

He told me after Neville recovered, they built a life together, one filled with hope and second chances. Neville and Susan married in a small chapel near the hospital, the ceremony simple yet profound. They went on to have two children."

Rose's breath caught in her throat. Her father remarried. The words echoed in her mind, colliding with the cherished memories of her mother, the woman she had adored, the mother she had lost.

Rose felt as though the floor had shifted beneath her.

"I'm sorry," Zach said softly. "I wanted to tell you sooner, but I thought it best to let you process things slowly. You deserve the truth, not half-truths or secrets."

She swallowed past the lump in her throat. "No, don't be sorry. You were right to tell me. I want to know everything, I need to. If I'm going to find him…" She trailed off, her voice unsteady.

Zach nodded.

"He was a free man," she continued, blinking back tears. "Why shouldn't he remarry?" And yet, deep inside, sorrow pressed against her chest. The image of her mother, her sweet, beautiful mother flooded her mind.

Zach hesitated before speaking again. "Neville s-suffered from combat stress disorder. We were lucky to escape when we did. So many soldiers never got the chance. Some were put on trial, even executed. They called it weakness. To them, those men were no good."

A shadow crossed his face, one of unspeakable sorrow. A look of a man who had seen things no human being should ever witness.

Rose reached for his hand. "I'm sorry you had to endure such terrible times, Zach," she said softly, her heart aching for him.

For a long moment, they sat in silence.

Over the next few months, Rose became relentless in her search for her father.

Every night, after finishing her long workday, she combed through dusty files hidden away in forgotten cupboards, searching for any new information that might bring her closer to him. She knew the risk; if she was caught, it would mean instant dismissal. But the thought of finding her father gave her the strength to continue.

She never left the office early enough to relax and never allowed herself the luxury of a quiet evening. Because somewhere, buried in records and forgotten papers, was the answer she was searching for.

And she wouldn't stop until she found it.

At the end of a long day, after the office staff had left, Rose found herself drawn to the mysterious locked room. The keys, mostly labelled, hung on a hook nearby. Curiosity tugged at her, urging her forward. She hesitated, then reached for an unmarked key, trying several before one finally clicked into place. The old door creaked open, revealing a room untouched since she had started working there.

If she were caught, her search for her father could come to an abrupt and devastating end. Fired, and possibly worse, suspected of wrongdoing. She had always planned to visit the archives office officially, to inquire about her father's disappearance while serving in the army, an event that had led to the assumption of his death. But finding a position here had been a stroke of luck, an answer to her prayers. And now, she had to take the risk.

Stepping into the darkness, she fumbled for a light switch but instead found a torch. She turned, making sure no one was watching, then flicked it on. The beam of light swept across towering shelves, their contents lost in shadow. A ladder rose toward even more shelves near the ceiling, enhancing the impression of a historic collection.

So, this is where they store the old records, she thought, her pulse quickening.

The walls and floors were built of cold stone, the air damp and musty, carrying a faint scent of mildew. Boxes lined the shelves, each labelled with a range of dates and locations, their labels faded but legible. Carefully, she pulled several down, searching for anything between 1939 and 1943. An hour passed with no luck, and the cold began to seep into her fingers. Frustrated but determined, she thought, "I can't give up now," she thought. The chill in the room grew more intense, and she reluctantly decided to return another day, despite the setback.

But just as she turned to leave, her gaze drifted upward. More boxes sat high on the top shelf, in a section she hadn't yet searched. A nagging feeling pushed her forward.

THOSE MISSING YEARS

Gritting her teeth, she grabbed the ladder and climbed. Each step groaned beneath her weight, and the higher she went, the gloomier and more unsettling the room became. A crack in the wall let in a howling wind, sending a shiver down her spine.

Then, she froze. A sound. A rustle, just below.

Heart pounding, she strained to listen. A mouse. Maybe a rat. She tried to convince herself, but her grip on the ladder tightened.

Moving quickly, she grabbed a folder labelled *1941*. But as she shifted her weight to descend, her foot caught in the ladder.

Panic surged through her. "Ouch," she gasped, barely containing her voice. Her eyes darted to the shadows. Was something there?

Ignoring the sting in her ankle, she freed herself, clutching the folder tightly. She scrambled down the ladder, not daring to look back. Without another glance behind her, she slipped out, locked the door, and hurried away.

That evening, Rose arrived at Zach's, her mind still spinning from what had happened.

"My manager has given me a two-week deadline for an urgent project from Texas," she told him. "I won't be able to see you for a while."

She hated the disappointment that flickered in his eyes, though he nodded in understanding.

"That's okay," he said. "I can help in the meantime by looking through the folder you took from the store cupboard."

Relief washed over her. "Thank you," she said with a warm smile. "I'll collect it as soon as I can before anyone notices it's missing."

As he walked her to the door, something about her struck him profoundly, the way the dim light caught her face, the quiet strength she carried.

"I'll be here when you're f-finished," he said honestly.

The war had left him with scars, both visible and hidden, but Rose's presence had become a solace. Each day, he found himself waiting for her visits, longing for them.

Early the next morning, Rose awoke, got dressed quickly, and sat at her small wooden table, absentmindedly spooning cornflakes into her mouth. Her thoughts drifted to her daughter in Yorkshire.

On the bus to work, she accepted the thick file on Texas from Mr Simons. The pages were crisp and smelled faintly of vanilla. The day was a blur of arranging meetings, typing confidential documents, and meeting deadlines. By the time she arrived home, exhaustion weighed on her.

But she had one more thing to do. That evening, she wrote another letter to Cosuda telling her how much she missed her and how she longed for even a few lines in return.

Please, just let me know you're okay, she wrote.

Then, she wrote a separate letter to the matron, pleading for a response. Had Cosuda even received her letters? Was something preventing them from reaching her? In darker moments, she wondered, was this God's way of punishing her for leaving her daughter at the orphanage?

She had always felt guilty, like a bad mother. But she had justifiable reasons, hadn't she? The war, the dangers, the uncertainty. Still, the thought of anything happening to Cosuda was more than she could bear.

THOSE MISSING YEARS

And the silence was becoming unbearable. The only thing that kept her going was the hope that one day, she would receive a reply, a sign that her daughter was safe and well. Until then, she would continue to write, to hope, and to endure the waiting.

Chapter 13

During the day, Zach worked steadily through the pile of paperwork until he came across a couple of familiar names, men who had served in the army alongside him and Neville. He was disappointed not to hear from Rose for a few days, even though she had told him she would be busy with an urgent project.

Just under a week later, Rose decided to stop by Zach's on her way home from work to lift her spirits. Most of the staff, including Rose, had been working double or even triple shifts due to a critical meeting with the City Council in Texas. She was certain he wouldn't mind her dropping in, especially since he had told her she was always welcome. Besides, they could continue the search for her father together.

When he opened the door, she could tell instantly that her visit wasn't an inconvenience. She was right, he was pleasantly surprised to see her. She had wanted to check in, see how he was, and find out how he was getting on with the documents she had left him to look through.

"It's good to see you, Rose. I'll put the kettle on. I'm sure you'd like a cup of tea?"

"I'd love one, thank you." She told him she wouldn't stay long, as she was exhausted after several long and busy days at the office and had another early start ahead.

He leaned back in his chair, studying her. "Tell me how work has been going since I last saw you."

She told him about the overseas project she was working on and the immense workload involved.

He listened attentively, sipping his tea, his eyes never leaving hers.

The clock ticked away, an hour, perhaps more....

As she finished her tea and prepared to leave, he leaned forward and reached across the table for a piece of paper.

"I found something," he said, handing it to her.

On it were the names of two soldiers—brothers, Alfred and Kenneth Clarke, who had served in the same battalion as him and Neville. Both had been stationed in Normandy. They came from a small village in Wales, and their family had lost their farm during the Blitz.

"I remember meeting them on the battlefield, where Neville led us," he added.

Rose felt a surge of excitement. These were their first real leads, and she was eager to investigate them as soon as possible, though she had to be careful not to draw attention at work.

"I'll return the file and hopefully have the opportunity to retrieve another one."

"Please take care," he advised.

Rose thanked Zach for his help and company and promised to try to see him after work the next day.

When she arrived home at 8 p.m., she found a letter on her doormat. Heart racing, she tore it open and scanned to the end. It was from the matron.

Dear Mrs Douglas,

We trust this letter finds you in good health. Your daughter, Cosuda, is thriving here at the orphanage. She excels in her studies and everything she does. There is no cause for concern, Cosuda is happy.

We advise you to continue your search for her grandfather, as returning too soon could disrupt her academic progress.

Yours sincerely

Hilda Jones
The Matron
St. Patricia's Orphanage

Though she felt relieved that her daughter was doing well, she was also disappointed by how brief and impersonal the letter was. She longed for direct communication from Cosuda but reminded herself to be grateful that the orphanage was taking care of her.

Clutching the letter, she dozed off on her bed until 10 o'clock, before finally settling in for the night.

As she lay there, Zach crossed her thoughts. She hoped he wasn't too upset that she had to leave so soon. Oddly, she realised she missed him.

She had a quick snack, took a bath, and decided it was too late for dinner. Climbing into bed, she reread the letter, her mind filled with thoughts of Cosuda.

The next morning, Rose rushed to the office, barely catching her bus before it pulled away. Huddling over her desk, she threw herself into the Texas project, uncovering hidden layers of history and piecing together fragments of the past.

THOSE MISSING YEARS

As she traced the inked paths connecting Normandy to distant shores, echoes of war lingered in the documents before her. Her pulse quickened when she stumbled across coded messages—desperate pleas for freedom and reunion. The transatlantic threads wove tales of sacrifice, courage, and love.

That evening, Zach assumed Rose wouldn't be coming over. At 8 p.m., he closed his eyes, trying to rest, when a knock at the door startled him. Checking the clock, he saw it was 9 p.m.

Swiftly wheeling himself through the hallway, he opened the door to find Rose standing there, looking utterly exhausted.

"Rose, are you okay?"

Her coat was crumpled, and her hair fell in dishevelled waves around her face. Fatigue etched lines across her features, but her eyes still held a glimmer of determination.

"Long day?" he asked, rolling closer.

She nodded, a half-smile tugging at her lips. "You could say that."

He reached out and brushed a stray strand of hair from her forehead. "Shall we talk about it?"

She hesitated, the weight of the day clinging to her. "I'm sorry for calling in so late. I didn't realise how late it was when I finished at the office. And then I went back to my room to eat...." Her voice trailed off as she looked away, as though unable to meet his gaze.

"I should have stayed there, but I needed to talk to someone," she admitted.

Relieved, and happy to see her, he nodded. He could see she wasn't her usual self. "I'm glad that someone was me. C-come in,

Rose. Tell me how today went. Did you find anything on the brothers?"

"No, I didn't have any luck, I'm afraid."

She had done a quick search, but as always, they seemed to hit a dead end just as things started to look promising.

He sat beside her, the wheels of his chair creaking. "Tell me," he said gently. "Whatever it is, you can share it with me."

She exhaled deeply and told him how disappointed she felt about the letter she had received from the matron. Though it brought good news, the lack of details left her uneasy.

In an attempt to remain upbeat, Zach tried to reassure her. "The letter seems like good news," he said. Don't worry too much."

But her expression told him otherwise and hinted at what she was thinking.

He had never had children, so how could he possibly understand? *How would he know what it was like?* she thought.

"You're probably right," she said eventually. "It sounds like she's doing okay."

The conversation turned to their investigation. Zach urged caution about sneaking into the storeroom at work. Rose admitted it wouldn't be possible tomorrow, but she needed to figure out the best time to do it. There *had* to be something—it was just a case of searching without being seen.

Zach offered to help, suggesting they wait until after work when the office was empty. But Rose shook her head. It was too risky. He agreed. The last thing either of them wanted was for her to lose her job.

As she reached for the doorknob to leave, Zach hesitated.

"Would you like to go out for a drink or something?" he asked. "You've been working so hard, that a break may be good for you."

She smiled softly. "Thank you, but I'm happy just sitting here with you. It's nice not to be alone, worrying about Cosuda. Although the matron's letter may have been brief, it reassures me that she's okay and happy."

After spending a couple of hours with Zach, she realised it was getting late and she needed to return to her room. She glanced back at him, and his eyes were filled with concern. He was right, she had been pushing herself too hard.

Thanking him for listening, she said goodnight, hoping to see him again soon.

"Could you come over tomorrow after work?" He didn't want to appear over-eager, but he did want her to stay again.

She said she would love to, but on one condition, she would bring dinner with her.

"It's a deal," he said, happy to have her company. "But, Rose, sometimes healing begins with a simple step. Let me take you out. Just a drink, even for an hour."

Rose hesitated. Maybe Zach was right; a break was what she needed.

"Okay," she said. "Just an hour."

The following day, after finishing work, Rose stopped by the corner shop and bought beef sausages and potatoes for their dinner. When she arrived at Zach's, she knocked on the door and waited. It seemed to take a while before he opened it. He looked up at her and said, "I'm so happy you're here."

"Are you okay? Has something happened?" she asked, concerned.

"Nothing has happened," he replied, his voice a mixture of relief and sorrow. "I'm just happy to see you."

He glanced down at his missing legs, the cruel aftermath of war etched into his very being. Memories flooded back: the faces of fallen soldiers, the deafening explosions. How terrible those times had been.

Sensing his unease, Rose tried to lighten the mood. "I told you I'd be here this evening to cook, and here I am." But she could feel his nervousness.

He admitted he didn't want to discuss the war tonight. Instead, he suggested they talk about their families and get to know each other better. She always let him share his wartime experiences in his own time, and she was especially eager to hear about his time with her father.

As promised, they went to the corner pub for drinks. Between them, there was a comfortable silence, a respite from memories that weighed heavily.

When they returned to Zach's, Rose prepared dinner. While it was cooking, they sat down and spoke of simpler things: childhood escapades, family stories, and future dreams.

Rose waited for the right moment before asking about his combat disorder, aware of how deeply it affected him. That evening, they learned a lot about each other, sharing laughter and conversation. It was a welcome distraction for them both.

Zach spoke about his own family and childhood—a life marked by loss and heartache that left scars. His parents, once the foundation of his world, had crumbled. The memories of his mother, a beautiful and extraordinary woman, had filled their neighbourhood with laughter. He had adored her, and the thought of her still brought tears to his eyes.

His father, on the other hand, had been a tempest—a man consumed by jealousy, perhaps worsened by the camaraderie he witnessed among fellow soldiers or by how his own family had changed in his absence. Then the war came, tearing Zach from home.

In 1942, at just 21 years old, in the trenches of France amidst the chaos, Zach received news of his mother's death. Six months later, another letter arrived, bearing yet more sorrow—his father had passed away too.

Zach stood at the crossroads of grief, carrying the memories of his mother's warmth and his father's stormy nature. In quiet moments, he allowed himself to mourn, tears tracing the contours of love and longing.

He believed his father had died of a broken heart, unable to go on without her. As an only child, with both parents gone, he was utterly alone. His mother had always supported him in every way she could, and he never stopped thinking about her. The war had taken not just his comrades but everyone he had truly loved. To him, every embrace carried the promise of loss—anyone he cared for would eventually be snatched away by fate's cruel hand.

Despite the relentless march of time, the pain remained a constant companion that shadowed his every step.

Later that evening, after they had finished dinner, Zach poured Rose a glass of wine and set it on the wooden table beside the sofa while he washed the dishes. He lit the fire and urged her to relax, knowing she had a busy day ahead.

The warm glow of the fire lit up Rose's cheeks, and Zach thought how beautiful she looked.

It was getting late when he noticed her eyes were closed. She had fallen asleep.

"Rose, don't go home—it's late. P-please, stay. Go to bed, and come back after work tomorrow," he said softly, gently waking her.

"Thank you. I will do just that," she replied without hesitation. Rising from the sofa, she reached out, touching his face gently before placing a kiss on his cheek.

"I'll see you tomorrow evening," she said, thanking him for a lovely night before heading off to bed.

Rose climbed the stairs, her steps heavy with the weight of unanswered questions. She had a shared pleasant evening, yet the ache of not hearing from her daughter lingered, a quiet shadow in her heart. Tomorrow would come, but for now, all she could do was try and rest.

Chapter 14

It was November 1962, six years since Rose had left Cosuda at the orphanage. Despite the heartache, she believed she had made the right decision, reassured by the regular letters from the matron describing how well Cosuda was doing. She remained confident that, one day, they would be reunited as a family.

When the bus failed to arrive, Rose pulled her coat tighter around her and set off on foot. The biting cold gnawed at her exposed cheeks, turning them bright pink, and she watched her breath fog up in front of her with each exhale.

As she walked, Rose's thoughts drifted to Cosuda. Hearing about her wellbeing helped her put on a brave face, but deep down, she missed her real home. She often wondered when she would finally return.

That evening, Zach had made up his mind to ask Rose to move in with him. It made sense, given their shared goal of investigating Neville's disappearance and his awareness of her financial constraints. By living together, she would save on rent, and they could spend more time on their search.

Determined to have the evening free, Rose worked tirelessly throughout the day, even skipping lunch. At 5 p.m., Zach was surprised by a knock at the door. He hadn't expected anyone, least of all Rose, who had been working late to complete a project. When he opened the door, there she stood—a delightful surprise after a long day.

"I apologise for arriving early," she said. "But I've decided to take the evening off. The project is nearly finished, and my manager praised me for the extra effort."

"You are always welcome, any time," Zach replied with a warm smile.

Later that night, Zach gathered the courage to ask if she would consider moving in, temporarily, until she was ready to return to England. Rose was taken aback at first but quickly realised it made perfect sense.

"Yes, I'd love to," she responded enthusiastically. She reasoned that paying Zach rather than a landlord was far more practical. They got along well, and she trusted that living with him wouldn't be an issue. Besides, he had spare rooms, and she could use the money she saved for more important matters.

For the first time in a long while, Rose felt happy. Knowing that her daughter was thriving brought her immense relief, even though she still longed for a personal response to one of her letters.

That evening, she took charge of the kitchen, preparing roast chicken with vegetables and potatoes. Over dinner, they discussed moving some of her belongings from her rented room.

"I'll speak to my line manager tomorrow," she said. "With any luck, I'll be able to leave early. I'll also stop by to give notice to my landlord."

After clearing up, they settled in to watch *Gone with the Wind*. When the opening credits rolled, Rose helped Zach move from his chair to the sofa.

"I love a good romantic film," she said.

Zach smiled. "Me too."

As the evening wore on, they reminisced about their lives before the war had shattered their world. Laughter flowed freely, soothing old wounds.

Zach could only imagine how much Rose was juggling, her daughter, her job, and the search for her father. Yet tonight, she looked relaxed. He was painfully aware that she would one day leave for London, and he would once again be alone in Normandy. He hoped they could keep in touch, but the vast distance between them made it feel like an impossible dream.

"Do you ever wonder what life would have been like if the war hadn't happened?" Rose asked.

"Sometimes," Zach admitted.

"Thank you for a lovely evening," she said, her voice softening. "I haven't had a night like this in a long time, just having dinner, watching a film, and relaxing with…" She hesitated, then added softly, "…such lovely company."

A shyness in her voice and the subtle hesitations in her movements only made her more endearing to him.

It was late when she realised the time. She stood up, looking forward to bringing over some of her belongings the next day.

"It's a good idea to start moving things in gradually," Zach said. "Over the notice period. I'll have dinner ready?" He added with a playful smile.

She nodded. The idea of leaving her cramped rented room made perfect sense. Working on the investigation together would be much easier.

Before she left, she instinctively helped Zach from the sofa back into his chair.

"Thank you," he said, accepting her kindness without hesitation.

As Rose arrived back at her rented room and closed the door behind her, she thought about moving in with Zach. It would allow them more time to find her father. But could she and Zach navigate their uncertain path together? Only time will tell.

Zach went to bed feeling happier than he had in a long time.

The next evening, after work, Rose went to see her landlord to give notice. Despite her spotless record of paying rent on time and keeping the place immaculate, he was disappointed. He informed her that leaving early would mean forfeiting her deposit. Since she couldn't afford to lose the money, she reluctantly agreed to stay until the end of the month.

During the following weeks, Rose's commitments kept her busy, which meant she didn't see much of Zach.

Finally, after a long month, she moved into Zach's house, bringing everything she owned, though it wasn't much. A battered suitcase held a few changes of clothes, an old, faded photograph of her parents, and one of Cosuda. Everything else had been left behind with Tom. Travelling to France had made it impossible to bring more. She had no regrets; material possessions meant little to her now.

The room Zach had given her was small but charming. The faded floral wallpaper whispered of decades past. A small window let in the soft morning light. A green rug lay beside the single bed, and a worn armchair sat in the corner, its upholstery showing signs of age. Despite its simplicity, the space felt like a sanctuary, where memories lingered, and time stood still.

When she asked about paying rent and bills, Zach waved her off. Money wasn't important to him, and he knew she was struggling financially.

"We can talk about it another time," he assured her.

THOSE MISSING YEARS

The following morning, Rose woke early, feeling happy about the move as she left for work. Moving in with Zach had been the right decision—it would help them both.

And, though she wouldn't admit it outright, she enjoyed his company. Even if it meant late nights poring over old documents together, she was grateful not to be alone anymore.

Rose returned some of the files to their designated spots as the office emptied that evening. She then picked up another batch for Zach to review the next day. Their teamwork was relentless; they followed every lead, no matter how faint, piecing together fragments like a jigsaw puzzle.

The trail often led back to the time Zach and her father had spent in France during the war. Letters and every visit to an informant ended in frustration. Dead ends seemed to multiply, but Rose refused to give up. Somewhere, she was certain, she would uncover the truth, one that could change everything.

Zach's days were filled with the rustling of paper. He found solace in his work, sifting through documents of the past. But it was when Rose returned from work, weary yet determined that his heart truly stirred. Their connection was platonic, yet Zach harboured deeper feelings. He wrestled with the fear of confessing them, afraid that doing so might jeopardise their friendship.

In the evenings, the two of them would sit by the fireplace, discussing the day's findings and their personal histories. One evening, as they spoke about their lives, Rose asked him about the moment he had received the call to go to war. Even though it was part of the help she needed, Zach was glad she had asked—it showed she was interested in him.

"There's not much to tell," he began. "I was nineteen when I received my call-up papers for the military. My mother was devastated when they sent me to France, but she understood I had no choice. My father was called up at the same time, which made it even harder for her. I was an only child, and suddenly, we were both gone.

Life in France was harsh. The constant threat of enemy attack, the scarcity of supplies, and the haunting images of destruction took o toll on all of us. But amidst the chaos, there were moments of camaraderie that kept us going. My father and I served together for a time, and it gave me a sense of purpose to know I was fighting alongside him."

As Zach spoke, Rose felt a deep pang of empathy for the young man he had been and the trials he had endured. Their loss and hardship had forged a bond between them, even if they hadn't yet acknowledged it.

"After two years, I received a telegram informing me that my mother had died. She had fallen ill with pneumonia. A fellow soldier handed me the crumpled telegram. 'Your mother has passed away,' it read. The news hit me hard, and my father felt the weight of grief just as deeply."

They had been deployed into combat immediately after completing their training.

Zach had been a qualified chef and had hoped to avoid being drafted, but unless you worked in a reserved occupation, you had to fight.

"What is a reserved occupation?" Rose asked, feeling a little foolish—but how would she know?

"It's an occupation the government considered essential to the country's functioning, like coal mining or many engineering trades. Your f-father was always very good to me—he looked out for me, probably because I was so young. Discipline and order were drilled into us daily, but it served us well in the years ahead."

They were learning more about each other with each passing day.

After spending two years in Germany, Zach had developed a stutter. It worsened when he was anxious.

He glanced at Rose, but she remained silent, listening.

"It's like I forget to breathe, and I can't get my words out," he admitted. "Sometimes I cut conversations short and just listen because it's easier. The cruel part is that when I'm alone, speaking to myself, I'm perfectly fluent. I've always wanted to connect with others but never had the energy for verbal conversations."

Before meeting Rose, he had never shared his life with anyone. But there was something about her, an unspoken understanding that put him at ease. Perhaps it was their shared experience of loss, but he found himself opening up, revealing the past he had buried deep within.

He was becoming more aware of his feelings for her. She was easy to talk to, with no hidden agenda. She was here to find her father and would soon return home to her daughter.

Rose struggled to hear the pain in his voice, afraid that if she responded, she might burst into tears.

"You've never mentioned your scar," Zach said hesitantly. "Do you mind if I ask what happened?"

She remembered the day she had run away from Joan and John as if it were yesterday.

"In the aftermath of the war, after I left my host family, I was brutally attacked on the streets by a gang. They stole the few coins people had given me to survive. I sheltered under a bridge in London, suffering from pneumonia, when they set upon me—kicking and punching. My vision blurred, and I looked up to see a young boy pulling out a knife.

As he came towards me, I remember feeling blood trickling down my face…" Her words seemed to freeze, suspended in that chilling moment.

"Everything went dark. When I woke up, I was in hospital, with no memory of how I had got there. The pain from my injuries was overwhelming, and my memories were a jumbled mess. The staff told me that an elderly lady had brought me in and that she had saved my life. But I never got the chance to thank her. The hospital wouldn't reveal her address."

Zach listened, feeling a deep sadness for her. "I'm so sorry for what you went through," he said quietly.

As the days had turned into weeks, Rose often wondered about the woman who had risked her own safety to help a stranger. She imagined a guardian angel and promised herself that if she ever found her, she would thank her properly. Her kindness had pulled Rose back from the brink of death. But time had slipped away, and after she was discharged from the hospital, she had been thrown into the chaos of a youth hostel. She had always hoped that fate might one day reunite them.

Yawning, she stretched and sighed. "It's time for bed. It's been a long but wonderful night."

She leaned over and kissed Zach's cheek. "Goodnight, Zach."

He lifted her hand and kissed it gently. "Goodnight, Rose. Sleep well."

They went to bed, content with how the evening had unfolded.

Chapter 15

Cosuda's 15th birthday had come and gone, but the cough that had once been dormant had returned with a vengeance over the past two weeks, each day leaving her weaker.

That fateful day arrived when Cosuda suddenly felt unwell during her dance lesson. A wave of fatigue washed over her, and she began coughing loudly, prompting the other girls to pause and check on her. She felt as though she was moving awkwardly, stumbling mid-pirouette, her legs giving way beneath her. The room fell silent as she became delirious and slowly drifted towards the floor.

The girls gathered around, with Lucy right at the front. Cosuda lay motionless, appearing unconscious. Lucy was attempting to revive her when the matron walked in and hurried over.

"What is going on here?" she asked loudly, her eyes widening when she saw Cosuda on the floor. "Mrs Brown, why didn't you send for me?" she demanded.

"Have you called anyone, an ambulance or a doctor?" she asked, her face filled with worry.

"It only just happened. I was about to call the doctor when you appeared," Mrs Brown replied.

"Okay, do that now," the matron instructed firmly.

Lucy explained that they had all been dancing when she noticed Cosuda looking strange before she fell, almost in slow motion. The matron knelt beside her, placed a hand on her damp forehead, and noticed her eyes flickering—a sign of fever.

"Cosuda, can you hear me? How long have you been feeling unwell?" she asked urgently.

Cosuda mumbled, "I want to get up... I want to... I need to... change into my cleaning clothes."

After checking her pulse, the matron turned to Lucy. "Run and fetch Johnny as quickly as you can. We need to get her into bed."

Lucy sprinted down the corridor, nearly colliding with a ladder before spotting Johnny at the top.

"Quick, Johnny!" she shouted. "It's Cosuda! Something's wrong—she's not well, and the matron needs your help!"

Johnny climbed down in record time and rushed to the dance studio.

"Lift her carefully," the matron instructed. "Carry her to the dormitory." He nodded, adrenaline kicking in. Having trained for emergencies, his First Aid at Work certification took over. Kneeling beside her, he noted how pale and clammy she was. Gently, he slipped his arms under her shoulders, cradled her head against his chest, and carried her out of the studio, his steps steady and sure. The matron followed closely, her footsteps echoing through the corridor.

In the dimly lit dormitory, Johnny laid Cosuda gently on her bed and draped a loose cover over her. Lucy and the other girls stood at the foot of the bed, their faces etched with worry, whispering among themselves.

Cosuda's eyes fluttered open, settling on the silent group gathered at the end of her bed. As she closed her eyes again, the matron turned to the girls. "Back to the studio and resume your lessons," she ordered, her voice steady but urgent.

"Johnny, bring a jug of water and a glass, quickly," she added.

When she tried to help Cosuda drink, she was too weak to take a sip. The matron remained at her bedside, watching over her until the doctor arrived.

As time passed, Cosuda's condition worsened. She drifted in and out of consciousness, her persistent cough racking her frail body. Memories of her childhood surfaced—had she been happy? Had her mother worried about her enough? She remembered the warmth of her mother's arms and the lullabies she had sung. In her feverish haze, all she longed for was her mother's presence.

The matron paced anxiously, speaking to Cosuda to keep her conscious, but her words seemed to fade into the background.

"Stay with me, Cosuda. Don't sleep. The doctor will be here soon," she murmured, wiping the sweat from the girl's forehead. But Cosuda's vacant eyes showed little recognition. Her fever burned fiercely, and her breathing became increasingly shallow.

The wait for the doctor felt endless. Cosuda moaned softly in her sleep, unresponsive even when the matron touched her. She had become so still and pale that it was difficult to tell if she was breathing at all.

At last, Dr Andrew Ellis stepped through the wrought iron gates of the orphanage, his medical bag heavy in his grip. Adjusting the wire-rimmed glasses perched on his nose, he took in the fading sunlight before entering the building.

The matron met him at the door, relief evident on her face.

"Thank you for coming, Doctor. I'm Mrs Hilda Jones, the matron here."

"Good evening. I'm Dr Andrew Ellis. Please, tell me everything from the beginning." He exuded a calm yet urgent presence, his voice steady but with concern.

She recounted the events: how Cosuda had been dancing, seeming almost entranced, before collapsing. She also mentioned the persistent cough Cosuda had suffered from over the past fortnight.

Dr Ellis listened intently, his brow furrowing.

Johnny and Lucy stood nearby, their faces tense with anxiety. Johnny's mind raced with thoughts of Cosuda's condition, while Lucy fought back tears, looking at her friend's pale face.

Examining Cosuda, he checked her pupils and listened to her chest. His concerned expression did not go unnoticed by the matron.

"Pneumonia," he murmured to himself. "This coughing may be more than just an infection."

The matron's face tightened, her knuckles white as she gripped the edge of the bed.

"How old is she?" he asked, adjusting his spectacles.

"She's fifteen, Doctor."

Dr Ellis scribbled down some notes. "Has anyone else in the village fallen ill recently?"

"No, not that I've heard."

He sighed. "We'll do what we can."

Although he didn't want to alarm the matron, he felt compelled to express his concerns.

"But she's strong, Doctor! She's an incredible dancer. This will destroy her, dancing is her life. You have to help her," the matron pleaded.

"I understand," he said gently. "We'll do everything we can. But we need to get her to hospital as soon as possible. Tests are necessary to determine the cause, and she needs treatment immediately."

Everything was happening so fast. The matron's heart pounded as she feared for Cosuda's life.

The doctor called for an ambulance, and it wasn't long before the siren pierced the evening, piercing the cool air. Inside, they fitted Cosuda with an oxygen mask and secured her onto a stretcher. The matron accompanied her, holding her hand tightly as they sped towards the hospital.

Upon arrival, she was rushed to Accident and Emergency, where a doctor quickly assessed her condition before transferring her to a specialist unit. There, she was immediately started on antibiotics, but the battle for her recovery was just beginning.

The door opened, and the middle-aged doctor stepped outside to where the matron was waiting. His greying hair framed a stern jawline, and he wore a crisp white coat, stained from past surgeries.

Dr Mark introduced himself to the matron and asked her to wait in the waiting room while they examined the patient.

"I'll go with her," she said, her voice steady. "She's like my daughter," she added with equal determination.

Dr Mark raised an eyebrow, his tone firm. "No, you have to wait."

Reluctantly, she stepped back. Following the examination, they admitted the girl to the intensive care unit. The sterile white walls seemed to close in on her as she lay in the narrow bed. Fluids were administered intravenously via a drip, and she required breathing assistance through a ventilator.

The doctor's fears were confirmed: pneumonia. The constant coughing had caused her eardrums to rupture, resulting in nerve deafness. Dr Mark immediately contacted a specialist ear, nose, and throat doctor to assess Cosuda's hearing. Nurses bustled around her, monitoring her vitals. As the fluids dripped into her veins, her eyes fluttered shut, willing her body to heal.

And then, as if summoned by her silence, she opened her eyes and asked, "Am I dying?" She was too weak to speak aloud.

The matron's heart sank. She squeezed Cosuda's hand. "No, my dear," the matron replied, her voice a gentle. "There's nothing to worry about. You're not dying, you're a fighter. We're all here for you. You'll be fine in a few days; you just need to rest. You've been working long hours, and it's been too much for you."

Dr Mark leaned in closer. "We're doing everything we can. Rest now, and let us help you heal."

Cosuda simply looked at her. She could see her lips moving, but she was unable to hear. The matron was unaware of the tears running down her own cheeks as she observed the girl.

"Why are you crying? Please speak up. I can't hear you," Cosuda mouthed her frustration evident even in her weakened state.

Her fever blazed, her body frail, but her eyes fierce.

"I can't miss my class tomorrow," Cosuda whispered, though she could hardly hear herself. The matron, lost in the fear of losing her, did not respond. She stayed by her side, willing her to hold on and fight for another day.

"Mum, please come back for me," Cosuda mumbled, her voice barely audible. Her words were a desperate plea, reaching for a past that felt impossibly distant, leaving behind memories and unanswered questions about her mother. Her thoughts drifted in and out of focus, the world around her a blur of white and worry.

Her fever had risen steadily over the past few hours, leaving her weak and disoriented. Her eyes remained red-rimmed and vacant.

"We'll get you better," the matron said soothingly.

Cosuda looked up at her and attempted to speak again, but the words failed her. With a sigh, she closed her eyes, surrendering to exhaustion.

The following morning, Dr Mark returned and attempted to give her a drop of liquid to drink, but she was too weak to take it.

"How is she?" the doctor asked. He had seen many sick patients over the years, and pneumonia was a ruthless killer. However, he could see first-hand how swiftly the illness had ravaged her in just 24 hours. Reading through the previous doctor's notes, he examined her and took her temperature, which remained dangerously high. It confirmed what he feared, her hearing had been affected.

He paused, choosing his words carefully. "Prepare for the worst."

He turned to the matron with a bleak expression, the weight of the diagnosis heavy in the air. His gaze lingered on the frail figure in the bed, wondering if she had the strength to fight this battle.

"Please don't say it," the matron whispered, her voice breaking. "I've grown so fond of her… she's like a daughter to me." She collapsed into a chair, her hands covering her face, terrified of what he might say next.

"The hospital is doing everything it can to keep her cool and bring down her fever. You can help by making sure she drinks plenty of fluids, even if you have to force them down." His tone was gentle but firm. He didn't want to give her false hope.

"We can only pray for her now," Dr Mark said.

Immediately, the matron began applying damp flannels and offering Cosuda water. The girl was unaware of the people surrounding her, lost in her own world of feverish dreams.

Some of the other girls from the orphanage arrived at the hospital, but they weren't allowed into her room for safety reasons. They stood outside, staring in shock through the glass window, unable to comprehend how she had deteriorated so quickly.

Cosuda was the orphanage's first case of this illness, and there had been no previous reports of an outbreak in the area. Dr Mark checked her temperature again, his expression growing more serious.

"How is she now?" the matron asked.

"She's the same," he replied grimly. He stared at her for what felt like an eternity. He knew she couldn't last much longer unless the fever broke.

"What's her situation? I understand she's in your care at the orphanage, but does she have any parents? If so, they need to be informed," he said firmly.

The matron hesitated. "Her mother left for France in a hurry eight years ago, promising to return as soon as possible, but that could mean years. She never provided an address, so we have no way of contacting her. I expected to hear from her with a forwarding address, but I'm not sure Cosuda will ever see or hear from her again," she said, concealing the painful truth. "I'm the closest person to her, and I'm happy to help with anything she needs."

Dr Mark's expression remained unreadable. "What about her father?" he asked.

"There was no mention of her father."

"There is not a lot we can do in that case, but since she is under your care, I will consult with you directly. I have to leave for another emergency, but I will be back in the morning. If anything changes during the night, or if you need me, please call."

"Thank you, Doctor," the matron said gratefully. They left the room, and she walked down the corridor alongside him.

"I wish I could give you more hope, but there's nothing more I can do for her right now. We must continue praying," he said softly. "I see how much she means to you."

"What is the cause of her illness, Doctor?"

"It could be one of several reasons. The most common is that it can be spread by someone sneezing or coughing, with tiny droplets carrying germs into the air that someone else can inhale. It can also be transmitted through contact with contaminated surfaces, where germs are transferred by touching the mouth or face," he explained.

"Yes, she means a lot to me," the matron said, her usual sternness giving way to a rare moment of vulnerability.

"I can see that," Dr Mark replied, gently tapping her on the shoulder.

"I will call you if necessary," she said, closing the door behind him and quickly returning to Cosuda.

The hospital allowed the matron to stay the night, and although exhausted, she barely slept in case she was needed. The hum of machines and the sterile scent of antiseptic filled the room creating an atmosphere of tension.

Dr Mark returned early the following morning, as promised, and took Cosuda's temperature, which was slightly lower. As he examined her, she stirred, the dim light blurring her vision. Her head throbbed as she struggled to make sense of her surroundings. The matron's face came into focus.

"What's happening? Where am I?" Cosuda's voice was raspy, her throat parched.

"I'm here, Cosuda. Everything will be fine," the matron reassured her.

"Why can't I hear you? You are not my mother," she murmured, her mind still foggy. She tried to sit up, but weakness pinned her to the bed.

"No, dear, I'm your matron from school. You were dancing—do you remember?"

Cosuda looked confused, the strain of trying to understand adding to her exhaustion. Her memories felt fragmented, like distant stars, and she struggled to make sense of her surroundings. The doctor had said that sleep was the best remedy. Perhaps, in her dreams, she would find answers.

For two weeks, Dr Mark checked on her, monitoring her fever and assessing her condition. Then came a glimmer of hope, her temperature had finally dropped, and she felt cooler. However, the doctor remained cautious. Her hearing, it seemed, had suffered during her illness, but refrained from revealing the severity until the necessary tests were completed. Now that her temperature was nearly back to normal, the tests could be performed.

She opened her eyes, squinting the harsh light. "What time is my next lesson?" she asked, looking directly at the matron.

"No lessons today, Cosuda. You need to stay in bed and get better."

Cosuda frowned, wanting her to speak louder, but she lacked the energy to ask.

The matron was overjoyed at Cosuda's progress, albeit slow. However, Dr Mark did not want to celebrate too soon, as there was still a long way to go. He left to see his other patients, promising to return with a specialist who could perform the necessary hearing tests.

The next morning, Dr Mark arrived with Mr Stanley, the audiologist. The sombre expressions of those around him revealed that her condition hadn't improved since Dr Mark had contacted him.

Despite her continued weakness, he was relieved to see how much Cosuda had improved overnight. Her fever had subsided, but he advised the matron to be prepared for the outcome.

"It is a very quick and painless test, and we will know the results right away," he reassured.

"Thank you," the matron replied.

He inserted an earpiece containing a microphone and speaker into each ear. As he adjusted them, the matron's mind raced. The doctor's suspicions were confirmed—both ears had been affected.

"Cosuda's hearing has been severely impaired," Mr Stanley told the matron. "The illness she contracted has left her with little hearing."

"No, it can't be! Her dancing is her life. How will she ever dance if she's deaf?" she demanded, her tone more severe than intended.

Mr Stanley explained that there were options and assured them that he would speak with the staff, as well as Cosuda, to explain everything, but only once she had regained more strength.

Cosuda looked up at the doctor and those gathered at the foot of her bed.

Dr Mark felt a surge of relief as he observed her progress. The fever had finally subsided, and she was on the mend. Looking directly at her, he promised to see her again soon.

The matron's emotions were a whirlwind, grateful for Cosuda's rescue, yet fearful that her newfound deafness might hinder her dancing dreams. She had so many questions, but she chose to wait until she heard her options. She couldn't help but think how close they had come to losing her. It felt like a miracle that she appeared to be recovering. She nodded curtly at the doctor in gratitude.

He told her, "This is why I became a doctor. I only wish I could cure everyone, but unfortunately, that isn't always possible."

"She must be extraordinarily strong-willed to have begun pulling through this," he added. "But if I'm being completely honest, I didn't expect her to."

"Can I dance soon, Doctor?" Cosuda asked.

He shook his head. "Not for a while, Cosuda. You need to be patient a little longer," he said, smiling gently.

It was too early to tell her about the impact of her hearing loss. As she was still very weak from the fever, he wanted her to rest before giving her any further news. The matron asked about the next steps, and he was honest with her, telling her that it would be a long time before she could dance again. They couldn't yet say how long she would need to stay in the hospital, but she would remain under his care. Her body was frail, and her illness would take a long time to heal.

A week later, Dr Mark and Mr Stanley scheduled a meeting with Cosuda and the matron to discuss her future.

Cosuda looked at them, unsure of what to expect. Mr Stanley met her gaze and explained that someone who is deaf can still detect sounds through vibrations. Depending on their level of hearing, they might even be able to feel and dance to the beat of the music.

Sitting beside her bed, he sketched a drawing of what the implants would look like.

Cosuda watched intently, her heart heavy with a mix of hope and fear.

"With cochlear implants, you may be able to hear some of the lower notes in the music," he said gently.

She sat in silence, absorbing his words, which she perceived only as a whisper. Sensing her uncertainty, he assured her, "With your determination, you will dance again."

"We need to run more tests to determine the extent of your hearing loss, which will help us decide on the best procedure," he explained to both Cosuda and the matron.

After the appointment, her fears eased slightly, and she hoped she would be a suitable candidate for the implant surgery. The thought of dancing again flickered in her mind like a distant dream. She wondered how much of her life would change and if she could adapt to a new way of hearing.

Though the matron was incredibly grateful that Cosuda was alive and gradually improving, she knew how devastated the girl would be once she fully understood what this meant for her future.

As she walked back to Cosuda's bedside, she gazed down at the sleeping child, surprised by her own emotions. Never before had she grown so attached to a child—yet her reasons remained shrouded in secrecy. The matron gently brushed a stray hair from the girl's forehead, her thoughts drifting to memories of her past.

Chapter 16

One evening, while going through files, Rose discovered a lead that pointed to Arthur Briggs, a former prisoner of war.

"I don't remember him," he admitted. "I worked with Neville in 1939 but wasn't called up until the following year. Maybe Arthur had been transferred out of France by then."

According to the file, Arthur would now be sixty years old. Rose noticed he had a contact address in Paris. Since this was her first genuine lead, she needed to speak to him as soon as possible.

She told Zach that if the company didn't allow her to take time off, she would rather resign than miss this opportunity.

"I need to return this box of information in the morning and discreetly put it back in the locked storage room. Then I'll speak to my manager about taking leave," she said.

The next morning, she arrived early to ensure she could return the box unnoticed. The office was quiet, and no one was around, so she quickly placed the box back in storage. However, as she was locking up, she spotted one of the administrators watching from a distance.

Muttering under her breath, she said, "That's exactly what I don't need right now."

She removed the cover from the typewriter and immediately began typing a message to her manager, apologising and requesting an urgent meeting. After a moment's hesitation, she walked over to the secretary's desk and placed the letter in the post tray.

By now, someone had likely reported her for entering the archive storeroom, and she feared the inevitable consequences. Despite wanting to keep her job, she knew she would have to explain her actions to her manager. The job was only temporary—her real goal had always been to return to England once she found her father. That had been the purpose of this entire trip.

Later that afternoon, she received a reply instructing her to attend a meeting with Mr Simons at 4 p.m.

When she arrived at his office, she knocked and waited. A smartly dressed young man in uniform opened the door.

"Follow me, Mrs Douglas."

She had never been to this part of the building before and was struck by how formal everything appeared. A row of chairs lined the hallway outside his office.

"Take a seat and wait to be called," he said in a crisp, professional tone.

Moments later, she was led inside, where Mr Simons and Miss Lacoste were seated opposite her. The atmosphere was serious, and she assumed she was about to be dismissed.

"Sit down, Mrs Douglas," Mr Simons said.

"I will be taking notes during the meeting," Miss Lacoste informed her.

Rose's fingers tapped nervously on the table as words tumbled out in a rush.

"I'll resign," she said, her voice wavering but determined. She glanced around the room, finally meeting their eyes. "I told you my reason for being here in Normandy was to find my father," she continued, searching their faces for understanding. "I have to take a leave of absence. I don't know how long I'll be gone."

Mr Simons held up a hand to stop her.

"You've been doing an excellent job. Everyone has been singing your praises since you started."

Her shoulders relaxed slightly.

"Thank you, Mr Simons. I'm pleased to hear that."

"We don't want to lose you," he continued, leaning back in his chair. "Over the years, we have seen how hard you work and how dedicated you are to your job. While we understand your reasons, we can't let you go indefinitely."

She nodded, a small smile forming on her lips.

"I appreciate that. I completely understand and will keep in touch."

"Come and see me when you return. If there's a vacancy, we will gladly offer you a job," he said sincerely.

"Thank you."

As she left his office, she couldn't help but think about the incident in the archives. It hadn't been mentioned, so perhaps it had gone unreported. The meeting had left her with a sense of satisfaction, yet a bittersweet awareness lingered; soon, she would return to England for her daughter.

The staff wished her well and encouraged her to keep in touch. As she made her way home, she reflected on how much she was appreciated. Her thoughts drifted to Arthur, wondering how he had fared in the years since the war ended.

Together, she and Zach made the necessary travel arrangements. However, Rose gently explained to him that the four-hour train journey to Paris would be much faster if she travelled alone. Though Zach felt a pang of uselessness, he understood her reasoning, it would slow her down considerably if he accompanied her. The weight of responsibility rested heavily on her shoulders, but she knew it was the right decision.

The next day, Rose was packed and ready to embark on her journey, hoping to return with good news.

"I'll write as soon as I arrive to keep you updated. I'll be back as soon as possible, depending on how things go with Arthur," she assured him.

"Please be careful," he said, looking straight into her eyes. "I will m-miss you. And yes, please let me know when you've arrived safely," he added, his voice filled with concern.

"I will," she replied with a smile, embracing him tightly. "I will miss you too."

After boarding the train, she dozed on and off throughout the long journey, her thoughts drifting between memories of Cosuda, her father, and Zach. As the countryside blurred past the window, she recalled her daughter's gentle smile, her father's stern but loving guidance, and Zach's unwavering support. Each memory was a bittersweet reminder of what she had lost and what she still hoped to find.

The matron responded to most of her letters, keeping her updated on Cosuda's health and ballet progress, something she was always grateful for. However, she often wondered why she had never heard from Cosuda herself. She imagined what her daughter would look like now that she had turned fifteen. The ideal solution would be to find her father and then return to England to bring her daughter home. She would miss Zach, he had become a close friend and a part of her life but she couldn't dwell on that now. Despite their growing friendship, her father and daughter remained her top priorities.

THOSE MISSING YEARS

Meanwhile, Zach decided the day after Rose left for Paris that he would finally tell her how he felt when she returned. He had kept his emotions hidden for a long time, but he needed to be sure she wouldn't run. In the meantime, all he could do was search through files, write letters to some of his contacts for leads, and have a meal ready for her when she got home from work. She was a remarkable woman, relentless in her search. If only he could ease her distress over losing contact with her daughter but that was beyond his control. He just wished she would finally receive a personal response from Cosuda.

As he sifted through the files, his mind wandered to the day he first met Rose. Her determination had captivated him instantly. He longed to be the one to bring her some semblance of peace.

That evening, Zach sat sipping his tea with the TV on mute, his thoughts consumed by Rose and how much he missed her. He was falling in love with her. While he believed the warmth was reciprocated, he had no idea how she truly felt. *Am I just a friend?* he wondered.

Meanwhile, Rose arrived in Paris, stepping off the train at Gare du Nord. She was exhausted but determined. First, she needed to find a safe place to stay before going to see Arthur. As she wandered through the cobbled alleys, the scent of freshly baked croissants made her stomach growl. She paused for a moment, allowing herself to savour the aroma.

She was about to enter a café when she noticed a small B&B. Pushing open the heavy wooden door, she was greeted by the scent of freshly picked flowers. As she walked over the creaky floorboards, she felt the warmth of a crackling fire. The tiny windows, draped with lace curtains, added to the cosy atmosphere. Rose felt a sense of relief wash over her as she stepped into the cosy interior. She had found a sanctuary in this foreign city.

She approached the reception desk, where the proprietor, Madame Daphne, greeted her with a knowing smile.

"Bonjour, mademoiselle. Welcome to La Maison des Fleurs. My name is Madame Daphne. How may I help you?" the woman asked in a lilting French accent.

Rose smiled back, feeling a wave of comfort washing over her. "Bonjour, Madame. I need a room for a few nights, please."

"That is fine. Have you travelled far?"

Rose's voice reflected her exhaustion. "From Normandy, by train."

"Ah, Normandy, a region of lush meadows and dramatic cliffs. It must have been quite a journey," Madame said.

She gestured towards a worn armchair by the fireplace. "Sit, my dear. Warm yourself. Tea?" she offered, already pouring from a delicate pot.

"Yes, please," Rose replied.

Rose explained that she wasn't sure how long she would be staying, but Madame assured her it was not a problem. She even offered to have dinner ready for 7 p.m. that evening. Leading Rose up the winding staircase, she showed her to a small room with a breathtaking view of the Seine before leaving her to unpack and freshen up. The décor was a harmonious blend of antique charm and modern comfort and featured an elegant writing desk beside a sleek modern armchair. It was the perfect place to stay within her budget.

THOSE MISSING YEARS

As they spoke later, Madame described the grandeur of Paris. "The Eiffel Tower stands like a sentinel over the city, shimmering with lights every evening."

Rose could almost see the tower's iron latticework glistening in the twilight.

Madame continued, "And the Seine winds through the heart of Paris, reflecting the golden hues of the bridges and the laughter of lovers strolling along its banks."

Rose imagined herself walking those very streets, the history of Paris woven into every cobblestone. She felt an unexpected sense of belonging as if the city was welcoming her with open arms. She thanked Madame for sharing Paris's beauty but explained that she was only there to meet an old friend. As beautiful and romantic as the city was, she had come solely for Arthur.

The next morning, she wrote a letter to Zach to let him know she had arrived safely, settled into Madame Daphne's bed and breakfast, and that everything was fine. Madame Daphne gave her directions to Arthur's address, which turned out to be a long journey through the Parisian public transport system, complete with cancellations before she finally reached her destination.

When Rose arrived, she hesitated for a moment before knocking on the door. A young woman answered and explained that she had bought the house just over a year ago. Regretfully, she added that no forwarding address had been left behind.

As their conversation unfolded, one of Arthur's neighbours, who had been tending to his garden nearby, overheard them. Noticing her disappointment, he approached and kindly invited her inside for a cup of tea. The neighbour, Mr Paul Clarke, was a gentle soul with a warm smile that conveyed kindness.

While they sat in his kitchen, sipping their tea, he shared what little he knew about Arthur. He described him as a private man who mostly kept to himself. Through the neighbourhood grapevine, he had heard that Arthur had fallen ill and, shortly after, had been taken away by a gentleman.

Mr Clarke mentioned, "This happened about a year ago. Arthur didn't have many visitors, but that gentleman seemed close to him. I always wondered if he was family. He never returned, and before we knew it, new neighbours had moved in."

Her heart sank slightly, but a spark of hope remained. Perhaps this gentleman knew where Arthur was now. She thanked Mr Clarke and made a mental note to follow up on this new lead. "You've been very helpful. It might be best if I go to the police station and see if they can help me find him."

That evening, after returning to the hotel, she wrote to Zach, informing him that Arthur no longer lived at the address she had for him. She had dinner at the hotel and retired to bed early.

The following morning, Rose was up bright and early, determined to make the police station her starting point in the search for Arthur. Upon arriving at the station, she introduced herself to an officer and explained why she needed to speak with Mr Briggs. The officer nodded and took her contact details informing her to return in 48 hours when they expected to have more information.

As she stepped out of the station into the morning sunshine, she decided to use the waiting time to explore the town. Her first stop was the local library. It was a charming building with ivy creeping up its stone walls. Inside, the musty scent of old books greeted her, bringing a sense of calm amidst the chaos of her mission.

She approached the librarian, a young woman with a welcoming smile, and asked if there were any records or newspapers from the war years. Her interest was deeply personal, driven by her search for her missing father, and she felt a connection to the history surrounding her. The librarian led her to a dusty archive room, where she spent hours sifting through yellowed pages and faded photographs. She was so engrossed in the stories they told that she barely noticed the time until she had to leave.

Afterwards, she stopped by the butcher's shop next door, where she spoke with an elderly employee whose eyes crinkled with age as he leaned on the counter.

"Excuse me, I'm looking for some information about a Mr Briggs," Rose began. "Arthur Briggs." Do you know him at all?"

"Ah, Mr Briggs," he said with a low hum. "A remarkable man, he was."

Rose, eager for any information, asked, "Sir, do you know where I can find him?"

The butcher's gaze drifted to the window as if searching for answers in the passing crowd. "His son used to live nearby. But it must be over a year ago that he cancelled his father's meat deliveries. Said he was moving because of illness."

"Do you know where he moved to?" Rose asked politely.

The butcher shrugged. "I don't know exactly, but I believe it's a care home on the outskirts of Paris. I heard his Alzheimer's had advanced to the point where he could no longer care for himself."

"I'm sorry to hear that, but thank you, you've been a great help."

Two days later, she returned to the police station, where they provided her with the address of a nursing home where Mr Briggs had been taken by his son fourteen months earlier. Although the home was not far from the B&B, the journey took just under two hours due to the need to transfer buses.

As she stepped off the bus, she saw the nursing home directly across the street. She pushed open the heavy wooden door and stepped inside. The air was thick with the scent of disinfectant and age. The receptionist took her details and asked her to take a seat while she spoke with a senior member of staff.

The care manager arrived thirty minutes later, introduced herself, and apologised for the delay, explaining that she had been dealing with an emergency.

"Good afternoon, my name is Rose Douglas. I'm looking for Arthur Briggs," she said. "I understand his son brought him here over a year ago?"

The manager led Rose into her office and made her a cup of tea while they discussed the purpose of her visit. She described Arthur's illness and how his dementia was progressing.

"He remembers very little now, so please avoid discussing anything that may confuse or upset him."

"I will be careful," Rose interrupted gently. "I'll only ask him about Neville, who was a close friend of his."

Grateful for the advice, Rose followed the manager to Arthur's room. The manager introduced her before leaving them to talk.

Rose approached him gently, offering a kind smile to put him at ease. She sat down in the large Victorian chair beside his bed.

"Hello, Arthur. May I tell you who I am and why I'm here?"

She could see the toll the illness had taken on him, and her heart ached at the sight. His frail figure and distant eyes were a stark reminder of the relentless march of time. She mentioned her father, hoping for a flicker of recognition, but his eyes remained distant. She spoke softly to him about life in general, sharing snippets of recent days, but there was still no response.

Although Rose realised her journey had been in vain, she took comfort in having seen Arthur, a man who had once worked closely with her father and played a significant role in his life. It had been a long but deeply important trip. She wanted to sit with him a little longer, hoping for any sign of recognition, but seeing him in such poor health saddened her.

After fifteen minutes, she decided it was time to leave. She leaned in and kissed his forehead, a gesture of compassion and farewell.

"Thank you for seeing me, Arthur, but I think you should rest now. Perhaps I will see you again soon."

Knowing she wouldn't be returning, she added, "Goodbye, Arthur. Please take care."

As she slowly walked towards the door, she turned to smile at him, when she heard a mumble.

"Your father was a great man."

"Oh, Arthur, thank you very much; that is lovely to hear."

She walked back to his bed, held his hand, and asked, "Do you want to talk about anything? Like what happened to him?"

In a whisper, he replied, "Yes, I do."

"That would be very helpful, but please stop if it becomes too much," she said softly.

"We were together until he was injured. He suffered for years and spent a long time in hospital. After he married his nurse, they returned to Normandy."

He closed his eyes, and Rose watched him, trying to take everything in. When he opened them again, he gazed up at her.

"Hello, I haven't seen you before. Are you new here? Everyone is nice."

Rose's emotions welled up. It was heartbreaking—just moments ago, he had spoken about her father, yet now, he didn't remember her. She felt a pang of sadness and helplessness, knowing that his memory was slipping away.

"Yes, I am," she replied, wiping away a tear. She embraced his hand, feeling the frailty in his grip. "I'll see you soon, Arthur,? She said, even though she knew it might not be true. When she looked back at him, his eyes were closed. Realising there was nothing more she could do, she left her contact details with the care home and returned to the B&B.

The following morning, after a quiet breakfast, Rose packed her case and set off for home. Before leaving, she made her way to Madame Daphne to say goodbye.

"Madame Daphne, I wanted to thank you for everything," Rose said warmly. "Your hospitality has been wonderful."

Madame Daphne smiled. "It was my pleasure, dear. Safe travels, and I hope you found the answers you were looking for."

After their heartfelt exchange, Rose set off. There was no time to write to Zach to tell him she was on her way, so she decided to surprise him instead.

As the train rattled along the tracks, she found herself lost in thought about the events of the past few days. The journey had been long and tiring, but hearing Arthur's words about her father had given her some solace and renewed determination to uncover more of his story.

When she finally arrived in the early evening, all she wanted was the comfort of home and the warmth of Zach's presence. She was eager to share every detail with him. This chapter had come to an end, but the next one was just beginning.

Chapter 17

Finally, home was in sight. She opened the front door, expecting to hear the wireless, but it was silent. Walking into the quiet, dark living room, she switched on the light. Zach jumped and turned around, startled to see Rose standing there. He wheeled his chair towards her with such speed that he nearly crashed into her. She wrapped her arms around him tightly.

"I'm so happy to see you," she said, meaning every word.

"I missed you so very much," he replied. Since meeting Rose, he had felt a sense of purpose in his life.

"Why didn't you tell me you were coming back? I would have prepared something special for you."

Rose offered a small smile, weary but warm. "Don't worry, Zach, I ate on the train. But how are you?" she asked, studying his face as though trying to read the emotions hidden beneath his cheerful exterior.

"I'm....better now that I'm s-seeing you," he said, beaming. He admitted he had been overthinking things lately, but now, seeing her again, he was overjoyed.

Her presence filled the room he'd missed, yet he couldn't shake the thought of everything he'd left unsaid.

"You must be exhausted from the long journey, and as much as I'd love to hear about your meeting with Arthur, you can tell me all about it tomorrow."

Rose was glad to be back with Zach and appreciated his suggestion to leave the conversation until the morning. She needed rest. "You're right," she murmured, stepping closer. As she walked over to say goodnight, she noticed him looking up at her. Leaning in to gently place a kiss on his cheek, she could almost feel his heartbeat. She quickly moved away, but before she could speak, he took both hands, his touch tender. He drew her close, brushing his lips to hers, and kissed her tenderly.

He had wanted to do that for a long time, and it finally felt like the right moment.

At first, she was too shocked to react, but then she gave in, melting into his arms. When they finally broke apart, she looked at him, dazed. "Where did that come from?" she whispered.

She surprised herself with how naturally she had responded. She couldn't remember the last time she had been kissed like that. Tom had stopped touching her as soon as Cosuda was born.

"It's because I love you, Rose," Zach said. "I've wanted to tell you for so long. Being with you feels more real than anything I've ever known. I didn't think it was possible to feel this way, but I know it's real."

A chill ran down her spine, grounding her in the reality of what just happened.

"There are so many thoughts swirling in my head; I can't think right now. I have a lot to process. I'm sorry, Zach... this is so much, so fast. I don't know what to say. I just... I need time to think." Her voice trembled, and she hesitated before looking at him.

Romance had been the last thing on her mind after her marriage with Tom fell apart. The wounds were still raw, and opening her heart again felt not only impossible but far too soon. She had never considered this possibility before. But with Zach, it was different. There was a quiet, unspoken spark that she'd kept buried beneath the pain of her past. He was a kind man, steady, and dependable, with strong morals that she admired.

As she looked at him, the flicker of disappointment in his eyes struck her deeply. Guilt welled up inside her, mingling with a pull towards him she couldn't ignore.

"I understand," he said softly, his voice steady but touched with sadness. "Let's get some rest. Tomorrow, you can tell me more about Arthur, and we'll begin a new search for your father."

At the doorway to her room, she paused, glancing back at him. A part of her wanted to kiss him goodnight again, but something held her back. Now didn't feel like the right time.

"Please s-stay with me tonight, Rose?" His voice was soft, vulnerable. "I just want to be close to you."

She took his hand and followed him. Soon, they were wrapped in each other's arms, finding comfort in their shared closeness.

His kiss had changed everything between them. The walls she'd kept so carefully in place had crumbled, leaving her exposed.

"I l-love you, Rose," he stammered.

She smiled, tears brimming in her eyes. "I love you, too, Zach." Her voice was steady, but her heart raced with a mix of fear and hope.

The silence between them was warm and comforting until they drifted off to sleep.

The following morning, they woke early and talked nonstop over breakfast about her time in Paris.

She told him that Arthur had remembered Neville marrying his nurse and moving back to Normandy, but beyond that, his memory was patchy due to his dementia.

THOSE MISSING YEARS

"The care manager said his son had brought him to the home, but visits only sporadically. He didn't leave any contact details because he currently has no fixed address. Since Arthur's wife died two years ago, his condition has worsened," Rose said. Arthur's memory isn't what it used to be. He remembered Neville, whom he called his 'war hero colleague,' but the details were patchy, slipping away as he spoke. He seemed lost like he was trying to grasp something that wasn't there."

She didn't realise the effect her words were having on Zach, the way his hands clenched at his sides as he listened.

"So many s-sad times." He closed his eyes, willing the memories away. But they clung to him like shrapnel, tearing through his soul. The tears came freely.

"Oh, Zach, I'm so sorry," Rose said gently. She reached for his clammy hands and held them in her own. "I should have been more careful with my words."

"No, you don't need to apologise," he said. I wanted to know how things went with Arthur. It's just…the flashbacks return when I least expect them," he admitted.

His eyes locked onto hers, the intensity in his gaze revealing the weight he carried. "I was there. I saw it all. The ones who limped home. The ones who never spoke about their demons. They're still with me," he said.

Rose reached up and wiped the sweat from his brow. She didn't need to say anything; she simply held him.

"Since meeting you," Zach said, the past doesn't haunt me as much."

Feeling drained, he closed his eyes, and Rose gently guided him to the sofa.

Whilst Zach rested, she sat nearby, her thoughts consumed by other ways to find out whether her father was still alive. Now that Arthur had told her he had moved to Normandy, she clung to the hope that he might still be there. She paced around the living room in deep thought, replaying the conversation from the night before and formulating a plan.

Determined to take action, she sat down to write a letter to her daughter, hoping for a reply, and another to the matron, thinking it might lead to more information. Afterwards, she occupied herself with household chores. Having spent a few hours cleaning the house, preparing dinner, and making some written plans, she felt satisfied with her day.

By the time Zach appeared in the kitchen, she'd prepared dinner and outlined written plans to search for Neville.

"How are you feeling, Zach?" Rose asked. She thought he looked pale, as if from the strain of revisiting those wartime memories with Arthur and Neville.

"I'm sorry for what happened earlier, Rose. It hasn't affected me like that in a long time… but I feel better now after the rest."

She nodded as she set the table for dinner. They ate in companionable silence.

"Are you okay?" Zach asked, concerned.

"Yes, I am," she replied, still thinking about the night before.

|After clearing the dishes, Rose turned to Zach. "I need to contact work," She said and grabbed her coat before heading to the phone box outside. The chilly evening air brushed against her as she stepped into the cramped booth.

She dialled the number and waited, her heart pounding. When Miss Lacoste answered, Rose explained that she had returned from

Paris and asked if they could meet. Miss Lacoste scheduled an appointment for first thing the next morning, leaving Rose with cautious optimism. But as she walked back home, uncertainty tugged at her. If they had no position available, she would have to return to the agency and begin the process of searching for temporary work all over again.

As soon as she arrived home, she told Zach about the call.

"I'm not surprised," he said reassuringly. "They told you how much they would miss you and to contact them if you needed a job." "There's no rush, Rose."

But Rose was a proud woman and insisted on returning to work.

The next morning, she took the early bus. Miss Lacoste greeted her warmly and, after a brief conversation, promised to discuss her situation with Mr Simons and get back to her soon.

Two days later, a letter arrived from Mr Simons. It explained that due to temporary staff leaving a backlog of work, they were pleased to offer her the same position, on the condition that she could start immediately. Relief washed over her, she was incredibly grateful and accepted without hesitation, ready to tackle the challenges ahead.

Meanwhile, Zach quietly supported her in his own way. He placed an advertisement in the local shop window: "If you've heard of Neville Azpax, please contact Mrs Rose Douglas, care of the local post office." As he pinned the notice, he hoped it might bring them closer to answers.

Back at work, Rose quickly realised how much there was to do. She stayed late most evenings, determined to make up for the time she had been away. Her line manager informed her that much of her workload had been left untouched. Temporary staff had tried to keep up, but it was clear that they hadn't been effective.

The backlog of administrative tasks was daunting.

One of her colleagues remarked, "One of the temps spent more time filing her nails and reapplying lipstick every half hour than actually working."

Rose laughed. "Perhaps that worked in my favour, it's probably why I got my job back so easily."

Late that evening, there was a heavy knock at the front door. Rose opened it to find a man in uniform standing there.

"Mrs Rose Douglas?" he asked.

"That's me," she replied, her voice cautious.

He handed her a telegram. "Please sign for this," he said, offering a pen.

"Yes, of course," she replied, taking the pen. He waited at the door while she signed, then took the paper back with a curt nod.

"Thank you, madam," he said with a serious expression before turning and walking away.

A sense of unease settled over her. Her mind immediately went to Cosuda. "Please, don't let anything have happened to Cosuda," she murmured, casting a worried glance at Zach.

Her hands shook as she tore open the envelope. Her heart raced, bracing for the worst. But to her surprise, the telegram wasn't about Cosuda, it was from Tom. He had filed for divorce.

Rose stared at the words for a moment, her emotions mixed. While she had left him a long time ago and had no intention of going back, the finality of it still lingered in the air. This was the official end of a chapter she had already closed in her heart.

THOSE MISSING YEARS

Given their years of silence, Rose assumed the process would be quick. While relieved that the telegram had nothing to do with Cosuda, a wave of sadness washed over her. She had always believed marriage was forever, but now she understood that sometimes, it was best to let go.

There was little in their shared home that she wanted, just as there was little left between them. She hadn't looked back since leaving Tom and felt no desire to claim anything from that part of her life. Six weeks later, the absolute divorce papers arrived from his solicitor. As she read through the documents, she wondered what had become of him and whether he had ever tried to contact Cosuda.

However, the matron had never mentioned him in her letters, which only confirmed what Rose already suspected—he hadn't been in touch.

She folded the papers neatly, placed them in a drawer, and lingered for a moment in thought. "It's over," she whispered, more to herself than anyone else. The words felt heavier than she expected, but also freeing.

Tomorrow would bring another step forward, and she resolved to keep searching for both answers and peace.

Chapter 18

The matron asked Johnny to prepare one of the private rooms for Cosuda's return from the hospital. He chose the prettiest of them, decorated in pink silk and lace. It was only used in exceptional circumstances, and this was one of those times.

After six long months, Cosuda was finally leaving the hospital. She was filled with excitement at the thought of returning to the orphanage to see her friends. As the ambulance pulled up to the gates, she could see a crowd gathered outside. The moment she was wheeled inside, a warm rush of joy and belonging washed over her.

Dr Mark spoke gently as he informed the matron that Cosuda needed complete rest and was to remain in bed until he deemed her well enough to resume lessons.

"She shouldn't be left alone, Mrs Jones," he cautioned. "Please make sure someone stays with her through the night, at least until she shows significant improvement. We need to ensure she doesn't relapse. I will visit her regularly, or one of my colleagues will."

The matron nodded, her eyes filled with understanding and concern. She assured him that Cosuda would be well cared for and accompanied him to the main door, thanking him for everything he was doing.

As soon as Cosuda was settled into bed, she drifted into sleep, with the matron sitting by her side. A gentle tap at the door was followed by it immediately opening. Lucy peered inside, delighted that her friend had returned home. She turned to the matron.

"May I see her?" she asked eagerly.

Understanding their close bond, the matron nodded and invited Lucy in.

"Of course. It will be good for her to see a friendly face," she said, touching Lucy's arm affectionately before leaving the room.

Lucy sat beside Cosuda for a couple of hours, offering quiet words of encouragement.

"You have to stay strong," she said gently. "I need you, and you have such a bright future ahead of you." She hesitated before adding, "I'll be performing in France soon, and I'll be away for a while. Hopefully, I'll see you before I leave."

Her friend lay still, her eyes closed, lost in a world of her own. Lucy wasn't even sure if Cosuda had heard her, as she had been asleep for most of the visit. She simply sat in silence, saddened by how quickly things could change.

When the matron entered, Lucy knew it was time to go. She gently squeezed Cosuda's hand before rising to her feet. The room felt heavy with unspoken words, bound by the doctor's strict orders.

The next morning, Cosuda woke to find the matron by her bedside.

Confused, she asked, "Can Johnny come to see me, please?"

"Johnny?" The request took the matron by surprise. "Of course. I will send for him right away."

She knew Johnny was always kind to Cosuda and that she regarded him as a good friend—nothing more.

Once Johnny had finished his duties, the matron called him over.

"Sit with her and do not leave her alone," she instructed firmly. "Let me know if you have any concerns right away, as I will be busy most of the day with meetings and phone calls."

She reiterated, "Do not leave her, Johnny. The doctor left strict instructions that she is not to be alone. I will arrange for the other girls to take turns sitting with her when you need to step away."

Johnny nodded, assuring her he would take care of Cosuda. As the matron turned back to glance at her before closing the door, he noticed an unusual worry in her expression. It was rare for her to show such deep concern for anyone.

When Cosuda opened her eyes, she found Johnny standing beside her bed.

"I'm so glad to see you—you scared us," he said, hugging her carefully so as not to hurt her.

She looked at him strangely. "I can't hear you. What did you say?" She giggled in her usual way. "You can talk to me, I'm fine."

Relieved to hear that infectious giggle but startled by her words, he hesitated before repeating, "I'm glad to see you."

Since no one had told him what was wrong with her, he was afraid of saying too much in case he upset her, or got into trouble with the matron. Unsure of what to do or say, they sat quietly for what felt like an eternity. He tried his best to comfort her until the matron returned, but pretending everything was fine proved difficult.

When the matron finally walked in, she immediately noticed Cosuda was upset. Pulling Johnny aside, she asked, "How has she been?"

"She couldn't hear my voice," Johnny said politely, concern in his tone. "What's wrong with her, ma'am?"

THOSE MISSING YEARS

The matron placed a reassuring hand on his shoulder. "Thank you, Johnny. She will recover, so don't worry. You can leave now."

The worry in his eyes lingered as he glanced back at Cosuda before stepping out.

The matron could see how much Cosuda had enjoyed having Johnny there. Her eyes followed him as he left, though she remained silent. He smiled and waved before gently closing the door.

The way he looked at Cosuda, with such gentle care revealed his kind nature, a trait he extended to everyone. Yet, the matron couldn't bear the thought of losing Cosuda to anything that might pull her away from ballet. As she blossomed into a beautiful young woman, the matron hoped she had taken her advice to heart when she had first invited her to join ballet classes.

She could never have both. It was ballet or boyfriends. Cosuda was hers now, and nothing would take her away.

At the next appointment, the doctor carefully assessed the severity of Cosuda's hearing loss and spoke about the potential success of the surgery. Her initial reaction upon learning of her deafness was blind panic. The doctor's lips moved, but the words were swallowed by silence. She could feel the vibrations of her own breath, shallow and rapid, but the sound was lost to her.

"I'm going to recommend that we schedule another appointment with Mr Stanley," the doctor said, looking at her with a reassuring smile. "He will assess whether you're a suitable candidate for a cochlear implant."

"Thank you," she replied nervously.

That evening, Johnny was allowed to visit her again, but only after completing his duties. Before he entered her room, the matron explained the extent of Cosuda's deafness and advised him to be sensitive towards her. Not that she needed to. She knew Johnny would be nothing but kind. He was a good person, and she had great respect for him. He had come a long way since arriving at the orphanage. The matron demonstrated how to communicate with Cosuda, using slow and deliberate gestures to ensure Johnny understood.

Later that evening, Johnny knocked gently on the door before stepping inside.

Cosuda lifted her head and met his gaze. For the first time, she noticed how tall he was, how his grey-blue eyes softened when they met hers, and how his blonde hair fell effortlessly to his chin.

"Hello," Johnny said, suddenly self-conscious. Did he look stupid in his smart corduroy trousers and blue jacket? After giving her a caring hug, he sat down beside her bed.

Looking directly at him, she said, "You look smart. Are you going somewhere?"

He hesitated, reluctant to admit he had made an effort for her. "No, I was working in the garden and got a little muddy, so I just threw this on," he said casually, trying to downplay it.

Cosuda nodded, but her eyes didn't quite meet his. She glanced at his lips, then back at his eyes, her brow furrowing slightly. He noticed her fingers tapping rhythmically against her thigh, a habit she had picked up recently.

As they sat together, she handed him a pamphlet. "Cochlear implants," it read. Her fingers traced the words as she spoke, her voice steady despite the slight tremor in her hands.

"If I'm suitable, the surgery could be in six months," she explained. Then, with a strained smile, she added, "Until then, you need to look at me when you're talking."

"That's great news," Johnny said, his enthusiasm genuine. "The matron called me into her office earlier. She gave me a schedule of when I'm allowed to visit, usually after my duties. She told me about your hearing loss but said that once you've had the operation and recovered, you'll be able to continue your dance lessons." He paused, then added with a playful smirk, "I'll help you as much as I can and when I'm allowed to, of course."

"We'll get through this together," Johnny said, trying to sound optimistic.

Cosuda found his kindness touching and couldn't help but notice how much he cared. She admitted that her brush with death had terrified her, but she was determined not to let it interfere with her passion.

"I will get through this. I will dance again. Nothing will stop me," she said with fierce determination, despite the weakness in her body.

"You will. You are stronger than you think," Johnny said.

A moment later, she shifted uncomfortably. "Johnny, I need the bathroom. Can you help me?"

"Of course," he replied without hesitation. He moved to her side and gently supported her as she tried to sit up. She winced, a painful reminder of the pneumonia still ravaging her body. He carefully slid an arm under her shoulders, suddenly realising just how frail she had become. The weightlessness of her frame startled him, and he carried her with a tenderness that spoke volumes.

"I'm glad you're here," she murmured as they reached the bathroom door. "I couldn't do this without you."

"And I'm glad to help," he said sincerely.

He waited outside, leaning lightly against the wall. bathroom and closed the door behind her. "Shout when you're ready," he called out. When she was done, he helped her back to her chair, adjusting the cushions to ensure she was comfortable.

As she watched him speak, frustration flickered in her eyes; she struggled to understand his words.

Johnny noticed immediately and smiled, his eyes lighting up with an idea. "Let's try to guess what each other is saying," he suggested.

They turned it into a game, laughing as they exaggerated their words and expressions. The shared fun lifted their spirits, replacing frustration with laughter.

As promised, Johnny helped her whenever possible, and they spent more time together with each passing day. Just his presence boosted her confidence. Despite her deafness, her voice remained melodious and clear. Over time, she grew so proficient at lip-reading that she often forgot she was doing it.

The matron arranged for Cosuda to have sign language lessons and agreed that Johnny and Jane could also attend. Once they decided to join, she organised a tutor to teach them once a week, but only after their lessons and during their free time. Johnny liked the idea, and Lucy, who was often away, agreed to join in whenever she returned.

Miss Paxman, the dark-haired sign language tutor, visited the home twice a week. She instantly took a shine to Cosuda, always bringing her extra materials to read and offering a kind smile. Within a month of starting, Miss Paxman informed the matron that Cosuda had made significant progress. She had learned many signs, including the alphabet, and her efforts were further boosted by her hearing friends, who enthusiastically joined the lessons. Their willingness to learn sign language spoke volumes about their genuine friendship, which strengthened Cosuda's confidence.

At 5 o'clock that evening, the BSL lesson had finished. Cosuda returned to her room, feeling the need to rest before dinner. An hour later, Lucy appeared with her meal. She had been asked to stay with Cosuda and help her prepare for the night. They spent the evening together, engaged in easy conversation. Lucy was diplomatic when speaking about her time away, aware of the challenges Cosuda was facing and how they had affected her dancing. Her tactful words and warm presence made the conversation light and comforting, a welcome distraction for Cosuda.

The next morning, Cosuda woke early, her emotions in turmoil as she awaited her hospital results. Suddenly, the door opened, and the matron stood before her, holding a letter.

"You have been accepted for surgery, Cosuda," she announced, beaming.

"YES!" Cosuda shouted with joy.

After six long months, the time had finally come for her implant surgery. Anxious but prepared, she packed her belongings, looking forward to hearing again. Although she was stronger now, Dr Mark had recommended she be taken to the hospital by ambulance. Her friends wished her good luck and handed her a handmade green four-leaf clover. She missed Lucy, who had left for a performance in London before they had the chance to talk. Johnny had the biggest smile as he waved with both hands; he desperately wanted to hug her but thought it best not to draw attention to his feelings. As the ambulance door slammed shut, she tried not to focus on Johnny, waving instead at her friends.

Sitting beside her in the ambulance, the matron watched her closely.

"You will regain your strength, and your friends will be there to support you when you do," she assured her.

As Cosuda was led into the operating theatre, her nerves became apparent. Attempting to calm her, the doctor told her to count backwards from one hundred—it would be over before she knew it.

Two hours later, she slowly opened her eyes, the soft blur of the matron's familiar face coming into focus. The matron was sitting beside her, her presence a quiet comfort. Shortly after, the doctor entered, his expression was calm and reassuring. "The operation went well," he informed her. "You'll need about four weeks to recover before seeing your audiologist to activate the implant sound processor."

Relief washed over her as she absorbed his words. She managed a weak but heartfelt, "Thank you," her gratitude apparent in her eyes.

As she left the hospital, emotions overwhelmed her, and tears spilt freely down her cheeks. Learning that she would be practically deaf for the foreseeable future was devastating. Accepting her new silent reality had been difficult over the past year, but she clung to the promise that the implants would eventually restore her hearing. The past year had been an uphill battle, adjusting to her silent world.

However, her relationships with her friends had also suffered. One-to-one conversations were manageable, as long as there was no background noise, and she could maintain eye contact and pay close attention. Still, it left her feeling distanced from the group dynamics she once loved.

Upon their return back to the home, the matron guided Cosuda to her room, ensuring she was settled comfortably.

"Johnny is here to see you," she said, watching for a reaction.

It was 7 p.m., and Cosuda hadn't expected to see him until the next day, making the surprise all the more welcome. Smiling, she realised she had overreacted with excitement and quickly said, "Thank you."

The matron reluctantly left them alone, knowing that Johnny was the person Cosuda wanted to see the most.

"Hello," Johnny said, stepping inside with a shy smile. "I just finished work and wanted to check on you, see how everything went today and how you're feeling. I guessed you might be a little lonely, being back in your room alone."

Cosuda nodded, "I am, a little," she admitted. "I wish I could be in the dormitory with the girls, but the matron is looking after me well, so I really can't complain."

"They said my hearing would be difficult at first and that I wouldn't be able to hear natural sounds right away. But they promised it should improve gradually."

"It will take time, I'm sure, but you'll get used to it," Johnny reassured her. "As soon as you're feeling better, you'll be back in the dormitory. And yes, I agree that the matron is being exceptionally kind." He smirked slightly, finding it out of character for her to be so pleasant.

He sat beside her bed and watched as she drifted in and out of sleep.

"I'm so pleased you came to see me," she murmured, smiling at him.

He seemed to understand exactly how she was feeling without needing to ask. "I'll be visiting you more often," he promised.

Now that the matron had given him a proper schedule for visits, it would be much easier to spend time with her.

The matron knew how much Johnny's presence meant to Cosuda. However, she also felt the need to keep a close eye on them. She had once told Cosuda that there was no room for romance if she was ever to pursue her dreams of becoming a dancer. And she truly believed that Cosuda's dancing ambitions meant more to her than any boy ever could.

Cosuda noticed Johnny's tired appearance. "You should go and rest. Your days are long and I don't want you wearing yourself out."

She was enjoying his company more and more each day and couldn't wait for the next time he came to see her.

"The doctors said you'll be able to go for short walks soon, and I'll take you as soon as you feel ready, that's if you'd like me to, of course?"

"Yes, for sure," she said eagerly.

Everyone cared about her and did their best to make her feel better.

As always, he hugged her gently and said, "I'll see you tomorrow after I finish work." He walked to the door, stopped, and turned around to look back at her, appearing hesitant to leave. "Will you be okay?"

"Yes, I'll be fine," she replied with a warm smile. "The matron has arranged for the girls to visit me, so I won't be alone for long."

"Okay." He waved and left.

Lucy arrived late from her performance, her stepslight with anticipation as she hurried straight to Cosuda'sroom. She had missed her so much, but her new life as a professional dancer often kept her away. They were overjoyed to see each other and exchanged kisses, hugs, laughter, and tears.

"I'm so sorry I couldn't speak to you before I left for Paris," Lucy said softly, holding Cosuda close. But I sat with you talking, just in case you could hear me.

Cosuda's eyes sparkled with the memory. "It's okay. I remember you being with me." She hesitated briefly, then added, "The matron has arranged sign language lessons for me, Johnny and Jane. You and Susie can join in whenever you're both back. Johnny asked the matron if it was possible, and she agreed right away. She arranged for a tutor to come in weekly and ordered a selection of books so we could all practise together. Johnny's been amazing—he's helped me so much. I'm not sure how I would have coped without him," she said, her face glowing with gratitude.

"It's nice to see Johnny visiting you and helping you so much," Lucy said curiously.

"It is, and I love seeing him. His visits have made such a difference."

They chatted for hours, and their bond deepened by the time apart. As the night wore on, Lucy placed a hand on Cosuda's shoulder. "I'd better let you rest now, but t I'll be back soon, I promise"

Four weeks passed before her doctor arrived to assess her recovery. "Your surgical wounds are healing nicely, just as expected," he reassured her. "Mr Stanley, your audiologist, will be coming this afternoon to fit the external parts of the device."

Cosuda had a mix of nerves and anticipation. When the device was finally fitted and switched on, she was deeply moved to hear the matron's voice—just the way she remembered it.

The audiologist trained her on how to use the implants, with the matron listening in.

"It may take some time, Cosuda, for you to interpret the sounds Mr Stanley explained gently, so don't be disheartened if it doesn't happen right away. With practice, it will get easier."

"There are a few crackles, but it's amazing. Thank you so much," she said gratefully.

"You're very welcome," Mr Stanley replied. We'll see you again at your next appointment."

Although she would return to her dance lessons, it would take time before she could perform as she once did. This was just one more challenge to overcome, and she was determined that her deafness would never stop her.

Chapter 19

As Rose's birthday approached, Zach decided to book a table at a champagne restaurant. She had never truly celebrated her birthday before. In the later years of her marriage, Tom never acknowledged it, so it no longer held any significance for her. It was simply another day.

Zach had spent some time planning, hoping to show her just how much she was loved. He couldn't undo her past pain, but he could try and bring some light into her day. He wanted this year to be special for her and could only hope he had made the right decision.

That morning, before she left for work, Zach kissed her cheek and wished her a happy birthday. "Do you think you could try and come home early tonight?" he asked.

Rose's curiosity was piqued, but she smiled and promised to be home as soon as she could.

"I l-love you," he said, the stammer weaving its way into his words.

Rose's expression softened immediately. She moved closer, taking his hand in hers.

"I love you too, Zach."

Zach noticed the flicker of a bittersweet smile tugging at her lips. It mirrored the emotions she carried, happiness tempered by the ache of missing her daughter and another year of unanswered questions about her father.

Rose finished work early, as Zach had asked, but she was curious about the surprise. When she arrived home, she saw Zach, dressed smartly, looking even more handsome than before. He told her that as soon as she was ready, they would be going out for her birthday. He had reserved a table at a restaurant.

"I should dress to match you, then," she said excitedly.

Aside from quick trips to the local shop, this would be the first time they were going out as a couple, and the fact that it was for a birthday dinner made it even more special. Smiling at him, she ran up the stairs, feeling like a little girl again, eager to get ready for their date night.

For the first time since she had known him, she made an effort with her appearance. She adjusted her dress, smoothing the fabric one last time before heading downstairs. She'd never gone out of her way like this before, but tonight felt different.

When Zach saw her, his mouth parted slightly, but no words came. Rose had an understated grace, perhaps because she was unaware of how truly beautiful she was. Nobody had ever told her. Simplicity defined her charm—her skin glowed, and her inner warmth lit up her eyes. Happy to be going out with him, she couldn't help but smile, and he gazed at her in awe.

He loved living with her because she made him feel warm and wanted, something he had never experienced before. After his injuries, he never expected to meet anyone. When he came home from the hospital and the weight of the wheelchair beneath him all those years ago, he had decided he wouldn't even try.

As the taxi pulled up to the family-run restaurant beneath the warm hues of the summer sky, the setting felt like paradise. The waiter took their coats and seated them at the most romantic table in the dining room, one tucked into a quiet corner, overlooking a spectacular view of the beach and the promenade.

Zach ordered champagne. When the waiter poured their drinks and left to give them time to decide on their meal, Zach turned to Rose.

"You have changed my life," he said, as he looked into her eyes.

He reached into his pocket, pulling out a gold velvet box. Opening it with care, he turned towards her, revealing a sparkling ring inside.

"Will you m-marry me, Rose?" His voice faltered as he reached for her hand, bringing it to his lips with a gentle kiss.

"I still remember the day you turned up at my door looking for your father. You didn't know it, but that day, you saved me."

Rose was at a loss for words, staring at the sparkle of the ring. It shimmered under the light.

"I was nervous, wondering if my plan was enough and if this was the right time… but I had to try."

For a moment, she was too overwhelmed to speak. Then her face lit up with a radiant smile. "Yes, I would love to marry you."

This was the love she had waited for, and she would cherish it for the rest of her life.

The ring had belonged to Zach's mother. Its gold band gleamed softly under the dim light, and now, through every joy and every struggle, it would symbolize their love.

He placed the ring gently on her finger.

"It's beautiful, and I will always treasure it," she said, her eyes filled with love.

After finishing their meal, they called for a taxi home. Over a nightcap, they talked quietly, lost in the warmth of the evening.

Later, as they lay in bed, Rose crept closer to Zach, feeling the steady rhythm of his breath, and he wrapped his arms around her.

"Holding you gives me a sense that I finally belong… that I am loved," he said.

"Meeting someone was the last thing on my mind," Rose murmured as she snuggled against him. "But I'm so glad I found you."

If she had her daughter with her and found her father, her life would finally be complete.

After their romantic evening, life resumed its usual rhythm. Rose was incredibly happy with the man she lived with, but a deep sadness still lingered. Her thoughts often drifted to the day she had left her daughter at the orphanage. She wondered what she looked like now, whether she ever thought about her.

Normally, Rose was quiet and private, but Zach could see the pain etched on her face during those quiet moments. Although the matron at the orphanage kept in touch with Rose, she had made it clear that returning too soon could disrupt her daughter's fragile sense of stability. Rose told herself she would go back for her. But as time passed, Rose feared going back. The matron's manipulative nature planned seeds of fear. What if returning only made things harder for Cosuda?

Her beautiful daughter had once had dancing eyes, a love for singing and dancing, and a kindness that endeared her to everyone. Rose could still hear her soft, melodic humming as she did chores around the house.

Rose had no regrets about going to France. It had been the right decision, a necessary journey to find her father. And now, with the knowledge that her father was living in Normandy, a reunion felt almost within reach.

Monday morning arrived too soon, and Rose was running late. Tugging on her coat and slipping into her shoes, she rushed toward the door. But then, her gaze fell on a letter lying on the mat. She scooped up the crinkling envelope, and as she ripped it open, her breath caught. The words on the page blurred for a moment before they came into focus: it was from Arthur's care home. He had passed peacefully the night before.

She called out to Zach, holding the letter in her trembling hands. "Arthur's gone," she said softly.

Zach appeared in the doorway, "Rose…are you okay?"

"Yes," she said, handing him the letter. But I have to go, otherwise I will miss the bus," her words hurried but her eyes heavy with emotion. "We'll talk later,"

Her mind swirled with thoughts of Arthur as she stepped outside. Rushing to cross the street, she barely had time to register what was happening. She didn't notice the car speeding round the corner towards her util it was too late - it struck her. There was no time to react. No time to think.

The impact sent her sprawling. The pavement was cold beneath her as she landed on her back. Her eyes fluttered shut, and she slipped into unconsciousness.

The ambulance arrived at the scene at 9:30 a.m. The paramedics moved quickly, their faces grim. It was clear she was in critical condition, and they rushed her to the hospital.

By early evening, Zach was starting to worry. He assumed Rose had stayed late at work, searching for more leads on her father.

He knew how desperate she had become, but he didn't want her pushing herself too hard.

As the hours passed, anxiety gnawed at him. His mind raced, trying not to think the worst, but negativity had become his defense mechanism since returning from the war. Something felt wrong.

Then it was just after 6 p.m. when a loud forceful knock on the door made his heart leap. His pulse quickened as he rushed to answer it.

When he opened the, he wasn't surprised to see two officers standing on the step.

"Good evening, sir," one of them said formally. "May I speak with Mr Zach George?"

"Yes, that's me," he replied, fear tightening his throat. "How can I help you?"

The officer exchanged a glance with his partner, hesitating before continuing. "We have reason to believe you know Mrs Rose Douglas… and that this is her address?"

"Yes, I do know her. W-what is this all about? What has happened? Please tell me," Zach stammered, panic tightening his voice as he ran his hand through his hair. "She is my fiancée."

The officer pulled out his ID and asked, "May we talk inside, sir?"

"I—I'm sorry, yes, of course," Zach replied, wheeling his chair aside to let them in. side.

"Thank you, Mr George. I think it's best if we explain everything indoors." The officers then explained everything that had happened.

"A witness who was looking out of her window reported to the police that it was a hit-and-run. She saw the car swerving erratically, going up and down curbs. She believed the driver was drunk. After the car struck Mrs Douglas, the witness ran down the road to the telephone box to call for an ambulance and stayed with her until help arrived. If she hadn't acted so quickly, the situation could have been much worse."

"Please tell me she's going to be okay. She's going through so much right now. And if you could give me the witness's contact information, I would like to thank her personally."

"Yes, that's not a problem," the officer replied.

Zach was in a state of shock. "How is she? What are her injuries?" he asked frantically.

"They stated that her injuries appear to be serious, but they haven't provided any additional details yet."

"How did you get my address?" Zach asked.

"She had a work address in her handbag," the officer explained. From there, we were able to obtain her home address," the officer explained. "I'm sorry it took so long to notify you."

Zach explained to the officers who Rose was and shared a little about her background. The officers listened and then offered to drive him to the hospital.

Zach hesitated, then nodded gratefully. "Yes, please. Thank you."

When they arrived, the officers walked to the reception desk and spoke quietly to the nurse. Turning back, one of them said. "They'll update you as soon as they can."

The wait felt endless as he wheeled himself around the corridor. Finally, a nurse approached him. Her face was calm but serious. "Mr George? Please follow me to the family room."

As they reached the room outside the surgery centre, the nurse briefly explained what had happened to Rose, though she didn't have many details yet. She handed him a coffee and asked him to wait for the doctor, who would be able to provide more information.

An hour later, Dr David, the neurosurgeon, entered the room. Tired from worry, Zach looked up sharply as soon as the doctor walked in. The expression on the doctor's face scared him.

"How is Rose?" Zach asked, his voice filled with concern.

"We are still assessing her injuries and don't yet know the full extent. It was a bad accident, and she remains unconscious."

"Is she going to be okay, doctor? Will she pull through?" Zach was distraught.

"We have reviewed her X-rays and full-body scan, and we will be operating this evening."

Zach's grip tightened on the armrest of his wheelchair. The doctor paused, noting how deeply concerned he was.

"Can I see her?" Zach asked.

The doctor nodded but cautioned, "It will have to be brief."

Zach wheeled himself into the ICU behind the surgeon. When the door opened, the sterile scent of antiseptic stung his senses, but nothing could prepare him for what he saw. Rose was lying motionless, a breathing tube taped to her face, while monitors beeped steadily in the background. Nurses moved with quiet precision, checking her vitals.

Speechless, Zach felt tears sting his eyes. He could barely recognize her—her face was swollen and bruised. One arm was heavily plastered, and bandages were wrapped tightly around her body. As he reached for her hand, her puffy eyes flickered open and closed, and he gripped her hand gently.

The doctor advised him to go home, seeing how exhausted and overwhelmed he was. He assured Zach that if there were any changes, someone would either visit him or call, and he could return the next day.

But Zach refused to leave. "I want to s-stay in the waiting room until she goes in for surgery," he insisted.

Since the staff were unable to change his mind, they offered him some food and a drink. Too anxious to eat, he only accepted a mug of tea.

Dr David returned, his expression composed. "Does Rose have any family we can contact?" he asked gently.

Zach rubbed his face, exhausted but focused. He repeated what he had told the police. "Sh-she has a daughter in England, but she was only supposed to be there temporarily. It's…it's a long story. Rose hasn't seen her in ten years, but she receives regular letters from the Matron of the orphanage, who assures her that her daughter is doing well. Other than that, she hasn't mentioned any family," Zach said, burying his face in his hands.

"I understand, Mr George, but I needed to ask." The doctor hesitated before continuing. "The results show she has suffered multiple broken bones and a fractured skull. The bleeding in her brain has caused her to fall into a coma. She needs surgery."

"Are you asking for my consent? Because I'm not sure I can give it. We're engaged, and we were planning to marry." He went on to explain how Rose had ended up in Normandy.

"As she is divorced and no immediate family has come forward, you are considered her closest relation. Therefore, we need your consent to proceed. I will need you to sign the consent forms. This surgery is critical, Mr George and we must operate as soon as possible."

"Does the surgery pose a risk to her life?" Zach asked, not just thinking of himself but also her daughter.

"There are always risks with any surgery," the doctor said calmly. "But in this case, the benefits outweigh the risks."

Zach exhaled shakily, running his hands over his face. "If you're asking me, then the answer has to be yes."

"I'll have the paperwork drawn up right away."

"Do you have any idea how long she will be in surgery, doctor?"

"I wouldn't like to put a time on it. It depends on what we find once we begin. It's a complex procedure, and this type of operation could take anywhere from ten to twelve hours. I suggest you go home and come back tomorrow. If necessary, we will get a message to you."

Zach thanked him and added. "Please.... look after her." Before leaving, Zach made his way to the ICU to see Rose one last time before the operation. He wheeled himself to her bedside, leaned over, and kissed her cheek gently. His eyes well up as he whispered, "I'll be right here, waiting for you. You can do this. I love you."

Returning home in the early hours of the morning, he grabbed a quick snack before collapsing on the sofa. He closed his eyes, thinking about Rose and praying that the surgeons could repair her injuries. For a long time, he had felt his life was pointless until Rose came along and gave it meaning. He drifted in and out of restless sleep before returning to the hospital later that morning.

He made sure the receptionist knew he had arrived. When she informed him there was no news yet, he said he would be in the waiting room. He sat, anxiously, waiting for any update, looking toward the door each time it opened.

An hour later, Dr David entered the waiting area and found Zach sipping coffee, looking fearful, and staring at the wall.

"How is she doing, doctor?" Zach's voice trembled.

Dr David offered a reassuring smile. "The operation was long and challenging, but it went as well as we could have hoped. We managed to relieve the pressure on her brain and stop the bleeding. Although her spinal cord has been damaged, it is repairable."

Relief washed over Zach. "Thank you for everything you're doing for her, doctor."

"She's in recovery but still in a coma. Given the severity of the accident, in some respects, she's fortunate not to be paralysed. Rose will be in the hospital for several months, which will be a difficult journey for her. Until she regains consciousness, we won't know the full impact of her injuries."

"Can I see her?" Zach asked quietly.

"Yes, I'll take you to her for a short while. The nurses are with her constantly, waiting for her to wake up."

"I—I would like to be there when she wakes up," he said.

"Of course," Dr David replied with a reassuring nod.

Following the doctor into the room, Zach felt helpless seeing her in that condition. Rose lay motionless, the faint hum of machines filling the space. The nurse explained that the breathing tubes and wires made her appear worse than she was and that once they were removed, she would look better.

Zach sat down beside her and took her free hand in his, holding it gently. As he gazed at her swollen, bruised face, memories of their time together came flooding back. The joy and how happy they had been the night he proposed. He spoke to her softly, "I'm here, Rose," watching for any sign of movement, but she remained still.

Moments later, a nurse approached the bed. "You should leave now," she said. "Rose is in some pain, and I need to give her something to help her sleep more comfortably."

Zach thanked her and kissed Rose's swollen cheek. "I'll be back, Rose," he murmured.

An hour later, he was home, the house feeling unbearably empty without her. He couldn't sleep, praying for her recovery. Every chance he got, he returned to the hospital, sitting beside her and holding her hand, hoping to be there when she woke up.

Chapter 20

After a few months of complete rest and attempting to figure out her device, Cosuda pushed herself to get out of bed and practice her dance. Despite the doctor's advice that it would take a long time before she could start dancing again, she decided to go to class and try, but it was a bigger struggle than she had anticipated.

As the matron walked past the studio at 3 p.m., she was startled to see Cosuda dancing. As much as she hated to admit it, Cosuda looked exhausted. The matron sighed and said she was taking her back to her room to rest.

"It's important you rest, Cosuda, and listen to the doctor," she told her firmly.

"I'm fine," Cosuda replied. "I enjoyed spending the afternoon in the studio. Just being there makes me feel better."

She lay down on the bed and fell asleep almost instantly. When she awoke, she blinked and turned her head to find Johnny sitting next to the bed, looking at her.

"I didn't want to wake you because you were sleeping so peacefully," he explained softly.

Propping herself up on an elbow, she began to tell him about her day and how the matron had been fussing and had taken her back to her room to rest, but she assured him she would never give up.

Johnny listened intently, leaning forward as though her every word was precious.

That evening, they sat at a small table in her room and had dinner together.

Their days together began to follow a rhythm; walking slowly through the gardens, talking, and learning sign language. At twenty-six, Johnny was nine years older than Cosuda. The matron thought of him as no more than a good friend. Yet her watchful eyes often lingered, a subtle narrowing of her gaze whenever their laughter rang a little too freely.

Cosuda had never had a male friend before Johnny. The only man she had known was her father, but she had no idea what had happened to him. She had never known her grandfather, either. He had gone to war in France when her mother was only seven years old.

During their time together, Cosuda told Johnny the little she knew about her parents and how her mother had travelled to France to find her grandfather.

"As time goes on, I worry about my mother and what happened to my father," she admitted. It had been ten years since her mother left for France, and she hadn't heard anything from her. But she still believed that one day, she would walk through the door and take her home.

"I'm sure they're both fine. There must be a good reason why you haven't heard from them," Johnny reassured her.

"I do hope you're right," she said, though her heart carried the weight of doubts she couldn't voice.

The conversation turned lighter as they began to talk about their families and childhoods. When she told him for as long as she could remember she had dreamed of being a ballet dancer, her face lit up.

"I don't want to get married young and have children, like my mother did. I want more than that." Yet there was a gap in her story she didn't know how to fill. She had no idea how her parents had met or what their circumstances were because it was never talked about.

Johnny was a good listener and always supported her. She felt much better after talking to him. He had a way of soothing her without even trying. Some of the girls at the orphanage talked about meeting boys and dating as soon as they left the orphanage. But not Cosuda. Her dreams were different. Before her illness, the matron, stern as she was, had told her, "You're becoming the perfect dancer." Those words had echoed in her mind ever since.

One evening, she hesitated before asking, "Have you ever wondered what will become of you?" She was afraid his answer wouldn't include her, though she couldn't quite understand why she thought that way.

"Talk to me about you, Johnny. I don't even know your last name," she said curiously.

"Yes, I sometimes wonder, too… especially when I'm alone in my room with my thoughts. It's McRea, by the way," he said, smiling.

Then he began to tell her his story.

"As soon as I came into this world, my mother sent me away as an evacuee to an orphanage in the countryside of Hull. She was young, unmarried, and her father, my grandfather refused to let her keep me. I was illegitimate, you see. For some reason, I was never adopted. I don't know why. I was five years old when they told me my mother had been ill and died very quickly. I never knew who my father was."

"I'm so sorry, Johnny. That must have been so hard for you."

Johnny shrugged, though his smile didn't quite reach his eyes. "The orphanage made sure I had a roof over my head, at least. Most of the boys generally had to leave and fend for themselves at fourteen, but they helped me find a job. It wasn't much but it kept me going.

"I worked for my keep at the orphanage, so they let me stay longer than most. Everyone was kind to me through the terrible times of the war, probably because I never caused trouble. I simply did what they told me. But when I turned sixteen, they said they couldn't keep me any longer because I was now an adult. I had to leave. They gave me the name of this orphanage and told me they were looking for staff, and fortunately, the matron took me on. That pretty much sums up my life," he said with a shrug.

There were many similarities between their lives.

Listening intently to his every word, Cosuda said, "I'm sorry you had to go through so much. Did you ever find out what happened to your grandfather?"

Johnny shook his head, "No," he replied. "I assume he died since I've never heard anything about him or my grandmother."

"So you hadn't been here long when I visited with my mother, had you?" she asked

"No, just six months. I remember you coming with your mother very well. You were so tiny and sad, and so I tried to make you laugh with jokes."

"And I remember, you did," she said, smiling. "You always did."

"So, for now, I'll continue to work here until something changes," he said.

She hoped nothing would change. The thought of him leaving scared her, though she wasn't sure why. With Lucy away most of the time, Johnny had become her anchor, the one person she could confide in while remaining innocent and harmless. She wasn't ready for that to change.

After talking well into the evening. "You look tired," Johnny finally said. "I think you should get some sleep."

As much as they both enjoyed their time together, Johnny never committed to a specific time for their next meeting, just in case something happened and he couldn't be there. He never wanted to let her down.

"I'm going to ask the matron if I can try the class again tomorrow," she told him.

"Well, please take it easy because you're very special." He smiled. "Goodnight, and sleep tight."

As he closed the door, she smiled warmly at her dear friend. She lay there, reflecting on everything they had talked about before drifting off to sleep, content.

The next morning, she awoke early and waited for the matron, who always checked in last thing at night and first thing in the morning.

Already dressed for dance class, she eagerly awaited the matron's knock on the door.

"I'll walk down with you, but you must take it slowly. You're still not strong enough for a full day," the matron told her. "Just practice for an hour at the back of the classroom. When you're ready, I've asked Johnny to walk you back."

Cosuda was making a particularly good recovery, but the matron didn't want her to overdo it.

When she walked into the studio, she immediately noticed an unfamiliar dance teacher standing at the front of the room, waiting for everyone to arrive.

The girls exchanged uneasy glances as Miss Olive strode into the studio, her posture rigid and her lips pressed into a thin line.

She introduced herself. "Good morning, my name is Miss Olive, and I am your new dance teacher. Please make sure you are always on time because I do not tolerate lateness."

Cosuda assumed Miss Olive was aware of her deafness, but when she failed to follow instructions, the teacher shouted at her.

"What is wrong with you? Are you deaf or something?" she barked, her tone laced with impatience.

Still feeling self-conscious, heat flushed Cosuda's face. Her fingers instinctively brushed against the implants hidden behind her ear, and a lump formed in her throat. The humiliation was too much. Cosuda burst into tears and bolted from the studio. Miss Olive, perplexed and unsure of what was wrong, called out her name and ran after her. Cosuda continued down the corridor until she reached the safety of her room. As she turned to close the door, she noticed Miss Olive behind her. Her expression softened by confusion.

At first, she was nervous about revealing her implants, but she knew she had to. She explained about her deafness, the implants she was still adjusting to, and how she practised lip reading whenever she had the opportunity. She admitted how much she struggled to keep up, always pushing herself to her limits.

Miss Olive, taken aback, apologised. "I...I had no idea," she said quietly. "That's no excuse for shouting at you. I'm sorry."

Cosuda nodded. "Miss Brown knew," she said. "When will she be back?" she dared to ask.

Miss Olive sighed. "She left suddenly because her mother is ill. She had to catch a flight to Germany and won't be returning."

Without another word, they walked back to the studio, the silence filled with an unspoken truce.

Over the months that followed, she eventually felt accepted as both a dancer and a deaf person. She learned to navigate the world cautiously, relying on her instincts while also finding ways to enjoy her own company. Slowly, her confidence grew, and she began to grasp things more quickly and precisely than some of the hearing dancers.

Self-advocacy became her strength. She began asking questions and speaking up when she missed something. At first, she feared that questioning others would irritate them. But, she came to realise that if she needed to know whether she was doing something correctly, it was their responsibility to tell her.

Her dancing flourished as a result, though she occasionally encountered scepticism from some of the more advanced dancers.

Determined not to let it affect her, she confided in Lucy and Johnny about the ignorance she faced. Despite her challenges, she navigated what often felt like an isolated world with quiet resilience.

"I've learned that if you want to be part of society, you have to strive to be bigger and better than a hearing person," she said. "Some people are impatient with me, and there have been times when I've felt like an intruder in their lives."

Lucy and Johnny could see how much she was growing, learning to cope with her deafness each day. Each day, she seemed stronger and more confident, and they were deeply proud of how far she had come in just over a year. They were incredibly proud of how far she had come in just over a year.

She had developed her own method of hearing music—feeling the beat through the floor and letting the bass hum in her chest, a pulse that seemed to sync with her heartbeat. To ensure she hit every cue perfectly, her dancer friends used eye contact to signal the beginning and end of solos. The vibrations of the music travelled through her entire body, making her feel like a bird soaring effortlessly through the sky.

She relied on both the sound and the vibrations of the music to shape her dancing, and the excitement overtook her. Her chemistry with her hearing friends was so strong that words weren't always necessary for communication.

This was her life now. She was born to dance, and nothing had ever brought her more joy.

After a long day, Johnny arrived to take her back to her room.

"You must be tired, you've had quite a day," he said.

"It's been tough," she admitted. But without my cochlear implant, I would have been lost in a world of silence. I'll forever be grateful for the operation that saved my life as a dancer."

He stayed with her and talked for a while until he reluctantly glanced at the clock and stood to leave. "I've got some things to take care of," he said. As he stepped towards the door, a staff member appeared with her dinner.

He turned back, offering her a quick smile. "I hope to see you soon." But that night, he chose not to return, he felt, with a pang of guilt, that he was becoming too fond of her.

Meanwhile, Cosuda tried to focus on her school assignments, but her thoughts kept drifting to Johnny. He was warm and kind, and she was grateful for his friendship. But she was beginning to expect him to be there.

THOSE MISSING YEARS

Later that evening, Lucy visited her. The two of them curled up on Cosuda's bed, reminiscing about their time at the orphanage. Lucy, now performing on top-tier stage productions, was travelling to different cities and making a name for herself.

Cosuda listened, filled with pride for her friend's success, even as a flicker of envy reminded her how far she still had to go.

Cosuda, soon to be eighteen, was stronger than she had ever been. She had worked hard to rebuild herself to push through the challenges life had thrown her way. But she never stopped wondering about her parents and whether she would ever see them again.

The next morning, the matron came to her room. "I was thinking about organising a small party for your eighteenth birthday. How do you feel about that?"

Cosuda's eyes lit up, a spark of joy showed across her face. But as she nodded, curiosity flickered beneath her excitement. Why would the matron go out of her way to do something like this for her?

"Thank you, that would be wonderful. I believe I am not too far from being back to myself, so I would love that," she said, her voice filled with gratitude.

"You are so much stronger than I ever imagined possible. I just don't want you to overexert yourself. I was very scared when you first became ill, but I am so proud of you," the matron said warmly.

Cosuda signed, "Thank you," using sign language, a habit she seized every chance to practice. The matron smiled and returned the sign, replying, "You're welcome."

Then Cosuda said something she hadn't mentioned in a long time. Feeling more confident, she looked directly into the matron's eyes.

"I have often wondered why I've never heard from either my mother or father," she began, "but I have always hoped and prayed. Now, I wonder if I ever will," she said sadly. "It would be nice if they showed up since this is a special birthday. I've never been certain my father knew where I was. I don't remember ever hearing them talk about it, and I'm sure he wasn't home when I left, so I never got to say goodbye."

She would always be grateful to the matron, especially for her kindness over the years, but she also needed to keep her memories alive.

"I'm so sorry, but I have never heard anything from her," the matron said gently. "As you know, she was supposed to contact me with a forwarding address once she found somewhere to live. We tried to find her several times. When you first fell ill, we even contacted the British Consulate and the local authorities in France, but we were never successful."

The matron, terrified of losing Cosuda, she had held onto this lie for years. Whatever her reasons, she held them close, her expression carefully composed.

"It's fine. Thank you for trying," Cosuda replied. Something about the matron's words left her unsure. Still, she forced herself to smile, unwilling to let her doubt show.

But she could never fully accept it. She often wondered if something had happened to her mother. She remembered her mother's unhappiness at home and her desperate need to find her father, but she also knew how much her mother had loved her.

The matron walked up to her hesitantly, then pulled her into an embrace, a rare display of affection. "You're like a daughter to me, Cosuda. And remember, whatever happens, I will always care about you and be here for you."

It was out of character for the matron to be so demonstrative. Though Cosuda was surprised by her emotions, she appreciated the kindness, just as she had with Lucy. There were times when she felt that the matron's affection leaned more heavily towards her than Lucy. This confused her, and she hoped it was only her imagination.

The matron knew she shouldn't have favourites, but sometimes the heart didn't listen to reason.

Cosuda continued to attend her classes daily, growing stronger both physically and mentally. Her studies became a refuge, and like a sponge, she absorbed as much knowledge as possible.

Later that day, Johnny visited her and suggested they take a walk in the gardens. The evening air was bitterly cold, and the grass stood stiff with frost. They wandered around the large grounds and through the trees until they came across a small wooden bench nestled in a quiet corner.

Cosuda, tired from the walk, flopped down onto the bench with Johnny.

Johnny looked at her with admiration. Their faces were close, close enough for Cosuda to notice the faint blush creeping up his cheeks.

"You know, you're very special, and... I think... I..." He hesitated, then quickly stood up and said, "Let's go back inside."

He was nervous about his thoughts. He loved being with her, and he loved her childlike humour and devotion to ballet. She had been through so much, yet she still managed to giggle and make silly jokes.

"Yes, you're right, I am," she said, laughing at him.

He put his arm around her shoulders as they walked back to her room. Neither of them noticed, it just felt natural.

"You've done so well, and I'm so proud of you."

That evening, he stayed and had dinner with her, as he had been doing more frequently. It was becoming a routine she had come to expect, and they were both at ease with it.

The following week, the matron arranged for some dresses to be delivered for Cosuda's birthday party. She had a room filled with wardrobes containing the most beautiful gowns, reserved for the best dancers' performances.

One of the maids arrived with a variety of dresses and was tasked with helping her try them on. After her illness, she was slightly smaller than before, but her favourite dress among them all fit perfectly.

It was a rose-pink gown with semi-embroidered fabric that accentuated her slender waist and showcased her figure beautifully. It also came with a matching shawl, adding the perfect finishing touch. She gathered her long, dark hair into a twist and secured it with a silver slide that had once belonged to her mother. She had slipped it into her bag when she left London all those years ago, cherishing it as a precious keepsake.

"The matron will be pleased that it fits perfectly. She especially wanted this one for you. You must be special— in all the years I've been here, I've never known her to let anyone wear this gown. It has always been well protected and stored in a secure place," the maid told her.

Cosuda was puzzled. Why had the matron specifically chosen this dress for her? It was undeniably beautiful, but she couldn't help but wonder about the story behind it.

She wasn't sure when the matron had first mentioned a party, but when the big day arrived, she could hardly contain her excitement. She rested for most of the afternoon, hoping to regain her strength.

Johnny arrived later and waited patiently while she finished getting dressed. By now, he felt quite at home in her room. When the bathroom door opened, he glanced up and smiled. She looked stunning in the borrowed gown.

"You look so beautiful," Johnny said, his voice full of emotion. There were moments when she seemed so grown up, yet at the same time, so innocent.

"You're very kind, Johnny," she said, doing a small curtsy, just as she had practised on stage.

There were no words to describe how he felt when he looked at her, she was so elegant and graceful. He was captivated by both her strength and her beauty.

"Shall we go?" he asked.

"Yes, let's, Mr McRea," she replied with a smile.

He helped her drape a shawl over her shoulders before they walked to the hall together. Her appearance radiated grace, and her warm smile touched his heart.

Inside, the hall was decorated in soft silks and brocades, with matching candles burning all around. In one corner sat a cake with her name written proudly on top—a beautiful rainbow creation layered with buttercream and sprinkled with colourful toppings.

Overwhelmed by the effort that had gone into the celebration, she felt a deep sense of appreciation. She had never received so much attention before. There wasn't an enemy in sight, yet a lingering emptiness remained, one only her mother could fill. Still, she was determined to enjoy the evening, knowing how much effort the matron had put into making it special.

Looking around the hall, she was delighted to see Lucy and her friends making their way towards her. They gathered around, fussing over her and complimenting how lovely she looked. Laughter and conversation filled the air as she enjoyed their company.

The soft, flowing fabric of her dress made her want to dance, each step turning into a graceful glide across the floor as though the music itself had taken hold of her feet.

Johnny couldn't take his eyes off her, something that didn't escape Lucy's sharp notice.

The celebration was lively, full of colour and energy, with everyone more excited than usual. Just before 11 p.m., the lights dimmed slightly, and the candles at the top of the cake were lit. The crowd gathered and sang "Happy Birthday." After blowing out the candles, Cosuda gave a heartfelt thank-you speech. She made sure to express her gratitude to the matron for arranging such a wonderful celebration.

Noticing how pale and tired she looked, the matron quietly asked Johnny to take her back to her room. As much as Cosuda had loved the evening, she didn't argue.

She smiled at Johnny. "Thank you for looking after me tonight."

"I had such a wonderful time, Johnny. Everyone was so kind and caring," she added.

Before leaving, Cosuda decided to find the matron to personally thank her. She found her in her office, the door slightly ajar. Knocking gently, she called out, "Excuse me, ma'am, I just wanted to thank you for making my birthday so special."

The matron looked up, startled, quickly wiping her eyes.

"I'm sorry for interrupting. Are you okay?" Cosuda asked, her voice soft with concern.

The matron stood swiftly, composed, "Yes, I'm fine," she said, her voice firm but wavering slightly. "I think I might be catching a cold."

Cosuda wasn't convinced. The tears in the matron's eyes told a different story.

"You should get some rest now, Cosuda," the matron insisted.

Reluctantly, she nodded and left, though her mind lingered on the matron's unusual behaviour. There was something in her eyes that made Cosuda wonder about the story she wasn't being told. But she knew better than to push.

Johnny was waiting for her outside. He gently draped an arm around her shoulder as they walked back to her room. Helping her remove her shawl, he stood close, and she leaned against him, feeling both exhausted and grateful.

As she looked up at him, she felt at ease, as if she could talk to him about anything. "I had the best time," she said.

"It was nice to see you enjoying yourself," Johnny replied.

As he turned to leave, he paused, a moment of hesitation. Then, taking a step back toward her, he met her gaze and said softly, "I feel so happy when I'm with you." She had been his best friend for so long, but now he realised that he had grown to love her. Before she could respond, he added, "I love you, Cosuda."

For a moment, she was startled. But then instinct took over, and she found herself kissing him back. Then, as reality rushed in, she pulled away abruptly, her heart racing. Fear crept into her eyes. "I'm only eighteen, Johnny. We can't… why did you do that?" she whispered, distressed.

Her mother had been the only person she had ever kissed or been kissed by. Johnny felt so warm, so gentle, and it felt right. And yet, she knew she could never allow anything to happen between them.

Johnny didn't know what to say. A deep dread settled in his chest as he wondered if he had just ruined everything. The thought of losing her, of being pushed away, was unbearable.

"When I first met you all those years ago, the matron asked me to show you around the orphanage. You looked so lost, so devastated after your mother left. Over time, we became good friends, and I saw how strong you were, even in the hardest moments. When you fell ill, I found myself falling in love with you. When I saw you lying there, I thought I was going to lose you. You were like an injured butterfly."

Cosuda listened, but no words came out. "Johnny...I didn't know you felt this way."

Smiling, he continued. "Since then, we have spent most nights talking. I've learned so much about you, and I've come to love everything about you, from your kind and caring heart to your unwavering determination."

She watched him closely as he spoke. Though her implants worked perfectly, she barely needed them as she could lip-read flawlessly. "But Johnny, what would the matron say?" she asked, her voice trembling with emotion.

"We cannot... we must not..."

"I've never loved anyone before, so I know this is real."

"How do you know you love me? And what is love?" she questioned, her eyes searching his.

"Please believe me when I say I know," he pleaded.

She paced the room, clearly agitated, and he feared what she might say. He couldn't lose her. He knew she felt the same way, he had felt it when she returned his kiss, even if she was too afraid to admit it.

"You must go, Johnny. I need to sleep. We'll talk tomorrow," she said.

He was upset and didn't want to leave her like this. "Please, let's talk…" He couldn't bear the thought of losing her. She cried but insisted he leave. He couldn't see her face as she spoke, but he ached to hold her.

"Good night, Cosuda," he said quietly, closing the door behind him.

She turned to look back, but he was already gone. Lying in bed, she replayed the night's events in her mind, his words echoing in her head. She knew she had feelings for him. But ballet was her life, and it had always been. She belonged at the orphanage, under the matron's guidance, and nothing could change that. There was no room for love or marriage.

The matron had told her time and again: *You cannot be a great dancer if you want to be in a relationship.* She had always insisted that Cosuda was special, gifted, and destined to perform on the grandest stages, but only if she sacrificed everything else. Until now, Cosuda had never questioned it. She had no interest in boys and no distractions from ballet, nothing to pull her away from her dream.

But Johnny…. Johnny has changed everything.

As much as she loved him, she couldn't let him give up his future, especially his dream of having a family. Her obligations were to her art and to the matron, the woman who had given her everything since her mother abandoned her. Dancing had to come first.

As she undressed, she sat on her bed, wishing none of it had happened. The evening had been wonderful, perfect. And yet, all she could think about was how she felt when Johnny kissed her.

At least with him working at the orphanage, they could still see each other. Perhaps they could remain friends.

The next day, she went to class, though she struggled to concentrate. Johnny was all she could think about. Desperate for advice, she asked Lucy to meet her that evening, hoping she would stay for dinner.

"Yes, I'll come by after my day ends," Lucy said, curious about what Cosuda needed to discuss.

But Cosuda couldn't focus. Every word spoken in class felt like noise. Listening intently was already a challenge; today, it was impossible. Fearing she would get into trouble for her lack of attention, she left early. Fortunately, since she was still recovering, she was allowed to rest whenever she needed to.

Johnny avoided her all day. He didn't go to the hall as he usually did. He kept his distance. And it hurt more than she had expected.

When Lucy arrived, Cosuda explained everything. Lucy listened, speechless. But it all made sense now, she had often noticed the way Johnny looked at Cosuda.

"Say something," Cosuda urged.

Lucy hesitated. "He's twenty-seven. What will the matron say if she finds out?"

"Yes, I know, and I told him it couldn't happen again. But you must keep it between us."

She trusted her friend completely. While Cosuda shared everything with Lucy, she kept one secret to herself, that Johnny had told her he loved her, and she felt the same way.

"I cannot jeopardize my dancing. I've dreamt of this all my life, and the matron has given me this opportunity. I had such a lovely evening; it just happened and it was a mistake, and it will not happen again." But as she spoke, a sadness crossed her face.

Lucy hugged her friend.

"I didn't see him today, which is unusual," Cosuda said. Maybe he'll show up tomorrow, or perhaps the matron gave him other duties."

"You need to get some rest," Lucy said as she stood to leave. She placed a kiss on her cheek before walking away, leaving her friend to her thoughts.

Four more days passed, and still, there was no sign of Johnny. Lucy had said she hadn't seen him either. Cosuda was desperate to ask the matron where he was but didn't want to raise suspicion, so she decided against it. Without his visits, she found herself pacing around her room, unable to sleep despite her best efforts.

By the end of the week, she couldn't take it any longer. She had to find out where he was. The most obvious place to look was the kitchen, but there was no sign he'd been there. Next, she checked the garden storeroom, where he usually spent his time gardening, but he was nowhere to be found. The thought of never seeing him again was unbearable. Was he angry with her? Did he regret kissing her and confessing his love?

Every night, she lay in bed, wide awake, wondering if he was ill or even worse. Had he left the orphanage altogether? She didn't know what to think anymore. Neither the matron nor anyone else had mentioned his name.

Two weeks later, Johnny finally came to see her.

He knocked on her door, but she didn't have her implants in. Carefully, he opened the door, unsure of how she would react. She hadn't heard him enter. With tear tracks on her cheeks from weeping, she turned, and there he was, standing by the door. Relief washed over her face.

"I've missed you so much," she said joyfully.

He hesitated, uncertain of what her words meant. Had she changed her mind?

"Where have you been? I've been so worried about you." She was smiling and crying all at once.

"I've missed you too," he said, his voice broken and hoarse. "The matron sent me to the Royal Opera House in London on an errand for her. While I was there, I caught a throat infection. She arranged for me to stay until I was no longer contagious."

He was happy to see her but did not attempt to repeat the kiss. He would rather be her friend than lose her altogether, but deep down, he hoped she would be the one to suggest a next time.

"I'm so happy to see you," she said. "But that sounds terrible, doesn't it? Here I am, relieved you're back when you've been sick this whole time. I'm just glad you're feeling better. So many thoughts ran through my mind."

It was a relief to know he had been ill rather than deliberately avoiding her. Shaking slightly, she fumbled with her sleeves, but her face beamed with happiness. She couldn't take her eyes off him. To her, he looked even more handsome now. But she knew they could never have what they truly wanted. The matron would never allow it—not if she were to become a professional dancer.

"Were you very ill?" she asked gently.

He was touched by her concern. "Not as sick as you were back then," he said. "But I'm certainly on the mend, and I'm no longer contagious."

"I thought you had decided never to see me again." Her voice was filled with genuine worry.

"That's never going to happen," he said, his tone leaving no room for doubt. He thought back to her party and the way she had looked so grown up in her beautiful gown. And now, in her fluffy lemon bolero over her dress, she appeared so youthful.

"Will you stay and have dinner with me?" she asked hopefully.

"I would love to," he replied.

They were both happy to be back together as friends, believing that would be enough. The past would remain their secret.

They spent the evening talking over dinner, laughing and catching up as if nothing had changed. Everything felt normal again. And just before he left, he promised to see her the next day.

That night, as she drifted off to sleep, she felt happy and reassured. Johnny was back.

Chapter 21

Rose remained in a coma for six weeks, but when she finally began to wake up, she was extremely confused and barely aware of her surroundings. Still believing she was married to Tom, she couldn't understand why he wasn't with her. Desperately trying to press the button for the nurse, she realized she couldn't move.

The nurse opened the door and was pleased to see Rose's eyes open. In a hushed tone, Rose asked where Tom was and whether Cosuda was outside. She had no sense of time and could barely speak.

"Dr David will come and see you later," the nurse told her. She noticed Rose looking vague and distracted and assumed she was asking about her family.

Meanwhile, Zach arrived at the hospital and was making his way to the ICU when he ran into Dr David.

"Hello, Doctor. How is Rose?"

"It's good news," he assured him. "Fortunately, the X-rays have revealed no internal damage. Her ribs will cause some temporary discomfort, but there's no lasting harm. She has been extremely fortunate. She's awake, which is a positive sign, though she was confused when she first came around. Even though it may not seem that way now, she appears to be strong. She's still young. We don't know how long her recovery will take, but we expect it to be slow."

The doctor could see the pain on Zach's face and reiterated that their focus was on rehabilitation. Zach thanked him and expressed his gratitude for everything he was doing for Rose.

"I'd suggest maintaining an upbeat attitude, it's what she needs for her recovery," the doctor added reassuringly.

Zach's eyes grew moist as he looked at the doctor. He had faced the unspeakable horrors of war, yet nothing compared to seeing Rose lying there, a pale shadow of her once vibrant self. The beeping of the machines was a stark reminder of life's fragility. Though he had proposed, he hadn't realized just how powerful his feelings for her had become. He couldn't imagine life without her.

After being sent home as an amputee, he had never expected to meet anyone and had kept his heart guarded. *"Why would anyone want me?"* he thought.

After his conversation with the doctor, he went to see Rose. He tapped on the door before opening it and noticed a slight improvement. Though mildly sedated for pain relief, she was awake and smiled when she saw him.

"Hello, Rose. How are you feeling?" Zach asked gently, standing beside her.

She occasionally winced but bore the pain quietly. Yet, there was undeniable strength in the subtle way she adjusted her position, a clear sign that she wasn't just surviving but adapting. Her resilience shone through the haze of recovery.

"You're looking so much better than yesterday," Zach said with a smile, hugging her a little too tightly. She blinked and smiled back.

He was relieved she recognised him, especially after the doctor had told him she'd been delirious and asked for Tom. He reassured her that he had just spoken to her neurosurgeon, who was pleased with her progress.

Months of dedicated physical therapy followed. Slowly, Rose regained her senses and recognized the hospital staff around her. She engaged with the nurses and responded to instructions, gradually rebuilding her strength. The cognitive therapy sessions were challenging, but she persevered, relearning speech and everyday tasks. The occupational therapist helped her sit up, then move to a chair, and guided her through daily routines from brushing her teeth to dressing herself again.

Each day, Zach sat by her bedside while she slept peacefully.

"It's so good to see you," she said one afternoon, smiling softly. "They told me they don't know how long it will be before I can go home."

Looking at her fondly, Zach wondered if she remembered his proposal before the accident. Was now the right time to put the ring back on her finger? He took it from his pocket, and as he did, he saw recognition in her eyes, she beamed.

"The doctor removed it the night of the accident and asked me to look after it until you were well again," he explained.

Rose's smile faded as she thought of Cosuda. "I haven't been able to write to her in two months. What kind of mother am I?" she murmured, sadness thick in her voice.

Zach's heart ached for her. "I can write to her on your behalf," he offered, eager to help in any way.

"Yes, I'd like that. I just wish Cosuda would reply instead of the matron." She sighed. "It's clear she doesn't want anything to do with me, but I'm grateful the matron keeps me updated on how she's doing."

She went on to tell Zach that once she was well, she planned to return to the UK to see her daughter and hopefully bring her back to Normandy. However, she doubted the matron would approve. Her letters always implied that it was best for Cosuda if Rose stayed away. Sometimes, in quiet moments, Rose sensed there was more to the matron's words than she let on.

As much as Zach understood Rose's need to go home, he was terrified she might never return once she did. His confidence still had a long way to go.

That evening, Zach arrived at the hospital with a writing pad and pen in hand, ready to help Rose craft her letter to Cosuda. Sitting by her bedside, he listened closely as she dictated.

She began with an apology for the recent silence between them. Life, she explained, had thrown an unexpected curveball. A recent accident left her confined to the hospital, and she spent the last three months healing, battling pain and uncertainty. But today, her doctor had brought good news: she was mending and would soon be released. She told Cosuda she was getting closer to uncovering the truth about her grandfather's disappearance during the war and was hopeful that she would soon return to her.

Dr David provided Rose with a roadmap to recovery, including a detailed home treatment plan that promised continued progress.

"We'll see you back here in a week for the operation," the doctor said, offering a reassuring smile.

As they prepared to leave, the nurses who had cared for her came to say their goodbyes. They each shook Zach's hand.

"Look after each other," they said, their voices filled with genuine kindness.

Zach nodded, feeling a mixture of gratitude and apprehension. He knew the days ahead would be challenging, but the support they had received gave them strength.

They gathered Rose's belongings, a nurse helped her into the car. The three-hour journey home felt like the start of a new chapter. The beginning of the long road to rehabilitation. They reminded themselves how lucky she was to be alive. Rose was grateful to be home and determined to work hard to regain her strength so she could return to work as soon as possible. Meanwhile, Zach dedicated every day to helping her with her daily physiotherapy and boosting her confidence with uplifting conversation.

A week later, Rose underwent critical surgery. Though it lasted longer than expected, the procedure was a success. The doctor reassured her that, in time, she would regain feeling and function in her back and legs. She spent 24 hours in the recovery room before being transferred to the ward, where she remained until her condition stabilized. Considering the severity of the accident, she couldn't help but reflect on how much worse it could have been.

One week later, she was finally discharged. It was late in the evening when the ambulance pulled up at their house. The paramedics carefully helped her into a wheelchair, guiding her inside and ensuring she was comfortable before leaving.

They joked about both being in wheelchairs, but Rose knew hers was only temporary. Zach manoeuvred her chair up the front steps and into the hallway, where she struggled to avoid bumping into everything. The countertops were at the wrong height, making everything feel unfamiliar.

As she turned her chair, her eyes fell on a familiar-looking envelope on the doormat. With trembling fingers, she wheeled herself closer and ripped it open. She clutched the letter tightly, her hand covering her mouth. "Oh no… this can't be happening," she cried, tears of fear spilling down her face.

Zach was at her side in an instant, his concern written over his face. "What is it, Rose? What happened? Tell me," he urged.

"She's run away! Cosuda has run away from the orphanage, and no one knows where she is. The matron said the police won't do anything because she's legally an adult. And there's a note from Cosuda… she says she wants nothing to do with me and that I shouldn't look for her."

She handed the letter to Zach, wheeling her chair back and forth anxiously.

"What can we do?" he asked. "We need to speak to the police and let them know who you are and why you're here. I'm sure they'll have some information," Zach suggested.

"They already know everything about me," Rose said, shaking her head. "And the police have made it clear that, at eighteen, she's an adult. There's nothing they can do here in France."

She sat with her head in her hands, staring at the stairs, knowing she couldn't manage them on her own. Zach helped her use the ramp instead. There wasn't much she could do in her condition, so she lay down, lost in thought. As expected, they barely slept that night.

The next morning, Zach helped Rose bathe and dress. Thankfully, the bathroom had been designed for his wheelchair years before, making the process easier. Afterwards, she carefully wheeled herself down the ramp, with Zach leading the way.

"I don't know what I would do without you, Zach," she said softly.

Moving closer, he looked into her eyes. "I can't imagine what my life would be like without you, Rose. Thank you for coming into it.... for saving me," he said.

Her eyes filled with emotion as she hugged him.

"So much has happened since we met," Zach continued, "but sadly, not what you came here for."

Rose nodded. She told Zach she wanted to return to England to search for her daughter. Since Cosuda was no longer at the orphanage, she assumed she might either be on her way to France or had travelled to London to look for her father. The matron's letter had offered little insight, only stating that Cosuda had been happy and thriving in her ballet training. She had no idea why she had run away and believed it would be pointless for Rose to come looking for her.

But Rose was convinced that if Cosuda had been happy, why would she run away? She must be heading to Normandy. Rose would wait for her. In the meantime, she would continue searching for her father. Otherwise, all of this would have been for nothing.

First, she wrote a letter to Cosuda, in case she returned to the orphanage.

My Darling Cosuda,

The matron told me you ran away from the orphanage, and my heart aches knowing you are out there alone. I have tried to contact you many times over the years, sending gifts and letters, but your silence has left me wondering if you no longer want me in your life.

Please know that I have never stopped loving you, and I never will. I am doing everything I can to find you and bring you home. If there's a way for you to reach out to me, I'll be waiting, but I won't give up.

Stay strong, my darling. I will see you again.

Mum xxx

Zach wasted no time. He took the letter and posted it immediately. And then, they waited, each day holding their breath for a response.

When Zach returned, Rose told him she needed to go back to work. Zach insisted it was far too soon and urged her to rest and take things slowly.

Days turned into weeks with still no word from Cosuda. The police had assured them they would call with any updates, but the silence was unbearable. Rose's frustration mounted daily, and though she remained hopeful, the waiting was suffocating.

One evening, she finally turned to Zach, "I'll go back to work tomorrow," she said. "I need to keep busy, to do something while we wait. If any news comes, you'll be here to let me know right away."

Zach saw the worry across her face and understood. He squeezed her hand, "You know I'll be here, Rose."

Even as she tried to focus, her thoughts remained tethered to the past and the daughter she so desperately hoped to find.

Chapter 22

Another year had passed, and the matron continued to lie about Cosuda's disappearance. Despite her happiness, Cosuda's smile never quite reached her eyes, a reflection of the joy that always seemed just out of reach. In her quieter moments, she thought about her past home life, before her mother left her at the orphanage. Now twenty, she often considered with the idea of leaving to search for her mother. Yet, her ambition of becoming a professional dancer remained her top priority, for both herself and the matron.

Dance was her sanctuary. She danced with passion, progressing to become an exceptional performer, and the matron was immensely proud of how far she had come. After rehearsing for a ballet performance, she received news that she had been selected to train over the summer at the Dance Theatre in London. The producers were unaware of her deafness, but with her cochlear implants, it was never a barrier. She often, in fact, found that she received instructions faster than other hearing dancers. Dance became her natural form of communication, and her success was proof of her abilities. Now performing on stage before large audiences, her dreams had finally become reality.

On the morning she was set to leave for London, parting from Johnny proved almost unbearable, but she reminded herself that they were only friends, nothing more. She promised to write to him as soon as she could. Trying to hide her emotions, Cosuda hugged him and whispered in his ear, "I'll miss you." Johnny, unable to watch her leave, turned away and walked back to the kitchen. He couldn't bear to watch her board the coach and leave.

Wishing things were different, she thought about him during the journey, but there was no point so she quickly brushed the thoughts away. They stayed in regular contact for the first two months, but their conversations gradually dwindled. Cosuda, busy starring in a major production of *Sleeping Beauty*, barely had time to dwell on it. It was everything she had dreamed of, and the producers adored her. Before she knew it, four months had passed, the production had ended, and it was time to return to Yorkshire.

Lucy had just returned from Paris after six months, where she had dazzled audiences as the lead role in *Swan Lake*. Eager to see Cosuda, she asked her friends about her whereabouts but was told that Cosuda had been away in London and was expected back later that day.

Later that day, after unpacking her bags, Cosuda made her way to the matron's office. She barely touched the doorknob when it swung open, revealing the matron.

"Come in, Cosuda," the matron said, motioning to the chair opposite her desk. "Tell me all about it," she added, trying to contain her joy.

Cosuda's cheeks flushed with happiness as she recounted her time in London. "I had the best time," she said, beaming.

Leaning forward, the matron smiled. "The producer called," she began. "He couldn't stop singing your praises and said you're on the path to great success. And now," the matron continued, her tone turning brisk but still warm. "I'm sending you to Paris next week as Lucy's understudy. It's an incredible opportunity, and I know you'll make the most of it."

Cosuda was overjoyed at the feedback. She was still absorbing the news when the matron continued.

"One more thing," the matron said, carrying an undertone that sparked Cosuda's curiosity. "I've given Johnny a few days' leave. He's been working tirelessly, and it's time he took a well-earned rest."

Cosuda couldn't help but why the matron was acting this way, there was a deliberate weight behind her words, as though they carried a meaning she wasn't fully sharing.

"You've been so dedicated to your work, it's important to stay focused on your path."

Cosuda nodded, but her heart sank like a stone in still water. She had hoped to see Johnny, to talk to him but fate seemed to have other plans.

As she left the matron's office, her thoughts drifted to Johnny. She couldn't shake the unsettling feeling creeping into her mind. Was he with his new girlfriend?

Her next stop was Lucy. The moment they saw each other, they ran into a tight embrace, excited to reunite after so long. They quickly fell into deep conversation, catching up on everything that had happened since they had been apart. Lucy had left two months before Cosuda learned about her opportunity to train in London.

"I played some lead roles, and I just received wonderful feedback from the matron," Cosuda shared, smiling. "My biggest and best role was *Sleeping Beauty*, where I played Aurora."

Lucy's face lit up. "That's amazing! I'm so proud of you, Cosuda! You've come so far."

Now that Lucy was a professional, she was frequently away, performing in some of the world's most renowned theatres, so they didn't see each other as often as they used to.

"I met someone in Paris," Lucy said excitedly.

"That's wonderful news! I'm so happy for you. You have to tell me everything. How did you meet?"

"I will," Lucy said with a grin. "But first, tell me, what's going on with Johnny?"

"Johnny and I are just good friends. He understands that the matron will never allow anything more."

Lucy raised an eyebrow. "He was besotted with you when I left."

"I was in London for four months," Cosuda sighed. "When I got back two days ago, one of the girls told me he was seeing someone," she said, trying to sound indifferent. "Anyway, the matron is sending me to Paris next week to take over from you as an understudy, so I have to forget about him."

Lucy shook her head. "You can have both. I did, so why can't you?"

"It's too late," Cosuda said, her voice laced with regret. "I haven't seen him since I got back, and my dancing is more important." Still, a pang of longing hit her. "I will see him before I leave for Paris. After all, he's my friend. Why shouldn't he meet someone else?"

Lucy gave her a knowing smile. "It's never too late."

Cosuda wanted to believe her, to cling to the thread of possibility. But for now, she had to focus on preparing for Paris.

"It's not going to happen, Lucy," she said finally, forcing a smile. The matron would never allow it, and she's been kind to me over the years, so I must respect her wishes." She forced a smile. "Besides, I'm doing what I love most in the world. I am happy."

Lucy wasn't convinced. Her arms wrapped tightly around her friend. "I love you, Cosuda. You're the best friend anyone could have."

Cosuda smiled, "I love you too." Their friendship was the anchor she could hold on to.

The week passed quickly, and Johnny was still on leave. Cosuda missed him more than she cared to admit and wished she could have seen him before leaving again.

Before her departure, the matron handed her a thick envelope, carefully sealed with everything she needed. "Inside, you'll find your schedule, passes, contacts, and choreography notes. Review them on your journey, as there's no room for error."

Cosuda clutched the envelope tightly, her heart pounding. "I won't let you down, Ma-am,"

The matron's stern demeanor softened. "I'm very proud of how far you've come, Cosuda."

"Thank you," Cosuda replied, her voice emotional. "I wouldn't be here without you. If my mother hadn't brought me here all those years ago, none of this would have happened. So, I have to be grateful to her for that." Her hands tightened around the envelope. "This is the greatest moment of my life. Being cast as the understudy for Odette in *Swan Lake* is a dream come true. I could never thank you enough."

The matron stepped forward and embraced her, but she kept her own secret close to her chest.

"Good luck, Cosuda. I have every faith that you'll deliver a perfect performance."

Always surprised by her affection, she fumbled slightly. "I will," she said. Stepping out of the office, she felt ready for Paris, ready to dance her heart out on the world's most prestigious stage.

She went to say goodbye to Lucy, who told her she would be amazing and should enjoy every minute of it. Lucy was taking a two-week break with Samuel before her next performance in London.

After finishing her packing, Cosuda glanced out of the window and noticed Johnny had returned from his leave. He was sitting in the garden with a pretty young woman, who looked radiant as she laughed and then she leaned forward to kiss his hand. However, Johnny appeared more serious, he stared down at the ground, his expression unreadable. A lump formed in her throat as she took in the scene. Heartbroken by what she saw, she turned away before he could notice her. The rumours whispered among the other girls now felt like a harsh truth she could no longer ignore.

Later, her friends and colleagues gathered to wish her luck, promising to see her in three months. Lucy joined them to wave her off.

As the driver pulled away, Cosuda looked back. She couldn't shake the image of Johnny in the garden. But she knew one thing, she needed to forget him. Paris was waiting, and so was her future.

Her opening performance coincided with her twenty-first birthday, making the night even more special. Under the bright stage lights, Cosuda poured her heart into every movement, her body effortlessly embodying the grace and emotion of *Swan Lake*. The applause that erupted as she took her final bow. It was the most incredible experience of her life.

The night was long and thrilling, filled with congratulations and celebrations that lasted into the early hours. Yet, in the middle of it all, her thoughts drifted to her mother. She wished she could see her now to share this moment of triumph. And despite herself, she couldn't help but wonder what Johnny was doing.

Before leaving Paris, she visited the audiologist to adjust her implant. With each modification, sounds became clearer, sharper, and more distinct. By the end, the muffled echoes she had experienced after the performance were gone. The doctor reassured her that the implant was perfectly reset for her journey home. Though the process of adjusting and training her brain to process sound had been slow, her hard work and determination had paid off.

Three months flew by. On Saturday morning, she packed her belongings and bid farewell to the dancers and actors she had come to know so well. The goodbyes were bittersweet; some friendships, she knew, would last a lifetime.

A chauffeur drove her to the airport, where she boarded a direct flight to Leeds. Upon arrival, her regular driver greeted her with a broad smile, his familiar presence instantly putting her at ease.

The entire ride back to the orphanage was filled with laughter and lively conversation. Cosuda eagerly recounted her time in Paris, as she shared every detail of the performance and new friendships she made.

"There you are, my dear, back safe and sound," the driver said as they arrived.

"I appreciate the conversation," she replied, her gratitude evident.

"It's been wonderful hearing all about it. And from what I've gathered, you've been missed," he added while helping her carry her bags inside.

The mention of being missed intrigued her, and for a fleeting moment, she wished it had been Johnny waiting for her.

THOSE MISSING YEARS

She headed straight to the matron's office to announce her return. Finding the door closed, she knocked, but there was no answer. As she turned to leave, a faint sound caught her attention—a quiet whimper. Hesitating for a moment, she pressed her ear to the door, careful not to be seen. She didn't want anyone to think she was eavesdropping, but concern overruled her hesitation.

Slowly, she pushed the door open.

The office appeared empty. She was about to step back when something caught her eye—a single shoe peeking from behind the desk. Her breath hitched.

Moving cautiously toward it, her heart pounded as she found the matron lying on the floor, the telephone cord tangled around her leg.

"No, no, no," she whispered, swallowing her fear.

Trembling, she knelt beside the matron and reached out to check her pulse. It was faint but steady. Blood trickled from a wound on her skull, and her eyes remained closed.

She needed to act quickly.

"I'll get help! Help! Help!" she called, her voice echoing down the corridor.

As she rushed out of the office, she spotted Johnny approaching.

"Quick, Johnny! It's the matron, she needs an ambulance!"

He looked up, startled to see her, but the urgency in her voice was unmistakable. Without hesitation, he sprinted after her to the office. His eyes widened at the sight of the matron's lifeless form.

"Quick, use the phone! It must have fallen when she collapsed," she urged.

Johnny grabbed the receiver and called emergency services while Cosuda remained by the matron's side. He then ran to find Miss Thompson. Bursting into her classroom, he briefly explained the situation. Maintaining her composure, Miss Thompson instructed her students to continue their theory work before hurrying after him. On the way, she spotted Ethel.

"Ethel, stay with my class until I return," she requested before continuing toward the office.

When they arrived, the paramedics were already rushing in. Cosuda quickly explained how she had found the matron, stepping aside as they examined her.

Miss Thompson introduced herself. "I'm her assistant and a senior staff member. If you need any information, I can help. I've worked with her for years."

"Thank you, but please step back while we tend to her," one of the paramedics instructed.

Johnny and Cosuda exchanged anxious glances, their silent prayers echoing in their minds.

The paramedics immediately began CPR. Each compression felt like a plea for life, stretching every second into eternity.

After fifteen gruelling minutes, one of the paramedics exhaled in relief. "We've stabilized her enough now," he said, and carefully lifted the matron onto a stretcher.

"She suffered a cardiac arrest," the lead paramedic announced. "We need to transport her to the hospital immediately."

Miss Thompson pushed the door open wider as they carried the matron out. Tubes and an oxygen mask obscured her face, making her look like a shadow of her former self.

THOSE MISSING YEARS

As the ambulance doors closed, Johnny reached for Cosuda's hand, his touch grounding her trembling fingers. "Please… don't let anything happen to her," she murmured. "I couldn't bear it."

They walked back along the corridor in heavy silence.

"It's nice to see you, Johnny," she said softly, her emotions wavering.

"You too," he replied, avoiding her gaze.

With nothing more to say, Cosuda returned and made her way back to her dormitory. Johnny stood in the corridor for a moment longer before returning to his duties, his steps slow and deliberate.

The room was eerily quiet, the only sound the gentle patter of rain against the old, wooden windowpanes.

She thought about the matron, a woman who had been a pillar of strength during her darkest days. Stern with most, yet gentle and understanding with her and Lucy.

Lying in bed, Cosuda closed her eyes, whispering a desperate prayer.

A plea for the matron's recovery, for the strength to hold on to hope.

Chapter 23

Rose found it hard to return to work after such an extended absence. While they didn't put too much pressure on her, she knew they needed the work done. Her manager informed her that Susan, the woman who had covered for her while she was away, would be stopping by the office at 9 a.m to collect her belongings and provide Rose with an update on the projects. The team had warmly welcomed Rose back, and although she was grateful, she couldn't help but feel nervous.

Susan's work had been impeccable, so much so that they had offered her another temporary position. However, she had to decline because she needed to care for her husband, whose illness had worsened,. As Susan stepped through the revolving doors into the office, she promptly introduced herself.

At precisely nine, Susan stepped through the doors into the office. She moved with an easy grace, her honey-blonde hair was neatly styled into a bob at the nape of her neck. She wore a simple but elegant navy blue dress paired with a well-fitted jacket and a string of pearls around her neck. She was a striking woman, someone who commanded attention the moment she entered a room.

"Good morning, you must be Rose," she said, extending her hand.

"Yes, and you must be Susan. Nice to meet you," Rose replied, shaking her hand. Susan's grip was firm and confident.

"I've organised everything on your desk," Susan said, gesturing toward the neatly stacked papers and files. "I've also left detailed notes on the current projects. I hope they'll help you get back on track."

"Thank you, Susan. I can't tell you how much I appreciate it," Rose said.

They sat down together, and Susan carefully explained each task, her words precise and thoughtful.

"I'm sorry to hear your husband is unwell. I hope he gets better soon," Rose said kindly.

"He's coming home tomorrow after three months of convalescing. Since I have contacts here at the archives, they asked if I could help while you were away. It was a bit of a break for me," Susan said, though her face was tinged with sadness.

They spent much of the day together. Rose found Susan to be a lovely woman, but she couldn't ignore the worry in her eyes. It was clear how much she loved her husband.

Before leaving, Susan collected her belongings. "I should get going. My husband's doctor will be visiting soon," she said, a hint of concern crossing her face.

"I hope everything goes well. Please let me know if there's anything I can do."

Rose walked with her to the main entrance and wished her well, and they exchanged addresses, agreeing to meet for coffee someday.

"Take care, Susan."

Late in the afternoon, Zach heard a gentle knock on the front door. The sound broke the quiet, and for a moment, he thought it might be Cosuda. Though he'd never met her, the idea of seeing her had lingered in his mind ever since Rose mentioned her.

As he opened the door, a young woman stood there, her gaze meeting his before darting away. She seemed taken aback as she noticed his chair, then quickly averted her gaze.

"I'm sorry, I didn't mean to stare," she said shyly, her cheeks flushing. "My name is Lily. I spoke to the post office about the card in the window, and they gave me your address. It said to ask for Rose. Could I speak with her, please?"

Zach offered a smile, seeing her nervousness. "Rose is at work right now," he explained. "But I'm sure she'll be eager to speak with you. Would you like to come in and wait?"

Lily hesitated, shifting her weight from one foot to another. "I'd rather come back another time," she said. She didn't reveal how she knew Neville and insisted on speaking only with Rose, since her name had been on the card.

"It will only be a couple of hours until she gets home. I can make you a drink while you wait?" Zach offered, afraid she might not return if she left now.

"Thank you, but I'll come back another time," she said, turning to leave.

Desperate to keep her from disappearing, Zach quickly blurted out, "I'm Rose's fiancé." Then added, "It would mean so much to her to meet anyone who knew Neville Azpax."

Lily remained unreadable, offering no clues. After a long moment, she finally nodded. "Saturday at 1 p.m., she said, pulling a small notebook from her bag and scribbling the name and address of a cafe. She handed it to Zach before walking off.

It left Zach alone with his thoughts. He stared at the note in his hand, curious about who Lily was.

THOSE MISSING YEARS

At the end of the workday, Rose gathered her things and stepped out into the cool evening air. When she arrived home, she found Zach waiting in the living room. She told him about Susan and her husband's illness.

Zach listened, nodding thoughtfully, but his excitement was palpable. "I'm sorry for Susan," he said, "but I need to tell you what happened today. This afternoon, a young woman came to see you. She introduced herself as Lily." He paused, watching Rose closely. "She saw the card I put in the shop window about Neville."

Rose tried to steady her voice, not letting the tremble of anticipation seep through. "And what did Lily say?"

"I told her you would be home soon and that she was welcome to wait, but she needed to leave. I asked her how she knew Neville, but she wouldn't say only that she would speak to you since your name was on the advert."

Zach handed her a slip of paper with an address.

"She asked you to meet her this Saturday at 1 p.m.," he said, beaming.

Rose's heart skipped a beat, her mind racing with possibilities. Could this be the moment she had been waiting for? Could this be the end of their search? She dared not fully believe it, at least, not yet. But as she sat there, watching the fire flicker and feeling Zach's hopeful gaze on her, she allowed herself a sliver of hope, a tiny flame she prayed would not go out.

Excitement, nerves, and fear swirled inside her. She couldn't wait to find out what it was all about. "I just need to get through the rest of the week," she murmured, wondering who Lily was and what she might know about her father.

The week dragged on, but at last, it was Saturday. Rose made an extra effort as she got ready, choosing a warm pink jacket paired with black casual trousers. She tied her hair neatly away from her face.

Zach kissed her gently, wished her good luck, and waved her off at the front door.

Sitting at the back of the bus, she leaned against the window, her mind racing with questions. Who was Lily, and what could she possibly know about Neville? The ride took forty-five minutes, and as the bus reached her stop, her stomach fluttered with nervous energy. She stepped off, scanning the area until she spotted the café.

She arrived at the perfect time, pausing for a moment before slowly crossing the busy road. Peering through the window, she saw only one person sitting at a table by the window, her back facing the street.

Swallowing her nerves, Rose pushed open the door and walked straight to the table. Wondering who had responded to the advertisement and what she might know about Neville.

"Excuse me, hello. I am Rose. Are you Lily?" she asked, hopeful.

The pretty, dark-haired woman in a nurse's uniform, her expression calm but with a flicker of curiosity in her eyes.

"Yes, I am. Please, sit down."

They ordered a pot of tea, and Lily began by asking Rose why was looking for Neville. Rose explained that she had come to France from England fourteen years ago in search of her father. She recounted that when she was seven years old, her father had been deployed to Normandy, which led to her evacuation. Lily listened intently but regarded her with a questioning look.

THOSE MISSING YEARS

"I'm sorry, I should have mentioned my father's name is Neville Azpax," Rose said. She went on to explain that her first lead in finding him had come the previous year when she discovered Arthur, one of his former lieutenants. Unfortunately, Arthur had suffered from PTSD and Alzheimer's, leaving his memories fragmented and unreliable. Sadly, he had since passed away, taking any further leads with him."

Before continuing, she studied Lily's expression.

"Lily remained silent, hesitant to speak. "You said Neville is your father?" Lily finally asked.

"Yes, he is. Do you know anything about him?" Rose repeated, her voice tinged with urgency.

Lily hesitated again, the seconds stretching. Then, with a deep breath, she said, "Neville is my father."

Rose froze, the words hitting her like a thunderclap, struggling to make sense of it.

"Your father? But my father has been missing and presumed dead for twenty-nine years." "But how? How is that possible? That would make us sisters!" Her eyes searched Lily's, desperate for answers.

Lily's expression remained composed, but her hands were slightly fidgety. Her mother knew nothing about their meeting, as she had insisted it was too risky, but Lily had always known this day would come. Meeting her half-sister for the first time was overwhelming, yet she felt it was the right moment, given their father's declining health. She needed to be certain Rose was genuine before sharing what she knew.

It was equally difficult for Rose, but because Lily had been young at the time, the subject of Neville and Rose had never been discussed openly in her family. And yet here they were, two strangers suddenly connected by a shared past and, perhaps, a shared future.

Lily took a deep breath, "My mother told me about you when I was four years old, but it was only that once. After that, they never spoke of you again. My father's PTSD worsened around the time I was born, and it became a subject they avoided completely."

Rose frowned, her thoughts racing. "Four years old? So, they knew about me... and just stopped talking about it?" she asked.

"Yes. During the war, my mother worked as a nurse at the hospital, that's where she met my father. She cared for him for a long time, and they fell in love. They married in the hospital."

Rose tried to process Lily's words. "And then you were born?" she asked.

"Yes," Lily replied. "I was born a year later, and my brother, Neville Jr., arrived two years after that. So yes, it appears you are my half-sister."

Rose's emotions swirled. "So... what happened to Neville?"

She was desperate to learn about her father but felt compelled to be patient and let Lily speak.

"I'm sorry, Lily, but how is he, our father? What happened to him?" she asked carefully.

Lily sighed, apologising for her initial coldness. Her heart ached as she listened to everything Rose had been through. She could see how much Rose cared and how anxious she was to know more.

"I'm sorry to tell you, but he's very ill. I'm sure you'd like to see him, but I need to speak with my mother first. I didn't want to upset her by telling her I had arranged to meet you."

"Yes, of course, but please, can it happen soon? I need to see him," Rose pleaded, desperation in her voice. "Thank goodness he's alive. I haven't known what happened to him all these years."

"You must prepare yourself," Lily warned. "He has difficulty concentrating, and he avoids thinking or speaking about the traumatic events of the war. The doctors say it's a kind of memory loss."

"I understand," Rose said. "But after searching for so long, I desperately want to see him."

Lily assured Rose that they would meet again after she had spoken to her mother. The sisters continued their conversation, briefly sharing details of their lives.

Lily had followed in her mother's footsteps and had been accepted into medical school at Sorbonne University. She had completed five years and was on track to earn her master's degree. She would be qualified at twenty-seven and planned to spend a year in England working in youth mental health before returning home to practice medicine. Neville Jr. was in his third year of studying to become a surgeon. Neither sibling had dated much, as both had been focused on their careers.

Rose, in turn, spoke about her childhood and how she had lost touch with her father and the years she had spent alone on the streets after the war. There was so much they needed to share.

After catching up, they left the café and went their separate ways, with Lily promising to contact Rose soon.

After years of searching, Rose was finally about to meet her father. As she caught the bus home, memories of her childhood resurfaced. She had never truly felt part of a family, and now she realized she had put Cosuda through the same experience.

She felt guilty but knew she had to do this. She had witnessed her mother's death when she was just seven years old, and shortly after, she had watched her father leave for war.

The bus jolted to a stop, pulling Rose from her thoughts. She stepped off, her heart pounding with a mix of excitement and apprehension. She had just met her half-sister as an adult, and their connection was through the man she had since fallen in love with.

All Rose needed now was Cosuda by her side. She had remained in constant contact with the police in both France and England, desperate to uncover what had driven her daughter to run away. But first, she had to see her father. The, she could return to England and finally uncover the truth behind Cosuda's disappearance.

She was excited to tell Zach the incredible news that Lily was her half-sister. Though their conversation initially was a cold start, it quickly became warm and amicable. They talked at length about their father.

She stepped inside, "Zach? I'm home."

From the living room, Zach called back, "Hi, how did it go?"

Slipping off her coat, she made her way to the sofa. She sat down across from Zach and began to recount her meeting with Lily.

"Lily said my father was ill but still alive," she told him.

Zach was happy that she would finally see him after so long, even though Lily had warned that he might have blocked out the memory of her. Ever the optimist, Zach couldn't help but wonder if the presence of an old war comrade might jog Neville's memory.

"I'll come with you," he offered gently. "Perhaps something familiar, something from our days in the war, might help him remember."

"Yes, that's a good idea," Rose said, hoping she wouldn't have to wait too long before Lily came around.

The following evening, there was a heavy knock at the door. Expecting to see Lily, Rose opened it, but to her surprise, it was Susan.

"Hello, Susan. It's nice to see you. Please, come in, and I'll put the kettle on. Have a seat. How's your husband?" Rose asked, noticing Susan's serious expression. She assumed it was due to her husband's illness.

Susan interrupted before she could continue. "I'm only here to discuss Neville."

Puzzled, Rose asked, "Neville? How do you know Neville?"

"I am Lily's mother and Neville's wife," Susan revealed. "Lily told me about your meeting, and when she gave me your address, I was surprised to see it was the same one you gave me when I left the office."

The kettle whistled sharply, cutting through the heavy silence. Upstairs, Zach had been on his way down when he overheard Susan's words. Sensing the weight of the conversation, he decided to stay upstairs, thinking that giving them space would make it easier for Rose and Susan to talk.

"On your last day of work, you told me your husband was very ill. Now Lily tells me that our father is ill," Rose said.

"Yes, that's right, he is," Susan responded, her voice heavy with pain.

"Lily said he has PTSD and may not recognise me. I'm so sorry, but where is he? Please, tell me everything. Can I see him?" she asked desperately. "I know it must have been a shock when Lily told you who I was, and I'm sorry, but I have been searching for him for many years."

Rose gestured for Susan to sit again while she made the tea. This time, Susan accepted. She visibly softened, looking drawn and tired. Apologizing for her abruptness, she admitted that her mind was constantly on her husband.

"I think I should start from the beginning," Susan said.

"I nursed Neville through the war, along with other soldiers, but there was always something special about him. He was kind, and always said nice things to me. He was cheeky and made me laugh, even through the terrible times. Over time, we fell in love.

"He talked about you in the hospital," she continued, "and said he was sorry for sending you away when you had just lost your mother. But he had no choice."

Although Rose didn't understand what was happening when she was seven, she did now. He was her father, and she loved him, but she remembered that, unlike her mother, he had never been kind.

"I'm sorry," Susan said gently, "but he hasn't mentioned you or his past since Lily was born. It's as though he has completely blocked it out. He still suffers from PTSD, experiencing smells and flashbacks that remind him of his time as a POW. On top of that, he's battling dementia, and his health is steadily declining.

Susan hesitated before continuing. "One of his lieutenants, a close friend, was in the hospital bed next to Neville. He had suffered serious wounds, and they never expected him to survive. When he woke up, he found his legs had been amputated. Like many other soldiers, he suffered from PTSD. Neville was devastated when he woke to find his friend's bed empty, he assumed he had died. He never really got over it."

Susan's story struck a chord. "What was his name?" Rose asked.

"I can't remember," Susan admitted.

Guessing it could be Zach, Rose asked, "Was it Zach, by any chance?"

Susan's expression changed slightly in thought of recognition. "Yes, I believe his name was Zach," she said, puzzled. "Why do you ask?"

Rose explained how she had met Zach years ago and how he had tirelessly helped her over the years to find her father.

Overhearing the heartfelt exchange, Zach finally descended the stairs. When he looked at Susan, his eyes reflected the same mix of sorrow and elation that filled Rose's heart.

Zach wheeled his chair forward, his voice soft. "Susan…"

Before he could say more, Susan crossed the room, breaking into one of disbelief and joy. Tears welled in her eyes as Zach opened his arms, and she embraced him tightly, his nurse, his friend.

"Neville's heart is fragile," Susan said. "The shock of seeing both his long-lost daughter and his closest friend might be too much. I'll prepare him for Rose's visit, to soften the impact of such overwhelming news."

By the end of the week, Rose was on her way to see her father. The combination of excitement and fear that he wouldn't recognize her was overwhelming. Zach went with her but stayed in the kitchen with Susan and Lily while Rose went into the bedroom to see her father first.

Susan made tea, and they sat at the table, catching up on the time they had spent together in the hospital, giving Rose as much time as she needed.

Zach shared memories with Susan, recounting the days he and Neville had spent side by side in the hospital. Though Susan's recollection of Zach was hazy, he had been one of many wounded soldiers she had cared for—she listened intently as he spoke.

As Rose gently pushed open the bedroom door, her eyes met Neville's, and a shared joy silently filled the room. A tearful whisper escaped her lips: "Hello, Daddy." He wrapped his weak arms around her tightly, and they wept together, speaking of the years once lost, now restored.

"I'm sorry, Rose, for sending you away," Neville murmured, his voice thick with emotion.

"It took me many years to understand what was happening, but I know now that you didn't have a choice. I'm just glad to see you after searching for so long," Rose replied with relief. Seeing her father's eyes light up with joy soothed her heart. She longed to share the news of Zach's presence, yet she hesitated, not wanting to overwhelm him.

When they pulled apart, "Rose," he began, "I've waited too long to tell you this…."

"It's okay," she replied. You can tell me what happened."

He told her that after leaving the battlefield, he was taken to the hospital with injuries. He had expected to recover and fly back to England for her, but illness struck, and depression weighed heavily on him. Determined to return, he attempted to leave, but doctors firmly forbade it, insisting he could not travel. He had believed he could heal and put the war behind him, but reality soon set in, he soon realised he couldn't.

During the dark hours, pacing around his hospital bed, he thought he was going to die. Then his thoughts turned to Rose, and the soldier in him refused to let go. He promised himself he wouldn't rest until he saw her again and found peace.

As Neville spoke, his voice trembled. "Rose, you kept me alive during those nights. The thought of seeing you again gave me the strength to keep going."

Rose squeezed his hand, her eyes brimming with tears, but she stayed silent, letting him continue.

After arriving home with Susan, he knew he couldn't go on like that, so he reluctantly sought help from a mental health professional. That's when he learned that PTSD was most likely the trigger for his depression. Knowing he needed support, he was prescribed medication to help manage his anxiety and function in daily life. With Susan's help, he connected with other soldiers who had experienced similar trauma, and they all shared the same struggle.

Neville's voice grew quiet, "I looked everywhere for Zach," he said. "but I couldn't find him. I had assumed the worst, that he hadn't survived the war."

Rose wanted to tell him that Zach was alive and outside, but seeing how much Neville needed to talk, she decided to wait for the right moment. "I'm sure Zach would understand, Dad. You did everything you could."

Listening to him remember so much was both heartbreaking and important. "It was hard to process everything, the deaths and the pain they had endured and witnessed. Many soldiers refused to seek help, fearing their superiors would see it as weakness and punish them by withholding privileges or subjecting them to harsher treatment.

Rose said, "That wasn't a weakness. You were all so strong just to survive what you went through."

"I saw the suicide rates rise," Neville confessed. "There were times when a part of me wondered if you'd be better off without me. I felt like a burden to the most important people in my life: my wife and children. When I close my eyes at night, I still see myself picking up the body parts of my soldiers or watching them die in my arms. I don't have any bullet wounds to show you because mine are the invisible kind, the kind we carry in our souls. I'm not ashamed of them; they're as real as wounds that bleed."

He couldn't stop looking at his daughter, his heart filled with relief and joy.

It hurt Rose to hear about his emotional pain, but she saw so much bravery in his words.

"We're here together now, and I'm listening to you," she reassured him. "But I want you to know that Zach is here. He's waiting outside with Susan to see you."

In disbelief, Neville's eyes filled with tears as raw emotion washed over his face. "Zach?" he whispered, barely able to form his name.

"I'll call him in," Rose said gently.

Moments later, Zach wheeled himself into the room. Both men's faces reflected deep emotion as they looked at each other. The years and their injuries, both physical and mental, had changed them. Neville's deep brown eyes remained the same, but his once-strong frame had become slender. For a moment, neither spoke; the weight of everything they'd endured and the bond they still shared said more than words ever could.

Their faces split into matching grins as Zach pushed himself forward and clasped Neville's outstretched hand, shaking it firmly and squeezing it hard. For hours, the two men sat together, their laughter and stories weaving together those missing years, years that had vanished without a trace since Neville was presumed dead in 1942. Now, the sound of their voices filled the room, binding them to the present with every shared memory.

Neville held Rose's hand tightly, "I couldn't be happier for the two of you." His words are simple yet heartfelt.

Later, Susan and Lily joined them, the gentle buzz of conversation and the occasional burst of laughter.

Neville smiled and said, "Neville Jr. will meet you both soon," he said his pride showing in the way he spoke his son's name. Summer isn't far now."

Rose watched her father. She had longed for this, for a chance to see him as the man he had been all along but whom she was only now discovering.

As the evening deepened, Rose stood near the door, her coat folded over her arm. The sound of voices around her, for the first time in years the house truly felt like home. Now that she lived nearby, nothing could keep her from visiting again and again—nothing would stop her.

"You'll be back tomorrow?" Neville asked.

"I'll be back. Nothing could keep me away now. Goodnight, Dad," she said, kissing his cheeks tightly.

It was difficult for her to leave after so many years apart, but she assured Susan she would be back the following day.

Stepping out into the cool night air, Rose glanced back one last time.

Chapter 24

Everyone was aware of how sick the matron was, but not all the girls were given the chance to visit her. Miss Thompson knew the matron had a special connection with Cosuda, so with her permission, she allowed her to visit the hospital.

One of the nurses escorted Cosuda to the ICU and gently warned her, "You should be prepared for how she looks. She is connected to monitors, has a breathing tube, and will most likely not respond, but talk to her, she just may hear you." The nurse informed her that she could stay in the room for only ten minutes.

When she entered the room, she saw the matron lying still, her breathing steady. Cosuda wanted her to know she was there. The hospital wouldn't allow her to stay overnight in the ICU, but because the matron was so ill, she was given a bed in one of the visitors' rooms, which were typically reserved for close family members of critically ill patients.

At 3 a.m., a nurse woke Cosuda. "Mrs Jones is asking for you. She's delirious, but I think you should come with me," she said.

Cosuda quickly put on her dressing gown and followed her. As she entered the room, she saw that the matron had been attempting to get out of bed. She stirred, appearing agitated. It was clear she was in pain. As her breathing grew heavy, the nurse administered morphine as needed. She then turned to Cosuda and said, "Press the emergency button if you need me for anything at all." With that, she left them alone, knowing the matron's time was running out.

The matron opened her eyes slightly. "I need to talk to you," she whispered, struggling to focus on Cosuda. She looked desperate, but Cosuda wanted her to rest. It was the second time she had shown such urgency as if she knew she was deteriorating.

"We'll talk tomorrow, so please rest," Cosuda said gently.

"No, it has to be now. It's important, we need to talk."

She refused to wait, and Cosuda didn't want to upset her. What could it be? Why couldn't it wait until the morning? She suspected the matron realised just how sick she was and needed to say something before it was too late.

"Please, listen to me," the matron pleaded, frustration in her weak voice, before closing her eyes for a few moments.

"Okay, I'm listening now," Cosuda said. Whatever it was, it mattered to her.

"What did you want to tell me?" she asked, holding the matron's hand and stroking it gently. Though afraid of what she might hear, she knew she had to listen. The matron looked desperately ill.

"I have never told anyone this before. I had to keep it to myself, but now I think you should know."

Cosuda couldn't imagine what she was about to hear. She didn't want anything negative to taint the kindness the matron had shown her over the years. In many ways, she had been like a mother to her.

Just then, the door opened, and the nurse entered. This time, she told Cosuda she could pull up a chair and stay with her. The matron drifted in and out of sleep, and in her dreams, she saw herself standing in a puddle. As she looked down at her reflection, she saw Cosuda's mother and herself growling at each other. They began shouting, and Cosuda called out for them to stop.

THOSE MISSING YEARS

At 5a.m, Cosuda, woke up abruptly, startled by the sound of the matron calling out in her sleep. She turned her head toward the matron, who lay still now.

"Are you ok, was the matron calling someone," the nurse said.

"I think she was dreaming… or having a nightmare, more like," Cosuda said.

"I am sorry… so very sorry," the matron murmured in her sleep.

The words struck Cosuda like ice, sending a chill down her spine, "What does she mean? Why is she apologising?" Cosuda asked.

The nurse withdrew a syringe from the cupboard and sedated the matron. "She needs rest," the nurse said firmly. "And so do you. Come back later. You'll have another chance to speak with her."

Cosuda nodded before slipping quietly out of the room, closing the door behind her. She lay in bed for a couple of hours, wondering if the matron would even remember their conversation when she saw her again. Struggling to sleep, she eventually approached the duty nurse. "I'm going home for a few hours," she said quietly. "Let me know if…if anything changes."

The hospital staff assured her they would call the orphanage if there was any significant change, but the nurse advised her or someone from the home not to wait too long before returning.

Back at the orphanage, Cosuda slept for a few hours before resuming her duties. She wondered if Miss Thompson would ask her to return to the hospital, someone needed to be with the matron.

Miss Thompson knew Hilda had a soft spot for Cosuda, but she also needed her back to continue with her chores. As soon as she saw her return, she called her into the office.

"The matron won't be leaving the hospital anytime soon, but they will keep us updated on her condition," Miss Thompson informed her.

"Carry on with your duties, Cosuda, starting with the matron's office," she instructed. It's a mess, there are papers scattered everywhere, and it needs a thorough cleaning."

Knowing how much the matron cared for Cosuda, Miss Thompson told her to finish her tasks as quickly as possible so she could return to the hospital. She relied on Cosuda for updates on the matron's condition.

Still wondering what the matron had wanted to tell her, Cosuda showered and put on her scrubs, as instructed, before heading to the matron's office to clean up after her accident.

She opened the door and found the office in the same state as the day before. Pens and paperwork were scattered across the floor. As she began picking everything up, she noticed an open box containing several bundles of letters, each tied with rubber bands. Some appeared to be unopened, while others had been torn open and returned to their original envelopes. The envelopes were addressed to Mrs Hilda Jones.

Puzzled, she placed them back in the box until she noticed her own name on one of the opened letters. Her focus sharpened. Should she read just this one? It felt wrong. But then, she spotted another bundle, this time with her name on every envelope. Most had been ripped open. This wasn't just curiosity anymore, these were her letters.

THOSE MISSING YEARS

As she read, tears streamed down her face. One letter began:

"My dearest Cosuda, I hope this finds you well. I miss you more than words can express."

Tears blurred her vision as she read about missed birthdays, lost milestones, and the ache of separation. The matron, who had always been kind to Cosuda, had kept these letters hidden. Why?

Her fingers trembled as she opened another bundle of unopened birthday and Christmas cards. She imagined her mother carefully choosing each one, writing heartfelt messages, and sealing them with love. A photograph slipped out, it was of her and her mother smiling together. On the back, it read that her father had taken it when she was three years old. Yet all of these memories had been tucked away in a drawer.

"Happy 18th birthday, my sweet Cosuda," one card read. *"May this year bring you joy, even in these difficult times."*

As she continued reading, emotions swirled inside her, a mix of gratitude for the matron's kindness, which had given her the chance to dance on the grand stage of the theatre, and sadness at the realization that her mother's letters had been hidden.

Why had they been kept from her? What secrets lay buried in this betrayal?

Then, she found a letter that mentioned her mother being in an accident. The weight of it all became unbearable. Her tears turned to anger. The shock of what she was reading overwhelmed her. She vowed to unravel the mystery, to bridge the gap between her past and present.

Surrounded by memories, Cosuda sat grieving for a mother she had never stopped longing for, questioning a matron with her own hidden sorrows and holding letters that contained the key to their intertwined destinies.

"Why wouldn't she tell me? And why would she tell my mother I had run away? None of this makes sense!" she cried aloud.

The office door creaked open. Johnny stood still, trying to locate the source of the noise.

"What's all the noise about?" he asked.

He looked down to find Cosuda lying in a heap on the floor, her body trembling with sobs. She neither heard nor saw him; she was too distraught. He knelt beside her.

"What is it? What's happened? Is it the matron?"

Surrounded by ripped-open letters and envelopes, Johnny had no idea what was going on. He held her gently, wiping her tears, but she remained unresponsive.

"It's fine," he reassured her softly. "There's no rush. Just tell me when you're ready."

Through her sobs, she finally whispered, "Oh Johnny, I can't believe it. How could she not tell me? Why?"

He was stunned as she explained that she had found letters from her mother hidden by the matron.

"I am so sorry she kept these from you," he said, shaking his head. "There must be a reason… but nothing excuses this. What will you do now?"

"I don't know," she admitted. "The matron is very ill. I don't know if I can be so cruel as to confront her. But now, I understand why she was so desperate to talk to me. I think she knows how serious her condition is… and that she may not have much time left."

THOSE MISSING YEARS

Now, as an adult, it was clearer to Cosuda just how much life had taken a toll on her mother. Johnny helped her gather the letters, and she took them to the dormitory, locking them safely in the small cupboard beside her bed. She would read more when she felt less overwhelmed.

But what would she do about the matron? Could she even return to the hospital? One thing was certain, she needed to contact her mother.

Johnny, sensing her turmoil, gently offered his support.

Surprised, she hesitated. She didn't want to interfere in his relationship with his girlfriend.

"Thank you, Johnny," she said softly.

"I would do anything for you, Cosuda," he replied. "But can we talk first?"

She knew what he wanted to say. And she knew she had to face it. The last few months had been difficult, knowing he had met someone. Yet, despite everything, he had never been far from her mind.

As they walked through the gardens, surrounded by rose trees and vibrant autumn leaves, she stole a glance at him. His strong upper arms and broad shoulders hinted at months of heavy work. He carried himself with newfound confidence.

As always, she felt at ease in his presence. But she had to remind herself that it was only friendship.

The golden hues of autumn surrounded them as they wandered in silence. Finally, they sat on a bench, and Johnny spoke first.

"How have you been?" he asked.

"I'm doing better," she admitted. "Much better than I was in London three months ago. But I'm still confused about the matron... I don't know how to handle it yet. Anyway, this isn't about me. You wanted to talk to me about something."

"Yes, I did," Johnny said. He took a deep breath.

He told her about Polly, a nursing student he had met while he was ill in London.

"I saw her at the surgery a couple of times. The doctor asked her to accompany me to the hospital for tests because I could barely stand. Later, she was sent to Yorkshire to finish her training... but she unexpectedly turned up to see me."

Cosuda frowned. "But I saw you sitting right here on this bench with her. You both looked so happy. I assumed you were together."

Johnny shook his head. "No. She liked me... but it became a little obsessive. I had to tell her the truth, that I was in love with someone else." His gaze locked onto hers.

Cosuda's heart pounded.

Johnny's love for her had never faded. Gently, he took her hands in his.

"My feelings for you haven't changed, Cosuda. They never will. I just need to know... do you feel the same?"

She had spent years suppressing her emotions, believing love and dance could not exist, just as the matron had told her. But she had fallen for Johnny despite it all.

Even the difference in their ages didn't matter.

"We'll have to admit it sooner or later, you know," he said, smiling.

THOSE MISSING YEARS

And this time, she didn't look away.

After a long pause, she realized she could have both, just as Lucy had said. She told him she had always felt the same way. It was as if all the awkwardness had melted away.

He leaned in and kissed her, and this time, it felt right. "I've wanted to do that for many years," he said passionately.

"Me too," Cosuda said smiling.

They had been falling in love with each other for at least five years, and now, their feelings were growing from a slow burn into a blaze. They had so much to look forward to, but there was also a lot to sort out.

"I understand you'll be going to your mother's, and you have another show in London. I don't want to hold you back."

She looked straight into his eyes. "Are you sure I'm what you want, Johnny?"

"Yes. I've never been more certain of anything. I didn't want to smother you." He took her into his arms and kissed her again. "You're my girl, and I love you, Cosuda."

"I love you too, Johnny."

And that was all he needed to hear.

She wanted to return to the hospital and see the matron, but first, she needed to think about what she would say. Right now, she had no idea how to deal with what she had discovered. As they walked back into the building, Cosuda fell silent, lost in thought as she made her way to Miss Thompson's office.

"Hello, Cosuda." Miss Thompson sat at her desk, surrounded by paperwork. "Is everything okay? Perhaps you should sit down." She could see how upset she was.

Cosuda explained that she had found the letters while cleaning the matron's office and, since they were addressed to her, had decided to read them. As she recounted their contents, Miss Thompson was astounded by the matron's decision to keep Cosuda's mother's letters instead of passing them on.

"I'm sorry you had to find them that way. I want you to believe me when I say she never discussed your parents with me. I know she was always fond of you. She once told me you reminded her of her own daughter."

"She had a daughter?" Cosuda asked, surprised.

"Not anymore, sadly. She had a daughter who died of a heart condition when she was seven years old. After that, she never spoke of her again until you arrived. It seemed as though you filled that void in her heart. Her husband died while she was pregnant, and she was devastated. But when her daughter was born, she devoted her life to her. And when she lost her, she changed. She became bitter and angry."

"Oh no, that's heartbreaking." It was all beginning to make sense.

"I remember her telling me that if I wanted to be a successful dancer, I couldn't have a boyfriend. Some of the other girls said she never told them that, but the matron was always so good to me that I never questioned it. Besides, I wasn't interested in boys."

She decided not to mention Johnny to Miss Thompson.

"I can understand why she wouldn't want you to be distracted," Miss Thompson said. "She always praised you as an extraordinary dancer with exceptional talent."

"I assumed I was just doing okay. I didn't think I was any better than that," Cosuda replied modestly.

THOSE MISSING YEARS

"She truly believed in you," Miss Thompson said.

"I don't know what to say except that I feel honoured she felt that way. I'll go to the hospital to see her before I leave for London next week," she said pensively.

"Take your time, you have my support."

Cosuda thanked Miss Thompson for her understanding.

How can I say anything to her now? she wondered.

Before leaving, she read more of the letters and was saddened to learn how desperate her mother had been to find her. One envelope stood out, it was addressed to the matron. She ripped it open, her eyes scanning the end of the letter to see who had written it. It was from her father.

In a lengthy message, he told the matron he was sorry for never visiting Cosuda after Rose had left for France. He explained that Rose had left a note saying Cosuda was in an orphanage in Yorkshire, but his life was now with his wife and daughter.

"What does this mean? My mother and I *are* his wife and daughter," she whispered, her voice trembling with disbelief.

Then she found another letter, addressed to her mother, c/o the orphanage. It had been opened. As she continued reading, her confusion deepened. It appeared her father had been living a double life.

After divorcing Rose, he had married his childhood love, with whom he had a daughter when Cosuda was just thirteen years old. He had met this woman before he had known Rose. When she became pregnant, he had wanted to support her, but her parents had refused, cutting off all contact. They had continued seeing each other in secret, and when the baby was born, she was just fourteen.

As soon as she turned sixteen, she rented a room, and Tom moved in with her, even though he was still married to Rose.

Cosuda's mind raced. How could my father have kept such a secret?

The letters painted a picture of a man torn between duty and love, a man who ultimately failed them all.

He and his childhood love had married immediately after his divorce from Rose was finalized. The letter ended with a hope that he might see Cosuda again one day, but just not now. He wrote that he would not be in contact again.

She had gone from being worried about the matron to feeling angry, confused, and heartbroken.

While she was getting ready to go to the hospital, Miss Thompson arranged transportation for her. Before leaving, she went to see Johnny and told him what she had learned about her father and her sister.

He was shocked and upset for her, offering to go with her for support.

"Thanks, Johnny, but I have to do this on my own. I'm not sure what I'll say to her, but I know I will as soon as I see her."

Cosuda was deep in thought about how to approach the matron when the driver pulled up at the hospital. She had no recollection of the journey. It was just a blur of streets and buildings passing by.

"I'll wait for you. Take your time," the driver assured her.

As she approached the reception desk, she noticed nurses hurrying toward the matron's room. A wave of anxiety surged through her.

THOSE MISSING YEARS

"What's happening with Mrs Jones?" Cosuda asked.

The receptionist motioned for her to take a seat. "We'll let you know when you can go in to see her," she said kindly.

A nurse rushed out of the room, and Cosuda recognised her from previous visits. She quickly stepped forward. "Is everything okay?" she asked.

The nurse's eyes widened. "It's good you arrived when you did," she said. "You should come in and see her right away."

Cosuda stumbled slightly as she followed the nurse into the room. The matron's condition had worsened, her skin was pale, and her breathing shallow. Cosuda took her frail hand and held it gently.

The matron opened her eyes, gazing into Cosuda's face. A flicker of recognition passed over her expression, and in a whisper, she murmured, Forgive me." Her eyes pleaded for understanding as her voice trailed off.

Cosuda leaned in, trying to catch the rest, but the weight of regret filled the air. The rhythmic beeping of the monitor seemed to echo the matron's longing.

"Quick, please! What's happening? Help her, please!" Cosuda pleaded desperately.

The nurse checked the matron and then turned to Cosuda, her expression solemn. "I'm so sorry. She's gone."

Sadness etched itself across Cosuda's face, but she had known how ill the matron was. And though she had never confronted her about the letters, she couldn't deny that the matron had shaped her into the person she had become. Despite her fears of the matron's strict ways when she first arrived at the orphanage, she had learned everything from her.

As Cosuda stepped out of the hospital entrance toward the waiting car, the driver looked up. "How did it go today?"

"Not so good, I'm afraid," she replied, then recounted what had happened. They drove back in silence.

Miss Thompson was not surprised by the news. The hospital had been keeping her informed daily about the matron's condition. Cosuda told her she would leave for London to perform before heading to France to see her mother. It was only for two nights, but she felt she owed it to the matron and the orphanage to carry on as usual. Once she packed, she would leave.

Now that she had the address from the letters, finding her mother wouldn't be too difficult.

In the garden, Johnny stood on a ladder, shears in hand, trimming the bushes and cutting the tops of the tall trees. Cosuda approached quietly, and when he turned, he greeted her with a smile, warm and familiar. He knew she was leaving for London, and then heading straight to France.

"How did it go with the matron?" he asked, stepping down from the ladder.

Cosuda told him the news, and sadness clouded Johnny's face. He had worked with the matron for many years and had always respected her, even though he disapproved of how she had kept Cosuda away from her mother. The loss weighed heavily on him.

"I'll return from London for the funeral," Cosuda said. "Then I'll leave for France straight after."

Johnny nodded. "I'll be here waiting for you when you return."

They were excited to be a couple, eager for the future that awaited them.

"I love you, Cosuda."

"I love you too, Johnny," she whispered before heading inside to pack a few essentials she'd need.

Cosuda's head was spinning. There was so much to think about, but above all, she felt relieved to have finally discovered the truth about her mother after all these years.

After saying goodbye to the girls, Cosuda turned to Miss Thompson. "I'll see you in a few days, after the show, for the funeral," she said. As she stepped toward the doorway, Johnny reached for her hand.

"I couldn't let you leave without a proper goodbye," he said.

The warmth of his touch reassured her. He leaned in, his lips brushing hers gently. "See you in a few days."

She waved at him one last time before stepping away. Her heart ached, full of love and uncertainty all at once.

As the train chugged toward London, her thoughts swirled. Cosuda stared out of the window. The landscape rushed past, blurring into muted green and greys. Her mind churned with tangled thoughts.

The matron's funeral was imminent, and she had promised to return. But another journey awaited her, one that would finally reunite her with her mother.

Chapter 25

Rose was aware that she and Zach hadn't spoken about their wedding since the accident. The weight of unspoken words hung between them. When they returned home after seeing her father, she shared some of what her father had told her with Zach, and he listened intently. His eyes sparkled with joy for her. He was overjoyed for her, and he was also happy to see Neville after so many years. But there was something else there too, an unspoken question, a hesitation. He wheeled his chair towards her, took her hand, and looked at her lovingly.

"Rose, I am so happy for you, and I don't want to sound insensitive, but this seems like the perfect time. Do you think we have waited long enough?"

"Long enough for what?" she asked him.

"For happiness. We've been through many years of sadness, perhaps it's our turn now. I've been waiting for you forever, and this feels like the perfect time."

Rose smiled, touched by his sincerity. Zach was kind and patient—whose love felt like a gift she didn't deserve after everything, and she was lucky to have met him. But as much as she wanted happiness with him, her heart ached. There was still one piece missing, a wound that hadn't healed. Cosuda. Her daughter. Could she embrace a future without finding her first?

She looked at him, her mind made up. "Yes, it is our turn for happiness." She reassured him that she was ready to marry again.

She no longer needed to look for her father. That chapter of her life was closed. But Cosuda was out there somewhere, and Rose couldn't rest until she held her daughter in her arms again.

Zach nodded, his expression softening as he placed his hand over hers. "We'll find her, Rose. Together."

The next morning, they sat at the kitchen table, talking about her trip to England.

"When are you leaving for England, Rose?" Zach asked, taking a thoughtful sip from his cup.

"As soon as I've booked a ticket," she replied, her eyes reflecting a mix of excitement and determination. Everything was falling into place, but she needed her daughter back to make it perfect.

They had made a good start on the wedding arrangements. Now, they just needed to set a date. It would be a simple, minimalistic wedding with family and close friends to celebrate their love.

Zach reached for her hand across the table. "I'll miss you," he said softly. "But I know you won't rest until she is with you."

Rose squeezed his hand. "I'll be back—and it will be with Cosuda," she promised, her voice filled with hope. "I love you, Zach, and I can't wait to marry you."

"I love you too," he replied.

He wrapped his arms around her and drew his chair closer.

"I hope you find her safe and sound," he said sincerely.

It was always expected that she would return to England for her daughter as soon as she had found her father, but now that she had met Zach, her life had changed. She was a determined and strong woman, and he didn't want to hold her back. The fight had been long and hard, but she was almost there.

Her day began at 6.30 a.m. the following morning with a meeting with her manager to officially resign. The office was quiet, the early morning light casting long shadows across the room. She took a deep breath as she explained everything that had happened, feeling a weight lifting off her shoulders. This time, she wouldn't be returning.

They wished her luck and said she would always be welcome to return to see them and that if she ever needed a job, one would be available for her. When they presented her with a beautiful bunch of mixed flowers and a glowing reference, she became quite emotional. Tears welled up in her eyes as she thanked them for always being so understanding.

The minibus arrived, and she was in a trance when the driver called out, "Are you getting on, madam?"

"Yes, I'm sorry." Almost missing the bus, she hopped on, paid him, and sat down with her flowers, thinking about everything she needed to do before going to England. The next step was to tell her father that he would be meeting his granddaughter very soon. That pleased her greatly, and they would soon be one big happy family.

As she stepped off the bus, Rose noticed Susan walking down the road towards her house, her face flushed and streaked with tears as she clutched a crumpled handkerchief and blew her nose.

"Is everything OK?" she called out, her pulse quickening.

Suddenly, Susan became hysterical, then broke into a frantic run. She flung herself at Rose tightly.

"Susan, what is it? Rose asked, panic rising in her chest. "Is it my father?"

She was shaking uncontrollably, unable to respond. Rose put her arm around her shoulder to steady her as she guided her to the front door.

"Zach, I need your help!" Rose called out as she led Susan inside.

Zach emerged from the kitchen, as he took in the scene. "Come in and sit down, Susan," he said, his voice calm and steady.

Rose sat beside Susan on the sofa, waiting as Zach disappeared to brew strong tea. The seconds dragged, and the only sounds in the room were the faint clicking of the teacups and Susan's choked sobs.

When Zach returned, he exchanged a glance with Rose. "Neville," he muttered under his breath, suspecting the worst but waiting for Susan to find her voice.

Rose waited and sat with her until she was ready to explain what was wrong. Zach made some strong tea while Rose tried to find out why Susan was so upset, but he suspected it had something to do with Neville.

"He's gone," she said. "He's gone," she repeated.

Rose felt a chill run down her spine.

"Gone? What do you mean, Susan?" she asked gently, though her heart was pounding.

But the look on Susan's face said it all.

"No, no, please, not my father. I have only just found him," she sobbed hard.

Zach tried to console Rose, realising that Susan was also struggling.

Through her tears, she told Rose how happy Neville was to have seen her. It was almost as if he had been waiting for her.

"It was late last night when he asked me to keep in touch with you. He said how sorry he was for leaving you again but he was happy that you and Zach had found each other. He spoke a little about his time with Zach and described him as a good man. I told him he could tell you himself since you would be coming the next evening. He smiled at that, said goodnight, and he never woke up this morning."

Zach, who had been quietly listening, placed the tea on the table and sat beside them.

"I am so sorry, Susan," he said. "Neville was a brave man."

Susan nodded, trying to hold back her sobs.

"He was. I can't believe he's gone. He talked about meeting Cosuda but knew he didn't have time," Susan said sadly.

Rose squeezed Susan's hand. "We'll get through this together. You're not alone."

Rose was devastated by what had just happened but grateful that she had managed to find him and had a lovely conversation with him, telling him about Cosuda and why she had been forced to place her in a home temporarily. There was little time for it to all sink in because the funeral needed to be arranged right away. Rose offered to help Susan, and she gladly accepted. Both women needed each other right now.

The military funeral service, held two days later, was predictably sad and emotional, just as it should have been. Only close family members and a few of Neville's soldiers, most of whom were still here but with some form of disability, were there to pay their respects to a great man. They were all proud that they could give him the send-off he deserved.

Nobody spoke except the minister, who delivered the eulogy.

Susan stood by the casket, her eyes red from crying, but she felt a sense of peace knowing that Neville was finally at rest. Rose stood beside her, offering silent support. The ceremony was simple but respectful for a beloved father, grandfather, and husband who had fought and given his life for his country. Afterwards, he was laid to rest at the Normandy American Cemetery and Memorial.

They returned to the village hall, where a small gathering was held. Friends and family spoke with Susan and Rose, while Zach offered his condolences. Some shared lovely stories about Neville that made them both sad yet happy.

Needing a moment alone, Rose stepped outside to get some fresh air and escape the crowd. As she stood in the freezing rain, her thoughts turned to her mother and the fact that her father would soon be joining her. It was heartbreaking to know she would never see him again, but she was grateful she had found him in time. A tear rolled down her cheek before she took a deep breath and went back inside to be with Zach.

As the evening drew to a close, the village hall gradually emptied. Susan, Rose, and Zach stood by the door, bidding farewell to the last of the guests.

"Thank you for coming," Rose said, her voice tinged with exhaustion and gratitude.

"You did well today," Zach said gently. "He knew you loved him, Rose. That's what matters."

Rose nodded, her thoughts drifting back to the stories she had heard about her father. Each tale painted a picture of a man she wished she had known better.

Later that afternoon, Rose promised to stay in touch with Susan, Lily, and Neville Jr.

Turning to Susan, she said, "I'm going to England to bring my daughter back. I'm not sure how long I'll be away, and I don't know what to expect until I arrive, but I will see you as soon as I return."

Susan handed Rose her phone number. "Let me know how you're getting on," she said. They arranged specific times for Zach to visit Susan's house to take Rose's calls. He would be welcome to spend time with them while she was away.

The following morning, Rose packed her bags, ready to leave. They were up early, and while she finished sorting out the last few things, Zach prepared breakfast. Sitting closely at the table, they had an emotional conversation.

They sat down for breakfast, their words were soft yet weighty.

"I'll miss you, Zach," Rose said, her voice full of emotion. "As soon as I'm in England, I'll contact Susan. I'll know more about Cosuda's whereabouts once I speak with the matron and find out why she left. I think…. I think she may be with Tom." She kissed him tightly.

Zach reached for her hand, "You'll find her, Rose. I know you will."

She hesitated, "I've always tried to do the right thing, but I can't shake the feeling that I have failed my daughter," she said.

"Please take care and be safe on your journey. I miss you already. I love you, Rose."

"I'll ring as soon as possible, and I love you too."

Susan arrived to take Rose to the station. When the whistle blew, she ran to open the door.

"Thank you, Susan," Rose called. "Take care. I'll call you."

THOSE MISSING YEARS

Once on the train, she pulled open the window and saw Susan standing alone, looking forlorn. As the train began to move, Rose waved frantically. Susan's figure grew smaller, but her presence lingered in Rose's mind.

Chapter 26

Rose sighed, her shoulders slumping as she heard the announcement. She sat down on a bench, clutching her small suitcase. The platform was bustling with people, each with their own stories. As she waited, her mind wandered to Cosuda, wondering what could have driven her to run away. What would the matron tell her? In about ten hours, she would find out.

She boarded the train and found a seat by the window, watching as Normandy disappeared. Green fields and small villages passed by in a blur. When the train pulled into the station in Paris, Rose gathered her belongings and stepped onto the platform. An announcement over the tannoy informed passengers that her train to Yorkshire had been delayed by an hour.

It was a quiet, foggy afternoon, and she suddenly felt alone. She reached into her handbag and pulled out a picture of her daughter, a reminder of how close she was to seeing her again. With time to spare, she looked for something to eat and drink. She noticed a small stall selling cups of tea and sandwiches. Sitting at a small table in the busy station, she quickly ate her sandwich before joining the crowd of noisy passengers heading to the platform. Rose hopped on just as the guard walked along, closing the doors.

The train pulled away into a cloud of smoke, chugging through the countryside towards Yorkshire. The familiar landscape greeted her, but she felt a sense of unease. By the time the train reached Northallerton station, it was early evening. Multiple diversions had made the journey longer than expected.

Years ago, she had flown to France, a journey much quicker by plane. However, air strikes driven by demands for higher wages and better working conditions had disrupted travel. It was hard for her to grasp how much had changed. Now, as she returned to find her daughter and understand why she had run away, the guilt from fifteen years ago resurfaced as sharply as ever.

She reminded herself that she had left Cosuda for the right reasons. Though she couldn't change the past, she could only hope for forgiveness.

Meanwhile, Cosuda arrived back at the orphanage, her heart heavy despite the applause that still echoed in her ears from her performance in London. The loss of the matron cast a shadow over her success, making each step back feel like a journey through memories, both sweet and sorrowful.

She found Johnny in the kitchen, his face lighting up the moment saw her. "Cosuda, you're back," he said, rushing to hug her. "I've missed you so much."

Her arms wrapped around him, "I've missed you too."

"How was London? And the performance?

"It was a challenge, but it was worth it. "But I'm glad to be back," she said smiling. "We have a lot to do now."

"We'll get through this together."

Together, they made their way to Miss Thompson's office. The matron's passing had left a void, and organising the funeral weighed heavily on them.

Miss Thompson greeted Cosuda with a warm but tired smile.

"Welcome back, Cosuda. I heard from London—it went well," she said. "Congratulations."

"Thank you," Cosuda replied. She then mentioned she would be travelling to France to see her mother after the matron's funeral.

There were a million things to do, but with Miss Thompson and Johnny's help, they would manage.

The following days were a blur of activity. Cosuda spent hours drafting a personal message for the matron's service, her mind drifting to memories of the woman who had been like a mother to her. She poured her emotions onto the paper, hoping to capture the essence of their shared journey.

The following weekend, Lucy returned from her tour to help with the funeral arrangements. Cosuda shared the shocking revelation that the matron had withheld letters from her mother and what she had uncovered after her accident.

Lucy was thrilled that Cosuda and Johnny were finally together. She couldn't contain her smile as she grabbed Cosuda's hands, squeezing them tightly. "I'm so glad to hear you're finally together," she said, her eyes shining with elation.

As Rose walked towards the orphanage, nerves settled in her stomach, but they were a sign of love and longing. That was what mattered.

She followed the familiar path she had taken fifteen years before when she had left Cosuda at the orphanage. The street lamps cast a soft glow that seemed to echo that moment, while the trees whispered secrets into the bitter wind. Nothing much had changed, yet everything felt different. Memories flooded back—the sight of Cosuda's hopeful eyes as she had promised to return.

When she reached the same wrought iron gates, she paused, took a deep breath, lifted the latch, and walked up to the front door. She knocked firmly on the heavy black knocker. The wait for an answer felt like forever.

THOSE MISSING YEARS

Finally, the door opened, and she found herself staring at a familiar face.

"He was just a boy…" she thought, not realising how much time had passed.

"Good evening, my name is—" she began, but before she could finish, the man cut her off, staring at her in shock.

"I know your name, Mrs Douglas," he said, slightly agitated. His heartbeat quickened, matching the pace of his racing thoughts.

"It's Johnny, isn't it?" she asked.

"I am," was all Johnny could say.

"How are you, Johnny? Can I speak to the matron, please?" Rose's voice was calm, though she sensed the icy welcome. She understood why.

Johnny hesitated before stepping aside, allowing her to enter. "Follow me," he said curtly.

"Thank you."

As they walked down the corridor, Rose noticed the silence of the orphanage—it felt heavier than she remembered.

They stopped at the matron's office, where Johnny turned and gestured towards a chair. "Take a seat, please," he said politely.

Just then, Rose noticed a young woman approaching—a pretty, slightly built girl carrying a large folder. Their eyes met, and both came to a sudden halt. Cosuda's hands trembled, and the folder slipped from her grasp, papers scattering across the floor. For a moment she stood motionless. Then, as if the weight of years caught up with her all at once, she put her hands over her face as a tear trickled down her cheek.

Johnny rushed to her side, catching her before she could fall.

Rose took a slow, tentative step forward, her voice barely above a whisper. "Cosuda... it's you. But I was told you ran away."

Cosuda didn't answer. She stood frozen, staring at the woman before her—her lips trembling as if trying to form words that wouldn't come.

"I am so sorry," Rose said softly.

Johnny's grip on Cosuda's shoulder tightened, offering quiet support.

Wiping away her tears, Cosuda whispered, "Mummy?" Her voice was small, fragile—like that of a child.

"Yes, my beautiful girl. I am so sorry." Rose reached out, smiling through her own tears. "Can you ever forgive me?"

Cosuda pulled back slightly, unsure of how to respond. Rose kept murmuring, "I'm sorry. I'm so sorry."

As Cosuda took a hesitant step forward, Rose's gaze flickered to the device behind her ear— a microphone and transmitter. But before she could process the thought, Cosuda flung herself into her mother's arms, holding her tightly.

"I always knew you would come back for me," she sobbed, clutching Ros tightly.

Rose held her daughter close, stroking her hair, and whispering, "I'll never leave you again."

"It's okay, Johnny. I need to speak with my mother," Cosuda said, her voice steadier now. "Don't worry—I'll be okay."

Johnny nodded, stepping back as Cosuda led Rose into a private room. They needed time—time to heal, to speak, to bridge the years that had separated them.

THOSE MISSING YEARS

For hours, they talked. But Cosuda needed to tell her mother the truth about the matron.

"I need to tell you about the matron," she said quietly, lowering her gaze,

"What about her?" she asked.

Cosuda hesitated, clasping her hands tightly in her lap. "She died…a few days ago."

Rose's face fell. "She died? She repeated in disbelief. When? What happened?"

Tears welled in Cosuda's eyes as she answered. "A few days ago. She always seemed so strong, but…"

"I'm so sorry, sweetheart," Rose murmured. "And I'm sorry I wasn't here sooner." Her voice trembled. "All I can ask is that you believe I was doing my best. That I loved you every single moment that I was away."

Cosuda exhaled shakily. "It's okay… Mum." The word felt unfamiliar, yet comforting.

For the next hour, Cosuda explained everything—the letters the matron had hidden, the discovery she had made after her accident, and the final days of the matron who had loved her like her own.

Rose clenched her fists, her voice raw and trembling. "Those letters were my lifeline, my hope. She stole my chance to reach you."

Cosuda looked at her mother and saw the pain in her mother's eyes—the regret and longing she had carried all this time.

"She was trying to replace the daughter she lost," she said. "I didn't have the heart to tell her how much she had hurt me before she died."

Rose caught her breath as guilt began to seep into her anger. She thought of the matron—the woman who had cared for Cosuda all these years. Had she acted out of love? Out of grief? Or both?

"I only just returned from London for the funeral," Cosuda continued, "and I was planning to go to Normandy straight after. I found your address in the letters."

Rose swallowed hard. "The matron answered a few of my letters—just enough to keep me from coming back. She told me it was best if I stayed away... And then, in the last one, she told me you had run away. That's when I knew I had to come. I should never have listened to her."

Cosuda sighed, conflicted. As much as the matron had cared for her, she had also taken something away from her.

"It makes sense now," Cosuda said. "She didn't want you to take me back because she saw me as a replacement for her daughter. She was good to me, but she robbed me of knowing you."

Rose saw the pain in her daughter's expression and gently changed the subject. She spoke of France—carefully choosing what to share, making sure the focus remained on Cosuda, not herself.

There was so much more to say. But that would come later. For now, all that mattered was this moment.

They spoke for hours, their conversation stretching well into the evening. Tears were shed, and voices rose in frustration as emotions surged between them. Though Cosuda now understood the truth, forgiveness did not come easily. For years, she had believed her mother had abandoned her—left her vulnerable and alone. The orphanage had been both her sanctuary and her prison.

"I need you to know," Cosuda began, her voice steady but filled with emotion, "as hard as it's been, I owe a part of who I am today to the matron. I spent years feeling abandoned, but her kindness kept me going. She taught me resilience and strength—qualities I never knew I had. But the pain of your absence never faded. I used to lie in bed at night, praying that you would change your mind and come for me. For so long, I believed you would. But when no birthday cards came, no letters… I started to wonder if I'd ever see you again."

As Rose wiped her tears, she hesitated before speaking. Her voice trembled as she said, "I know I failed you and I know my choices caused you pain, but please, let me explain—"

"No," Cosuda interrupted, her voice firm. "Let me finish, and then you can speak."

Rose nodded and listened, understanding that her daughter needed to release years of pent-up emotion. It wasn't just about the lost letters—it was the loneliness, the unanswered questions, the years spent in an orphanage while her mother searched for a father who never returned.

Forgiveness would take time, and Rose was prepared to wait. She would do whatever it took to mend what had been broken.

Cosuda stood at the edge of a precipice, knowing that moving forward meant letting go of the past. She was a survivor searching for peace. And in forgiveness, she found the sweetest kind of freedom.

Rose held out her hand. Cosuda hesitated, with everything unsaid, then slowly reached for it. And in that quiet moment, they began to rebuild what was broken.

That night, Rose called Zach, unable to contain her emotions.

"I've seen Cosuda," she said, her voice trembling with joy. "There's so much to tell you, but I'll explain everything when I get back."

Zach felt a surge of happiness for her. "I'm thrilled for you, Rose. I miss you, but take all the time you need."

"It's going as well as it could," she reassured him. "But I think I need to stay a little longer."

"That's why I love you so much," he said. "You always take care of everyone."

As he hung up, he felt an overwhelming sense of gratitude. He wasn't sure what he had done to deserve her.

Since meeting Zach, Rose had come to realise that her past notions of love had been mere shadows of what she felt now. Their journey to find her father had deepened their bond, revealing his unwavering support and quiet strength. Each passing day confirmed what she already knew—she wanted to spend the rest of her life with him.

A week later, the matron's funeral was held at St. Mary's Church in Kettlewell, North Yorkshire. The orphanage staff and children gathered. Their faces were a mixture of grief and solemn respect. The local vicar led the service before inviting Cosuda to step forward and deliver her tribute.

She rose from her seat and walked slowly to the altar, her hands trembling slightly as she unfolded her speech.

"My sadness over your departure is tempered by compassion and forgiveness. I know now that you were always destined to take the selfish path, but I never saw that side of you. To me, you were kind. And now, I understand why.

THOSE MISSING YEARS

The good times outweighed the difficult ones. You taught me to dance. Even when I became ill, you taught me how to love myself, It wasn't easy, but I did it.

Your love was a bittersweet gift, but it shaped me into the person I am today. Her voice wavered, but she continued. "Thank you. Now, be with your daughter and rest in peace. I will miss you."

Cosuda stepped back, full of things left unsaid but lighter all the same.

The matron, Hilda Jones, was laid to rest beside her daughter and husband, a quiet corner of the churchyard now holding the chapters of her life.

As the final prayers were spoken, Cosuda stood in silence, lost in a whirlwind of memories and emotions. In the distance, the faint murmur of voices drifted from the orphanage, where people had gathered to pay their respects.

In the weeks that followed, Rose and Cosuda focused on repairing their relationship. Slowly, trust was rebuilt, conversation by conversation.

When Cosuda revealed her illness and subsequent deafness, Rose felt the weight of guilt pressing down on her.

"I should have been there," she whispered, her voice thick with regret.

Cosuda reassured her. "The matron made sure I had the cochlear implants. Without them, I would have been lost in a world of silence. She gave me a future, and for that, I will always be grateful."

At the beginning, hearing people didn't let her into their world.

Looking into her mother's eyes, Cosuda said, "They didn't let me into their world of dance because I couldn't hear them. But I found my rhythm—my own way of dancing. Now, I want to show the world that silence can be just as beautiful."

Rose reached for her hand. "I'm so sorry for not being with you when you needed me. Can you ever forgive me?"

For a moment, there was only silence. Then, Cosuda spoke.

"Yes, I can. Because forgiveness means I can love again. It means I have a chance to start a new life—with only positivity."

As an adult, she understood why her mother had made the choices she did. But as a child, she had only known the pain of being left behind.

She could hear the relief in Rose's voice as she whispered, "Thank you. And I will keep saying sorry."

Cosuda smiled softly, feeling a weight lift off her shoulders. "Let's make the most of our time now, Mum. The past is behind us, and we have the future to look forward to."

Rose nodded, tears glistening in her eyes. "Yes, let's do that. Together."

Over the next few weeks, they learned a lot about each other, but it would take time to fix their relationship. One evening, Cosuda told her mother that Tom had written her a letter. Whilst she wasn't surprised that he had been having an affair, it was hard to know it had been going on throughout their marriage and even before was difficult to process. Worse still was discovering he had a daughter.

Rose offered softly, "Maybe you will see him and your sister someday."

"Maybe I will see my sister, and maybe I won't," Cosuda said. "But I am with those who love me, and that's all I need." She leaned in and kissed her mother's cheek, a small gesture filled with affection and reassurance.

The following morning, Cosuda was leaving for London to meet with the producers for another show. Before leaving, she reassured her mother, "I'll be back and forth for the next few months, but you should go home to be with Zach."

"Johnny is in the dining room. I think it would be nice if you two could talk over breakfast before you head home. I'll be busy packing, and once I'm finished, I'll arrange for a car to take you to the station."

She reflected on how things had changed—from the shy little girl she had left behind to the confident twenty-two-year-old stepping into a world of performance and independence. She hoped the time would come when her daughter would invite her to watch her dance, but she knew she would have to work hard to gain her trust again.

"Of course, darling. I will go and meet him now."

"I'm going to start my packing, and I will join you both after," Cosuda said. She then squeezed her mother tightly before she went to meet Johnny.

Rose's mind was spinning with happiness and fear, all rolled into one. As she walked into the dining room, she saw Johnny sitting at the table, waiting for her, with two cups of tea and biscuits on the table.

"Hello, Johnny. Thank you for the tea. It's lovely to meet you as my daughter's boyfriend. It's clear from talking with Cosuda that you make her happy."

"I love her, Mrs Douglas."

"Please call me Rose," she said, smiling.

He told her some of what it had been like for Cosuda over the years, particularly her deafness, and Rose thanked him for caring for her.

Johnny said, "She always knew you loved her and that one day you would come back for her."

"If only I had known she hadn't received my letters and cards. When I never received any replies, I assumed it was my punishment for leaving her," she said.

There was still so much she needed to tell Cosuda, but she knew she would have to do it gradually.

As they finished breakfast, she looked at Johnny and said, "I'm proud of you, you know. Both of you."

Johnny's eyes softened. "Thank you, that means a lot."

Cosuda carefully folded her last few beautiful dresses, slipping a photograph of the matron she had discovered in her office into her suitcase.

Rose, having finished packing her own suitcase, prepared to leave for home. Cosuda waited for her mother, and together they walked slowly down the long corridor towards the front entrance. The driver was already there, waiting to take her to the train station.

"Please keep in touch, will you?" Rose asked, her voice tinged with worry.

"Will you stay in touch?" Cosuda asked, her eyes imploring.

"I can't undo what I did, but I can give you as much time as it takes for you to forgive me. I always wanted to be perfect, even as a child, and it kills me that I failed, but I will never let you go again."

THOSE MISSING YEARS

"I will write to you as soon as possible, and I'll see you in Normandy in three months for the wedding," Cosuda promised her mother.

"You are my maid of honour, and I couldn't imagine anyone else by my side," Rose said, smiling. As they embraced, Rose whispered, "I'm proud of you, my darling."

And in a flash, Cosuda watched her mother disappear into the fog. For a moment, she stood motionless.

The scars of the past were still present, but for the first time, she felt better than she had in years and knew that this was the beginning of the rest of her life. And she was ready to face it.

Chapter 27

As the train rattled through the countryside, the landscape blurred into a tapestry of greens and browns. Rose had been travelling for twenty hours but hadn't noticed the time; all her thoughts were on the last three months with her daughter and what had happened since she left her at the orphanage. Her emotions were all over the place, but she kept reminding herself that she had been young at the time and would return for her daughter one day. The train's whistle blew, signalling the next station.

Zach was thrilled when Rose arrived safely back home. He could see the joy radiating from her face as she stepped through the door. They embraced tightly, the three months apart melting away in that moment.

Over a freshly brewed cup of tea, Rose began to tell him everything that had happened to Cosuda over the previous fifteen years. He listened intently, his eyes never leaving her face, absorbing each word. When she revealed how the matron had deliberately kept her letters and cards from Cosuda, Zach was at a complete loss for words. "How could someone do that? he finally asked, his voice heavy with disbelief. "She robbed you both of so much."

Rose, sensing turmoil, reached out and held his hand, reassuring him that everything was finally okay, and that they would face the future together.

There was now a glimmer of hope, a ray of sunshine, and a feeling she hadn't had in years. "It could be optimism and the anticipation of good things to come," she said to Zach with hope.

"Well, it's early days, but it sounds like she's going to be okay, and she's coming to the wedding, so that is a great start," he said, trying to reassure her.

She noticed a significant improvement in his speech, which was much better than it had been before she left for England.

"I've been checking in on Susan regularly over the past three months," Zach told Rose. He wanted to check on her after Neville's passing, and with each visit, he could see small signs of her recovery. She looked more rested, and Zach believed she was doing better recently. He also visited Susan when she invited him over, the aroma of freshly brewed coffee filling the air as they discussed Rose's calls.

After recounting the events of the past three months to Zach, Rose sat at the table and wrote a heartfelt letter to Cosuda, telling her how much she loved her and how proud she was of her. She posted the letter, and it wasn't long before Rose was delighted to receive replies in return. Everything was going better than she could have hoped for, and she prayed nothing would go wrong.

The following day, Rose made her way to see Susan. She felt the weight of emotions she hadn't yet processed but then knocked softly.

Susan answered, her eyes warm but shadowed by grief. "Rose, it's good to see you," she said.

"How are you?" Rose asked as they settled into the living room.

"I'm okay. I miss him terribly. Your father was a lovely man," she said, her voice tinged with sadness. Her gaze lingered on the framed photo of Neville by the window.

Rose nodded, her heart aching for the dual ache of her own loss and Susan's. Neville had been her father, a steady presence in her life that she hadn't yet fully come to terms with losing.

Changing the subject, Susan asked, "How are the wedding plans going?"

"It's coming together," Rose said with a smile. "It's only going to be a small gathering, nothing too elaborate. Zach has been working on the catering arrangements for the reception while I was away."

Susan nodded approvingly. "That sounds lovely. Your father would have been so proud," she said, reaching out over to squeeze Rose's hand.

Rose felt a lump in her throat but managed to keep her composure. "I hope so. I want it to be a day he would have loved."

"I think we are on track. Cosuda will arrive next week, and Johnny will come the night before the wedding. Do you think Lily and Neville Jnr will be back for the wedding? It would be lovely for Cosuda to meet her aunt and uncle," Rose said softly, her eyes reflecting the soft glow of the evening light.

"We will all be there, and we will not miss it," Susan replied with a reassuring smile.

The evening was filled with gentle conversation as Susan shared stories about her time with Neville.

Rose's excitement grew with each passing day. Cosuda's letter had brought a wave of joy, announcing her arrival in Normandy next week to help with the final wedding preparations. Johnny, though busy at the orphanage, promised to arrive the evening before the big day.

After Cosuda's production, she made her way back to the orphanage to pack before travelling to Normandy for her mother's wedding. Her first task was to see Lucy and give her the wedding details, followed by making last-minute arrangements with Johnny.

"I'm going to miss you," Johnny said as she threw her arms around his neck, hugging him tightly.

THOSE MISSING YEARS

Cosuda then made her way to the airport. Once there, she sat wondering how the matron could have kept her mother from her for all those years. Exhausted and emotionally drained, all she wanted to do now was sleep.

It had been a smooth flight, and aside from a brief moment of wondering what had happened to her father, she was looking forward to seeing her mother again. Zach had arranged for a car to pick her up at Caen-Carpiquet Airport. As they drove through the quaint town, she reflected on how her grandfather had once walked these very streets. She began to understand why her mother felt compelled to come here to search for him. Sadly, she would never have the chance to meet him, but being here felt like a connection to the past she had never known.

Normandy in spring was a beautiful time of year, and the thought of her mother's wedding brought a smile to her face. As the car turned onto a narrow, cobblestone street, Cosuda noticed the vibrant flowers spilling over the window boxes of quaint stone cottages. The air was filled with the scent of blooming lavender, and the distant sound of church bells echoed through the village. The car came to a gentle stop, and she stepped out, her heart racing.

Rose had made up the double bed for Cosuda's arrival that morning, ensuring everything was perfect. She looked around to make sure it was comfortable when she heard a car pull up. Looking out of the window, she saw Cosuda getting out of the car. Her movements were graceful yet carried a hint of urgency as she bounded toward the door. Her small hand pressed against the weathered wooden surface. Unable to contain her excitement, she called out to Zach, "I'll get the door."

"Okay, honey," Zach replied, guessing it was Cosuda.

Rose hurried downstairs, her heart pounding with a mix of excitement and nervousness. She opened the door, and there she was—her daughter, grinning.

"Hello, Mum," she said, throwing her arms around the woman who had once been her everything.

Rose could feel her heart beating as she drew her in closer. Her body shook as she cried for the lost time she would never get back, but her laughter filled the air, and the years melted away.

Tears blurred Zach's vision as he watched them embrace, the past and present colliding in a bittersweet reunion.

After introducing her to Zach, Rose went into the kitchen to make some tea. Zach was chatting to Cosuda, and she could see immediately that he was a nice man by the way he was with her mother. From the little memory she had, he was different from her father. Rose brought the tea in and watched them interact; it was going well. They spent the evening catching up, sharing stories, and making plans for the wedding. Cosuda felt a renewed sense of purpose and connection, knowing that despite the years apart, they were finally together.

Zach said he would make dinner while Rose showed Cosuda around the house and helped her unpack. He rolled up his sleeves and headed to the kitchen. Meanwhile, Rose carried Cosuda's case upstairs to her small, sunlit room.

"This will be your space," she said softly, opening the door to reveal a neatly made bed and dresser, and a vase of fresh flowers by the window.

Cosuda's eyes widened with gratitude. "It's lovely, Mum."

While Cosuda was unpacking, Rose helped her, tucking clothes into drawers and arranging a few belongings on the dresser.

She couldn't stop looking at her daughter and felt so proud of who she had become. When everything was neatly put away, they made their way downstairs., the smell of something delicious already wafting from the kitchen.

Cosuda followed her mother into the kitchen, her eyes scanning the counters and shelves. "That's amazing—you can reach everything," she said, marvelling at how perfectly the kitchen had been adjusted for Zach.

He turned to her, "Yes, I had it altered s-specifically a few years ago."

The aroma of roast lamb and fresh vegetables filled the air as Zach placed the dishes on the table.

"You're a good cook, Zach," Cosuda said, thanking him for the meal.

He nodded a hint of pride in his eyes. "Before the army, I worked as a chef. It was always my passion."

Cosuda took another bite, nodding thoughtfully. "Well, that doesn't surprise me—it's delicious."

"Thank you," Zach replied, his tone humble yet pleased. He moved to the kitchen, returning with a cherry pie and custard.

After the meal, Cosuda cleared the table, her mind drifting to thoughts of Johnny. The anticipation of seeing him again brought a smile to her lips. She hummed a tune as she washed the dishes.

Once everything was dried and put away, Rose couldn't help but smile as she watched Zach.

"Let's take a walk," he suggested. "

They stepped outside into the crisp evening air. Cosuda pushed Zach's chair as he led her down the path. The village was quiet, the only sounds were their footsteps and the distant chirping of crickets.

"This is the church where your mum and I w-will be married in a few days," he said. He glanced at Rose, his eyes filled with love and a hint of nervousness.

The old stone building stood tall, its stained-glass windows glowing softly from within. Rose slipped her hand into his, feeling the warmth and strength of his grip. Everything was ready—the flowers, the dress, the guests. Now, all that remained was to savour these last moments of calm before their special day.

Johnny arrived the next evening, and after all the introductions, they sat down to dinner. Cosuda and Johnny shared stories with Rose and Zach about their time at the orphanage, recounting how their paths had intertwined. The conversation flowed easily, their laughter and shared glances revealing the deep connections formed through their shared struggles.

As the night wore on, they all knew they needed to rest; the next day held the promise of a new beginning, with the wedding set for 3 pm. Rose kissed her daughter goodnight and put her arms around Johnny.

"Sleep well," she told them both.

Cosuda placed a gentle kiss on Zach's cheek, while Johnny shook his hand, the grip firm and reassuring.

Cosuda and Johnny went upstairs to the bedroom and unpacked his suitcase.

"I've missed you, Cosuda," he said, gently touching her face and kissing her.

She kissed him back as he pulled her closer into his arms.

THOSE MISSING YEARS

The room was filled with the soft glow of the evening sun, casting shadows on the walls. Johnny's eyes met Cosuda's, and for a brief moment, the weight of the past seemed to lift.

They sat on the edge of the bed, holding each other close, the silence between them filled with unspoken promises and the hope of a new beginning.

Cosuda's eyes met his, "We've come a long way, haven't we? she said.

Johnny nodded, "And we'll go further, as long as we have each other."

The silence that followed wasn't empty—it was filled with unspoken promises, shared strength, and the quiet hope of a new beginning.

Chapter 28

Rose and Zach exchanged vows the following day at the military chapel near their home. The ceremony was officiated by the kind-hearted military chaplain and was intimate and heartfelt.

Rose hired a vintage cream wedding dress that flowed gracefully to her ankles, adorned with a delicate layer of lace at the hem. She looked radiant, her hair elegantly swept to one side, held in place by her mother's ivory pearl crystal hairpin—a treasured heirloom from her wedding day.

In her hands, Rose carried a vibrant bouquet of the most beautiful bohemian wildflowers, which came alive in a flurry of yellows and oranges. The scar on her face was now softened by makeup. It reminded her of the journey she had endured and the pride she felt in overcoming it.

The sky was bright blue, and the sun shone. It was the perfect day.

As she stepped through the arched door into the church, her eyes were drawn to his. In that instant, a silent conversation passed between them. It was a real love story, which they put at the heart of their ceremony. They met as strangers, but thanks to her father, they had found each other and fallen in love. Their wedding was a celebration of their marriage, of course, but also of how they had experienced considerable heartbreak over the years before coming together. A heap of emotion was hidden behind his composed expression as he awaited the arrival of his bride. He had been fighting for his life after being blown up while serving in Leemdorf, but today he was marrying Rose—a fairytale marriage between the soldier and the woman whose love had saved his life.

THOSE MISSING YEARS

Coming so close to not being here and losing both his legs could have meant he was unable to stand at the altar. But while Rose was in England, he had poured every ounce of determination into hours of working with a physiotherapist to learn how to use prosthetic legs and eventually accomplished what had once seemed an impossible task. It meant they could look into each other's eyes and exchange their vows. He stood upright, nervously waiting for Rose to appear. The chaplain was already standing at the altar, ready to marry them.

As she paused at the entrance, her eyes travelled the length of the aisle. Her daughter linked her arm a smile lighting up her face as they stood side by side.

Walking down the long aisle, her jaw dropped as she noticed his chair at the side of him. She was stunned to see him standing tall at the altar, waiting for her. Her daughter proudly escorted her to Zach.

Cosuda looked stunning in a pastel blue gown that Miss Thompson had allowed her to borrow from the orphanage. The bodice featured a round neckline with a simple fold-over collar. She tied her hair neatly back off her face, softly reflecting the light from the sun, and held a posy in pastel shades of blue. Johnny looked smart in his dark blue suit, which complemented her outfit.

As Rose reached the altar, the smile on her face spoke louder than any words he could utter. When Zach saw that smile, it was the most beautiful thing, because he had always believed he would be alone for the rest of his life. She was everything he had ever dreamed of. He felt like the luckiest man in the world.

They shared pure love and happiness. He took her hands in his, his eyes brimming with emotion.

"I never thought I'd see this day," he whispered.

She smiled, her own eyes misty. "Neither did I," she replied softly. "But here we are, stronger than ever."

"How are you standing?" she asked him quietly.

Smiling, he whispered, "You accepted me as I am and loved every part of me. I have always dreamt of this day—when I could stand eye to eye with you as we promise our lives together."

"I will never forget this moment. I am so happy," she told him. She thought how handsome he looked as he proudly donned his uniform.

They were to be married in the presence of Rose's ex-co-workers and employers, with Susan and Lily as witnesses, and everyone was overjoyed for them.

Lucy looked stunning in a knee-length blue embroidered anglaise dress and peep-toe navy platform shoes, her golden hair cascaded down her back in gentle waves. Samuel, dressed in a smart petrol blue tailored suit, his eyes never leaving Lucy's face.

It was a simple, minimalist wedding—it was the oxygen needed rather than the fireworks.

For Cosuda, being there with Johnny felt like a dream. She had made a beautiful maid of honour, and Johnny thought how easy it was to love her. He was captivated by her beauty and dreamt of them doing the same one day. Cosuda moved through the church with a natural grace, as if she were born for the limelight. As she glanced around the chapel, she saw her mother beaming with happiness, Zach by her side. This sight filled her with joy, but she was mostly soaking in the atmosphere—the energy that kept her small body moving even when her feet were still.

THOSE MISSING YEARS

The music faded, and the chaplain stepped forward, holding the Bible. He thanked everyone for attending the wedding. After the prayer, he led them through their vows and the exchange of rings.

"I now proclaim you husband and wife."

The chaplain raised his hands, bringing the guests to their feet. Rose kissed Zach and smiled as they walked out of the chapel, followed by Cosuda and Johnny. The guests followed, stopping for hugs and congratulating the couple. Rose turned and threw her bouquet behind her. The few women collided to catch it, but it was Cosuda who emerged victorious, holding it up with a wide smile.

The reception, held in a small hall behind the chapel, was intimate and lively, with just twelve guests. Before entering, Zach adjusted himself into his wheelchair with practised ease. Rose wheeled Zach to the head table, their hands intertwined, their smiles beaming happiness. Zach gave a brief yet heartfelt speech, expressing his deep love for Rose and gratitude for their shared journey. The hall buzzed with excitement as guests chatted and danced, savouring the warmth of the beautiful spring day and the couple's special moment.

As the night drew to a close, the newlyweds bid farewell to their guests, thanking them for being part of their special day. Rose looked around the room, her heart full of gratitude for the love and support surrounding her. She knew that, despite their hardships, they were all moving forward together, ready to embrace the future with hope and determination.

They didn't want a big honeymoon and chose to spend two nights in Paris.

Rose had grown to love France, and now that she had Cosuda back in her life, why would they want to go back to England when it held so many bad memories? It was just a little painful saying goodbye because it was where she had lived with her parents—her mother especially, whom she adored. Her time in England was over, and she knew they could never make a life there. Cosuda would travel wherever her ballet took her, but Rose's home was now in France.

She had come here to find her father, and she was grateful that she did. She also had Susan, her brother, and her sister, from whom she could find some family comfort.

In just a day's time, she and Zach would board a train to Paris for their honeymoon. The mere thought of Paris filled her with joy; it was a city she adored, and now it symbolised a new beginning. They were in perfect harmony, both having so much to look forward to.

Rose's relationship with her daughter was growing stronger with each passing day. Cosuda's career as a dancer frequently took her to France, offering more opportunities for them to be together. She could see how deeply in love she was with Johnny and how he was equally besotted with her.

Cosuda cherished her time in Normandy with her mother. She got to know Zach a little more and thought he was a kind and good man. She felt reassured that he would take good care of her mother. Johnny was loved by everyone, and many commented on how good they looked together.

Rose told Cosuda that while she was on her honeymoon, they would be looking for a new home in Paris to begin their new life together.

It was time for Cosuda to say goodbye to Rose. She told her that after her many planned performances, she would take a break and visit her mother in her new home. It was an emotional farewell, but Cosuda promised to return as soon as she could. Johnny also bid farewell to Rose and Zach, expressing his gratitude for their warm hospitality and for making him feel so welcome.

Their honeymoon was everything they had hoped for. When you're with the right person, anywhere feels like the perfect place.

On their first day, they sat by the riverside, listening to the birds singing while they had their picnic. They talked about their dreams and the search for their first home together. Zach's disability compensation from the army, which he had once disregarded, now held new meaning. It allowed them to purchase their perfect home—a symbol of a fresh start. He had no interest in the money before, believing it would die with him.

The following day, they met with the real estate agent, who had two properties to show them. The first was a bit small and unsuitable for when the family stayed. However, the second property was perfect. The agent explained that the owner had relocated to one of his properties in America and no longer needed to be in Paris.

This property, a private estate brimming with character, was situated on the outskirts of an excellent neighbourhood in one of the most desirable Le Marais districts of Paris. The main floor featured a spacious reception room, an office, a dining room, and a kitchen at the back that opened onto beautiful gardens. The middle floor housed three bedrooms, one with an ensuite, and a luxurious master suite. At the very top was a self-contained apartment that spanned the entire width of the property. It boasted a further three bedrooms and a large hall that needed to be decorated.

"This is perfect, Zach," Rose said, seeking his opinion.

"I love it too," he said, clasping both of her hands.

After shaking hands with the agent, they sealed the deal and promised to see him again very soon. The next day, they returned to

Normandy, where Zach gave notice on his house. They had a few things to sort out before heading back to Paris. Rose went to see Susan and Lily to tell them about the move, assuring them they were always welcome to stay. Susan congratulated them and wished them the best of luck. Rose wrote to Cosuda, giving her their new address and hoping it wouldn't be too long before they would be able to move in.

Zach looked around the house he had lived in for many years, believing his life would end there. Before meeting Rose, his life had been a series of negative experiences.

"Are you OK, Zach?" Rose asked gently.

"It was never a home; it was always just a house," he replied, a smile spreading across his face. "But now, I've never been happier."

Cosuda wrote back to her mother, the words carefully chosen as she explained the unexpected news. She and Johnny had married after her performance in London, in a quiet ceremony arranged by the orphanage. It was the place where they had met and spent their lives with the only friends they had ever known. She hoped her mother wouldn't be too disappointed.

In the letter, Cosuda apologised for not telling her sooner but felt it was the right thing to do. She explained she didn't want to take the limelight away from them so soon after their wedding. "It felt like your moment," she wrote, "and I didn't want to overshadow it in any way."

When Rose read the letter, her hands lingered on the paper for a moment. Surprise and a twinge of disappointment, but also a quiet understanding. She couldn't deny that she had longed to be there, to see her daughter in her wedding dress. Ultimately, all she wanted was for her daughter to be happy.

She picked up a pen to reply, taking care to convey her love and support. "I'm so proud of you," she wrote. "I hope you and Johnny continue to find happiness in everything you do."

There wasn't a lot of packing to do, mostly clothes, because the furniture was old and unfit to be moved. Thanks to Zach's investment, they could start over.

They stayed in a little B&B in Paris, hoping their stay would be brief until their new home was ready. On their first night, they dined in their room, sharing so much love. The conversation flowed endlessly, leaving little time for sleep as they shared their hopes for the future.

Over the next few weeks, they kept busy searching for home furnishings. Finally, they received word from the solicitor that they could sign the paperwork and move into their perfect home. Rose and Zach offered Cosuda the self-contained top floor to start the ballet school she had always dreamt of. There was plenty of space for them to live there too if they decided it was right for them.

Standing at the doorway of their new home, Rose found herself reflecting on where it all began. So much had happened. She often thought of her mother, how quickly she had died after contracting pneumonia, her father, who had left to fight in the war, and those missing years without Cosuda. Then her thoughts turned to Zach and everything he had been through. She reflected on all those who had lost loved ones and how fortunate she was to have survived it all, despite coming dangerously close to death herself on more than one occasion.

Zach walked to her wearing his new prosthetic legs, something he had never felt the need to do before. He handed her a cup of tea and squeezed her hand, sensing her pain as he always did.

"Thinking about the past?" he asked, wrapping an arm around her shoulders.

She nodded, leaning into him. "It's hard not to, but I'm grateful for where we are now."

"Your father was a hero," he said softly.

Rose acknowledged his words with a knowing smile, but her chin sank to her chest as she thought about him. "He told me he was sorry for everything and said he was glad we found each other," she said through blurry eyes.

"If there's one thing this war has taught me, it's that time is short and every moment is precious," he said. Despite the occasional flashbacks that haunted him, his confidence had grown, and his stutter had almost virtually disappeared.

They went to bed early on the first night in their new home. Still carrying the faint scent of fresh paint and new beginnings. As they cuddled up together, their past ceased to exist as they fell asleep. Every day was a gift.

Chapter 29

Cosuda was going to be home for two weeks over Christmas, and Rose couldn't have been happier to be spending that time with her. She could hardly wait. Johnny would be following a few days later—he wanted her to have some quality time with her mother first.

The next few weeks passed quickly, and Cosuda returned home. This time, Rose felt more relaxed.

Zach had put up the six-foot-tall Christmas tree, carefully placing an angel on top. They neatly wrapped the gifts with ribbons and bows and placed them underneath. Rose strung sparkling Christmas lights across the ceiling of the living room. It looked perfect for everyone arriving for Christmas. Over the years, neither of them had much to celebrate, so this year was going to be special.

As the first snowflakes began to fall, Rose couldn't help but think of the harsh winters she had endured during her time with Joan and John.

Zach put the turkey in the oven along with the roast potatoes, and soon, the mouthwatering aroma of cooking filled the house.

Cosuda had asked her mother if Lucy and Samuel could join them for Christmas, and they were thrilled to accept the invitation without hesitation. They travelled from England together with Johnny.

Susan and Lily gladly accepted Rose and Zach's invitation to stay over for New Year. However, Neville Jr. was working at Great Ormond Street Hospital over the New Year and couldn't join them. His hard work over the years had earned him a promotion to senior consultant. His dedication and love for his job were evident to all who knew him.

Before the New Year celebrations, Neville Jr. and his girlfriend spent Christmas with his mother and sister. The living room felt both comforting and incomplete—filled with the familiar warmth of the crackling fireplace and the soft glow of fairy lights, yet marked the absence of their father. Despite her quiet grief, his mother decorated the tree with tender care determined to keep their family traditions alive. When they walked through the door, arms full of brightly wrapped gifts, the joy on her face was tinged with sadness, a reflection of their shared effort to find hope and happiness in the midst of loss.

While Susan found comfort in preserving family traditions at home, Christmas dinner at Rose and Zach's house had its own quiet reflection. It felt surreal as they gathered around the meticulously arranged table, the absence of Neville casting a quiet shadow over the festivities. Conversations and soft laughter filled the room as they sat down for Christmas dinner, the air thick with the scent of roasted turkey and mulled wine.

The mince pies and Christmas pudding disappeared quickly, leaving behind only crumbs and satisfied sighs. Samuel and Johnny poured the champagne, and the glasses were raised.

"Cheers, everyone," Cosuda said, her voice steady yet tinged with emotion. The response was softer, the room quieter as glass raised.

"To new beginnings," she added, a subtle but heartfelt note of hope—a promise to honour the past while finding the strength to embrace the future together.

When dinner was finished, everyone pitched in to clear the table. Some took on the task of washing the dishes, while others carefully dried and put them away.

In a quieter moment, Lucy turned to Cosuda with a soft smile. "I have something to tell you," she said, excitement in her voice.

As they stepped through the back door into the garden, Lucy continued, "Samuel and I are getting married. We're engaged." She held up her hand, the ring catching the light.

Cosuda's eyes widened with joy. "I am so happy for you both," she said, wrapping her arms around Lucy in delight. She had already noticed the ring during dinner, but seeing Lucy's happiness made her heart swell.

"It's been a long time coming," Cosuda said, clapping her hands and grinning.

"It would have happened a long time ago, but we've both been so busy with work," Lucy explained. If they weren't performing together, one of them was on stage somewhere else.

On Monday morning, Lucy and Samuel were packed and ready to head home. They thanked Rose and Zach for an unforgettable Christmas. The time had flown by, but it was a Christmas to remember.

Saying goodbye to Lucy was emotional for Cosuda, but they would be seeing each other again soon for the wedding.

"How did we get here? One minute we were scared little kids, and now we're grown-ups," Lucy said, hugging her best friend tightly.

"Goodbye for now, and remember that I love you," Cosuda whispered, her voice trembling with emotion.

"Love you too," Lucy replied, her eyes glistening with unshed tears.

The car pulled up to take them to the airport. Cosuda and Johnny went outside, waving as Lucy and Samuel drove away.

Overnight, the snow fell heavily, leaving a beautiful crisp white surface. It looked completely different from the snow in London, which had quickly turned to grey slush from countless footsteps.

It was wonderful to see in the New Year with Susan and Lily.

During their visit, Susan shared some unexpected news with Rose—her father had left a generous sum of money for her and Cosuda. Upon learning about Cosuda, he ensured his Will was amended by the solicitor. Susan, Lily, and Neville Jr. were also well provided for.

It had never crossed Rose's mind that she would inherit anything from her father's Will. But as Susan spoke about it, a wave of sadness washed over her, reminding her of how much she had missed him. Although Cosuda had never met her grandfather, knowing she was his granddaughter made Rose realise just how deeply she was loved.

After the New Year, Susan and Lily said their goodbyes. They didn't make any concrete plans for when they would next see each other, but both knew they would reunite someday.

Cosuda and Johnny returned to England, where they gave up their accommodation and jobs at the orphanage. They were thrilled to accept Rose and Zach's offer of the top-floor apartment in their home.

Three months later, they arrived in Paris and stepped into their new home. Moving through the spacious hall with its high ceilings and large windows, they envisioned the transformation that was about to take place. Soon, the old, dusty space would be filled with the sound of music and the graceful movements of young dancers.

They set plans in motion to accommodate between ten and twelve aspiring students. Builders and decorators arrived as soon as possible, ensuring the studio would be perfect when lessons began. With a separate entrance at the side of the house, stairs led directly to the top floor. Finally, they affixed a sign to the wall, proudly displaying their initials: *CJM Dance Studio*. The gleaming sign symbolised their shared dream, finally brought to life.

They worked tirelessly, transforming the space into a place of grace and discipline. As they finalized their plans, a deep sense of accomplishment washed over them. Cosuda invested her inheritance into the ballet school, determined to make her grandfather proud.

Back in the front room, Cosuda walked over to Rose. Taking her mother's hand, she gently placed it on her swollen belly. At that moment, the child kicked, as if sensing the presence of its grandmother.

The spare bedrooms would soon become a cosy nursery, ready to welcome the baby into the world. Cosuda imagined the laughter, the late-night whispers, and the lullabies that would fill those walls.

Within a year, Cosuda celebrated the grand opening of her dance studio. Ten regular students enrolled, including two who were deaf and two who had recently moved from England.

To ensure inclusivity, she hired Ann, a sign language interpreter who was born deaf but could lip-read to perfection. With her excellent references, Ann quickly became a valuable asset to the team.

Fluent in French, Cosuda worked closely with Johnny, who had studied business and accounting. Together, they watched the school flourish. Their passion for ballet and their dedication to their students quickly made the school a beloved part of the community.

Every day, the studio buzzed with activity. The sound of music filled the hall, bringing a sense of hope and normalcy to everyone involved. Cosuda watched with pride as her students mastered new techniques and formed friendships that transcended language barriers.

One evening, as she and Johnny tidied the studio, Cosuda turned to him with a smile. "Can you believe how far we've come?" she asked.

Johnny nodded, his eyes shining with pride. "It's amazing. We've created something truly special here."

He bent down and picked up their two-year-old daughter, Maggie. The little girl stretched her arms upward, eager to be lifted into her father's embrace. With her dark curls tucked under her chin, she was the spitting image of Cosuda at that age. Rose adored her.

Standing nearby, Rose found herself lost in thought. She reflected on all the people who had entered her life—those who had loved her and whom she had loved in return.

Aside from her mother and father, there was Mary, Nurse Valerie, Nurse Victoria, and the kind woman who had saved her life by taking her to the hospital. All of them had shaped her journey. A great sadness descended on her at the thought of them, their absence leaving an ache in her heart. But as always, Zach was there to love and protect her.

"Are you okay, Rose? You seemed deep in thought, he asked gently.

She turned to him with a soft smile. "Yes. I am happy," she said, realising just how lucky she was.

The war had taken its toll on all of them, but they had come through it stronger.

Life is for living.

About the Author

Jenny Rea was born in Chelsea, London, and now lives and works from her home in Bedford. She is the author of her debut novel, *Those Missing Years*.

A retired English, Maths, and ICT lecturer, Jenny has spent many years reading historical fiction and romance novels, as well as writing short stories across different genres. She holds qualifications in Creative Writing from the Open University and British Sign Language.

Her inspiration for *Those Missing Years* came from her fascination with World War II history and the incredible resilience of those who lived through it.

Made in the USA
Columbia, SC
01 May 2025

57423664R00187